lifestyles
of gods
& monsters

lifestyles of gods & monsters

Emily Roberson

FARRAR STRAUS GIROUX · NEW YORK

Farrar Straus Giroux Books for Young Readers
An imprint of Macmillan Children's Publishing Group, LLC
120 Broadway, New York, NY 10271

1   3   5   7   9   10   8   6   4   2

fiercereads.com

Library of Congress Cataloging-in-Publication Data

Names: Roberson, Emily, author.
Title: Lifestyles of gods and monsters / Emily Roberson.
Description: First edition. | New York : Farrar Straus Giroux, 2019. | Summary:
  In a reality TV retelling of the myth of the Minotaur, seventeen-year-old Ariadne
  fights to save her brother, Asterion, and make her own destiny in a world of celebrity,
  surveillance, and feigned authenticity.
Identifiers: LCCN 2018030123 | ISBN 9780374310622 (hardcover)
Subjects: | CYAC: Mythology, Greek—Fiction. | Ariadne (Greek mythology)—Fiction.
  | Minotaur (Greek mythological character)—Fiction. | Crete (Greece)—Fiction.
  | Reality television programs—Fiction.
Classification: LCC PZ7.1.R586 Li 2019 | DDC [Fic]—dc23
LC record available at https://lccn.loc.gov/2018030123

Our books may be purchased in bulk for promotional, educational, or business use.
Please contact your local bookseller or the Macmillan Corporate and Premium Sales
Department at (800) 221-7945 ext. 5442 or by email at
MacmillanSpecialMarkets@macmillan.com.

To Russell

lifestyles of gods & monsters

ONE

YOU WILL HAVE SEEN THEM, I SUPPOSE. THE GRAINY pictures, taken with a long telephoto lens. It has been fourteen years, but they still shock.

She has a face that everyone knows. Beautiful. Determinedly blond. Curated. The tabloid writers say, "Never a hair out of place."

In the series of paparazzi shots, she strides across the pasture. No Photoshop. No airbrush. No filters. It is a long walk, and the photographers got her from every angle. As always, she is trim, tanned, and toned (another favorite tabloid description). If her sheet of golden hair and blue eyes are familiar, her expression is not. Usually her face in pictures is cool and composed. Icy. In these, she is ravenous.

She never could hide how she felt about that bull.

That face alone would have been enough to sell all the magazines in a newsstand. Enough to crash any server. Even without the wooden cow. But there is a wooden cow. A cowhide-covered box with legs and a head.

When the white bull walked out of the sea a few months earlier, people called it a gift from the gods. They said it was a sure sign that Daddy was a good king of Crete; that he still had the favor of the gods, even after my older brother's murder. Our tragedy. That Daddy had been right to go to war with Athens. They called it beautiful. For myself, I don't see what's beautiful about a bull, white or brown. They look like livestock to me. Not my type.

It was beautiful to my mother.

There are lots of theories about my mother and the bull— some people say Daddy should have sacrificed it instead of keeping it. Daddy thinks that's ridiculous. The gods would not have handed him such a valuable thing only to ask him to kill it. Other people say it was because my mother was too proud and the gods wanted to take her down a notch. However, she's still proud, even after her abasement.

I think it's because the gods are jerks.

Whatever the reason, my mother fell in love with a bull and when the bull didn't return her affection, Daedalus, Daddy's architect, built her the wooden cow and brought it out to the pasture for her.

The paparazzi pictures of what happened next were taken

from so far away that if you didn't know what you are looking at, you wouldn't know what you are looking at.

Unfortunately, I know.

Eventually, the bull returned to munching the grass, and my mother went back to the palace.

When she returned to the paddock later, Daddy's people checked the trees for paparazzi, so there were no more pictures.

No one knows why she stopped going to see the bull. Maybe her infatuation ran its course, like an infection. Maybe the gods thought it had gone on long enough. Maybe she got tired of the whole thing. Eventually, life returned to normal. More or less. Mother went back to her royal duties and her social whirl, and if people moo when her name is mentioned, they do it very quietly behind closed doors. After a while, the world's attention moved on to the next big scandal.

The bull was never the same afterward. It went crazy, charging around, breaking fences, tearing up pastures. Daddy got so irritated that he had Heracles capture it and take it to the mainland. Let it be Athens's problem, Daddy said. Maybe it missed my mother. Who knows. Bulls can't talk.

My mother can talk, but she never talks about the bull. Daddy blocks access to the sites where the pictures are posted, but it's like the Hydra, always popping up somewhere else.

You'd think people would stop caring, but I guess it never gets old.

TWO

"ARIADNE, LOOK UP FROM THAT PHONE," MY MOTHER whispers from behind her smile. "The cameras are watching."

I don't look up. The cameras are always watching.

I am in the stadium VIP box with my relatives and the visiting dignitaries. My family holds the front row, of course, and the VIPs fill the three rows behind us. In the center of the stadium, a Jumbotron simulcasts the live feed.

The stately procession of competitors, newly arrived from Athens, will begin in a moment, but right now, the only thing the live feed shows is us. There's nothing like seeing your whole family broadcast one hundred feet tall, every feature blown up to giant size. I prefer to watch us on my phone.

My mother waves for the cameras. She is bringing it today:

a Chanel jacket, her tiara, her face so Botoxed that when she smiles, nothing but her mouth moves. The golden bracelet she always wears, with an image of my brother who died. She is ageless—icy and perfect. That is the only way I've ever seen her. If it wasn't for the photographic evidence, I wouldn't believe she could be another way.

Daddy is next to her, with his full beard and his three-piece suit. He takes up twice as much space as my mother. The golden sash across his chest and the heavy signet ring on his finger are the only outward signs of his power.

My parents look elegant and royal.

Elegant royalty sells.

Looking at them together, you can understand why their wedding still shows up on the list of the most-watched programming of the last thirty years. No episode of my older sisters' reality show, *The Cretan Paradoxes*, has ever broken the top one hundred. The first season of *The Labyrinth Contest* is in the top slot. Not that it's a competition.

The cameras turn now to my older sisters, the Paradoxes themselves, sitting together.

They have an uncanny sense of when they are being televised, and they both jump to their feet. Even that small action is greeted with rapturous shouts from the photographers and the crowd.

Since Acalle's best side is her left and Xenodice's is her right, they have a limited repertoire of poses they can do together effectively. There is also the small matter that what they are the most famous for is their bottoms, encased in Spandex, and it's really hard to get faces and backsides in the same picture. Though they do try.

The photographers yell, "Turn around, girls, turn around!"

Obediently, my sisters spin and wiggle. The camera zooms in, blowing up their tushes, larger than life. In the next frame, my mother glows with maternal pride.

Tushies sell.

Now it's my turn. My sisters are famous for their online makeup tutorials, but I could teach lessons in invisibility. I see myself, on my phone, slouching in my chair, staring at my phone, which holds a picture of me. It's like one of those paintings where someone looks at themselves in a mirror. An infinite loop.

I wish I was wearing jeans and a hooded sweatshirt to hide my face, but that is unacceptable to my mother and the fashion police. My mother would love to have her stylists make me fabulous, but I'm not interested. I don't want to be seen. Not like that.

So, we have compromised. I'm wearing a knee-length black dress with short sleeves and a square neckline. Pockets for my phone and the ball of silver thread I carry everywhere I go. Flats. I don't have any makeup on, and my long hair is down. I'm like the "before" picture in a makeover photo shoot. I seem tasteful and conservative. Like I'm going to the funeral of someone I didn't know particularly well.

Tasteful and conservative don't sell.

This fact doesn't keep the cameras from zooming in on me. I keep my eyes on my phone. I move my hair so they can't see my face. I wish I had my mask.

"Smile, Ariadne." Daddy's voice is a low rumble.

I flash a quick one. Nothing enthusiastic, but enough to get credit for it. No one cheers.

Then I get to see my face, blown up on the huge screen, one hundred feet high, broadcast to millions. I can feel all the eyes on me. I shiver.

Finally, the live feed cuts from us to the procession of competitors coming up from the harbor. Thank the gods. Now I can do my job. The reason I'm here.

Every year, my family holds a contest that is televised live worldwide. Fourteen Athenian teenagers, seven boys and seven girls, the bravest and most beautiful, come to Crete to face our monster, the Minotaur, in our maze. We are never short of competitors, even though it is a fight to the death.

The winner gets more money than most people see in a lifetime, and enough in sponsorships to support an entourage, but that's only a small part of why people enter. Killing a big-name monster is the fastest route to something even more valuable—fame, eternal glory, their name written in the stars, a way out of an ordinary life—the thing that everyone seems to be seeking.

Except for me. I'd be more than willing to accept a boring, ordinary life, if anyone was offering.

The Labyrinth Contest makes the path to killing the Minotaur clear, even if it isn't easy. First, move to Athens, since the only requirement to enter is that you be a resident of Athens at sixteen. Kids go there from all over the world for their chance to become one of the thousands who will be in the televised qualification round, where the biggest risk is that your trip through the obstacle course or bathing suit competition will go straight to the blooper reel. Qualifications run for two weeks and include obstacle courses and wrestling, a half marathon, a quiz show, and competitions in bathing suits and evening wear.

Finally, if you make it through and get chosen as one of the honored fourteen, you have two weeks of training in Athens, learning orienteering, weapons skills, and monster psychology, and end up here, in Crete, marching into the stadium in a blue-and-white tracksuit while you wave an Athenian flag. They are the bravest and most beautiful, and they know it.

None of them are thinking about the odds.

Which is a good thing, because the odds are terrible.

It's been ten years, and so far, the score is heavily weighted toward Crete—140 to zero. However, as the ads say, *The Minotaur is not immortal.* Any one of these competitors could hurt or kill him.

Which is why I'm here, in the VIP box, assessing the strengths of the competitors based on my previous experience with them. I am the Keeper of the Maze, in charge of leading the competitors to the entrance gate of the maze, where they will face the Minotaur. I'm also responsible for keeping him healthy and ready for each new run. So I rate the competitors. It may seem callous to think about them this way, but they signed up for this.

They have families and fans, millions of people to worry about them. The Minotaur only has me.

On my phone screen, I watch the competitors, looking at their faces and their body language, so I can see what they are hiding.

I choose a boy—small and compact with short curly hair— he was the acrobat, the one who flipped and twisted his way through qualifications. His kind of flexibility and explosive strength can be very useful going through the maze, but will he keep his head level enough to use them? I go in close on his eyes, ignoring his muscular torso and his smiling face. They flicker with fear. In my experience, panic is the thing that dooms competitors the quickest. If they freak out in there, the maze will get them before the Minotaur does.

Next, I look at one of the girls. She is supermodel beautiful, taller than the boy, maybe the tallest girl I've ever seen. She is Hippolyta, the Amazon, the only competitor whose name I remember from qualifications. She moved to Athens so she could be on *The Labyrinth Contest.*

Hard for me to imagine moving somewhere to sign your kid up for a battle that could end in death, but I don't think the person who leads them to the maze has any right to judge.

The Amazon is relaxed and athletic. Sure of herself as the highest-scoring competitor, but what do her eyes tell me?

Before I can look, I have a strange tingling at the back of my neck.

I glance up, keeping my face neutral.

Then I spot him, in the row behind me. A boy. About my age, looking at me with undisguised interest.

I check around me quickly, making sure he isn't looking at one of my sisters, but they are at the edge of the box, waving at the crowd.

His long legs are kicked out in front of him. He is broad across the chest, with curly hair and a nose that has been broken at least once. His eyebrows are dark slashes over bright eyes. He has a suit on, like the other men in the box, but he wears it differently, casually, with the tie loose at his throat, the jacket unbuttoned, his posture relaxed. Jiggling his foot like he is full of electrical energy, like he is ready to explode.

If I had a type, he would be it.

I wonder who he is. I have never seen him before in my life. The other VIPs are regulars, but he's new.

I look back at my screen, collapsing my shoulders and deploying the tricks of invisibility, but he doesn't stop looking at me, his eyes crackling with humor and intelligence.

Who is he?

I'm sure my sisters know. Or if they don't, they will soon. He's too cute for them to ignore. I tell myself I won't care, even a little bit, tomorrow or the next day, when a video is released of him in bed with whichever of my sisters gets her hands on him first. I almost believe myself.

No one has ever looked at me like this before.

He raises an eyebrow. At me. I am irritated with him for distracting me, and even more irritated with myself for the irrational impulse to lift an eyebrow in return. Gods. What is wrong with me?

I scowl instead.

His smile doesn't waver. But here's the thing—it isn't dumb or open-faced, like someone without a thought in his head. It's full of wry humor. Like there's a joke he's waiting for me to pick up on. And he'll take his time. He's inviting me to acknowledge the absurdity of this whole situation—the Spandex, the music from the speakers, the preening VIPs. Everything.

Then, I do it. Across the box, looking at someone I've never met before, I giggle.

When was the last time I did that?

"Ariadne," Daddy says, his voice breaking into my attention. "Get your head in the game. The competitors are almost out of sight."

I blush bright red. In the moment of looking at a boy, I'd forgotten why I'm here. Why we do this.

The Labyrinth Contest is divine vengeance for the murder of my older brother, Androgeous, who died when I was two. He went to Athens for their annual games, and he swept them, winning every event. Which pissed some people off. Late that night, after an evening of drunken celebration, Androgeous was stabbed to death. It isn't clear who did it. Some people say it was the other competitors, and some people say it was the king, Aegeus, himself. No one is telling.

Athens is a no-snitch zone, apparently, but Daddy and the gods believe in collective punishment.

So Daddy led a war against Athens, and won. Daddy demanded an enormous tribute in gold, and Athens paid it. It was still not enough to make up for the loss of my brother. They still had their games, so the gods brought us our own. They sent us the Minotaur and *The Labyrinth Contest* so we could keep making Athens pay.

The gods laid out the details, and it is up to us to follow them, each of us playing our part. Including me. With the gods involved, it could get way worse. Ask my mother and her wooden cow.

This year I am seventeen, the same age as the Athenians. I was a girl when this started, proud of my robes and my mask. Proud to be doing something so important for my daddy, for the gods, but I'm not proud anymore. I hate it.

That doesn't mean I can change it.

I pull my attention back to my phone, where the last of the competitors, a boy with bulky muscles and a crew cut, is parading through the crowd, smiling and waving. I don't even have to close in tight to see his fear. It's right there, on his face, for everyone to see.

Once the last of the competitors passes, we line up and leave the VIP box, my family first. My bodyguards form a circle around me, leading me out of the stadium, and I lose track of the boy. In front of the stadium, the line of long, black SUVs snakes down the hill and I wait for my car, ignoring the mingling VIPS around me and the crush of the crowd beyond the velvet ropes.

I'm not looking for the boy. Not one tiny bit.

It was nothing—a boy looking at a girl.

An ordinary thing that happens to people every day.

Just never to me.

On my phone, I scan the taped video of the other eleven competitors, the ones I missed while I was looking at the boy. Who I am not thinking about.

After watching and assessing everyone, two competitors stand out to me, Hippolyta and a blond boy named Vortigern.

Finally, my SUV pulls up. One of my bodyguards opens the door and lets me in before taking his spot with the rest of them in the tail car. I'm surprised—and disappointed—to find that I'm not alone. Acalle and Xenodice sit across from me in the rear-facing seats.

"What do you want?" I say, harsher than I mean to.

"We need a favor," Xenodice says in her breathy high voice, leaning forward while she flips her long hair and puts one of her French-manicured hands on my knee. I swear, Xenodice would flirt with a brick wall. She doesn't have another setting.

I take her hand off my knee. "You know, the word *favor* suggests some kind of reciprocity . . ."

Her plump, carefully-painted lower lip slides out into a pout. "We'd be *happy* to help you with *anything*, but you never want *our* favors."

I let that sit for a minute, deciding whether it's worth it to take the easy shot. Does she even know that *favor* has another, sexual, meaning?

"Now, *that* would send the viewing numbers through the roof," Acalle says, getting in there before I can. I laugh involuntarily. Acalle is straight-faced; anyone watching at home would never guess that there was any more going on inside her head than in Xenodice's.

"What? What's so funny?" Xenodice says, looking back and forth between us.

"Nothing," Acalle says. "It would take too long to explain it to you."

Out the windows of the car, the motorcade is making its slow way down Temple Row, the crowd pushing up against our car, trying to get a glimpse of who is behind the tinted windows. They'd be having a fit if they knew the Cretan Paradoxes were in the car.

"What do you want me to ask Daddy for?" I say, making my voice nicer. Because that's what I help them with. They get me to ask Daddy for things that he would say no to them about, and they help keep Mother away from me. Daddy disapproves of their show and their boys and their Spandex, and Mother disapproves of my hooded sweatshirts and video games. It's a fair trade, in my opinion.

"Shoes," Xenodice says. "I need you to talk to Daddy about shoes."

She holds out her tiny foot in its platform seven-inch stripper heels. "These are *so* over."

"Didn't I talk to Daddy about shoes two weeks ago?" I ask.

"Yes. That's the shoe shelf life," she says. "I will *not* be the subject of a magazine profile on the Cretan Paradoxes as shoe repeaters. We are not economy-class princesses."

"Okay," I say. "Shoes."

I turn to Acalle. "Is that what you want, too?"

"No, mine's harder." She has a businesswoman's look now. "I don't want them to bring Heracles here."

Xenodice spins and looks at her. "You didn't tell me that! You have to see Heracles! Everyone's been waiting on it! Do you look at your feed? Everyone is talking about #acalleandthelion, #roundthree . . ."

Last year, when Heracles came to visit my parents, Acalle and the great hero started a torrid affair—everything caught on tape, of course. It was great for everyone—Heracles had been out of the public eye for a while, so it got everyone talking about him again. For Acalle, it pulled her up into the A-list. It's one thing to be a pretty princess flirting and wearing hot clothes, but when she got the attention of the most famous hero in the world, that sent her into the stratosphere.

They fought and Heracles went away, then he came back in the winter, promising he'd changed. He hadn't. They fought and made up several more times before he left again.

"The ratings of every episode of *Paradoxes* with you and Heracles beat everything else at the same time, in every demographic," Xenodice says.

"I know," Acalle says.

"They're hoping to stop the ratings slide by bringing Heracles into *The Labyrinth Contest*," I say, adding my voice to Xenodice's.

The Cretan Paradoxes have always been wrapped up with *The Labyrinth Contest*. The contest was what first put my sisters on the map. In the first season, ten years ago, when Xenodice was fourteen, she was so beautiful that no one could miss her. A star, even then. My mother loved it. She welcomed the photo shoots and endorsement deals, invitations and opportunities that were coming for Xenodice and Acalle after that. Then they got their own reality show, *The Cretan Paradoxes*, five years ago, and now being famous is a full-time job for my sisters.

The Cretan Paradoxes generally goes on hiatus during the two weeks of *The Labyrinth Contest* because it wouldn't make any sense to be in a ratings battle with ourselves. Things change, though, because this time we are adding some Paradox energy to *The Labyrinth Contest*. My sisters will be involved in the makeover episode, and the plan is to have Heracles do some individual training for the competitors and color commentary on the runs through the maze.

However, the biggest ratings driver would be Acalle with Heracles. There are fans who would watch fifteen hours of blank screen if they thought they could find out what is going on with Acalle and Heracles.

"I know about the ratings," Acalle says, frustrated. "But I don't want to see him!"

"Why not?" I ask. "It seemed like you were into him."

"I am, when he's sober." Her voice is matter-of-fact. "When he's drunk . . ."

She looks at me, showing the fierce intelligence that she normally keeps hidden behind Xenodice-style doe eyes. "He scared me last time. It hurt."

"It was *hot*!" Xenodice says. "That's why everyone *loved* it."

"I didn't," Acalle says simply.

The car stops at the palace.

"Okay," I say. "I'll make sure they put you in a different plotline, one that you don't hate."

I can do that for my sister. Even though it will probably cost me something big. Nothing is free.

"Thank you," she whispers, squeezing my hand.

When the car door opens, Acalle's face is beautiful and sexy, what anyone would expect. She adjusts her skirt, pulling it up the millimeter necessary for the paparazzi to get the flash of underwear that they prepaid for, and she gets out of the car into the flashbulbs that follow my sisters everywhere they go. I give a few seconds for the cameras to trail them before I get out of the car and make my way inside.

I have to walk quickly, weaving my way through the crowd of VIPs, camera crews, and tourists; I don't want to be late for the debriefing meeting with Daddy. I'm not expected to stay long—I'll give my report on the competitors and he'll want to confirm that I have everything I need for tomorrow. But he hates it if I'm late.

* * *

When I get to the fifty-ninth-floor dining room, one of Daddy's bodyguards opens the door for me. The other one stands along the wall with his arms crossed, watching the doorway. The two priests stand against the back wall in their white robes, a cage of doves at the ready in case anyone needs to decipher the will of the gods at a moment's notice. My mother keeps lobbying in favor of the throwing of stones, since doves are a mess, but Daddy is a traditionalist.

Daddy is at the head of the big table, facing the plate-glass window that looks out at the sparkling city below, and my best friend, Icarus, is sitting beside him. Icarus is young, only nineteen, the same age as Acalle, but he's been working on our shows since elementary school.

He came here with his dad, Daedalus, from Athens when he was a baby, leaving Icarus's mother behind. Daedalus is a genius, an inventor, producer, visionary, but he's not the most practical person in the world. Daedalus says that before Daddy brought him to Crete, he could barely manage to keep the electric bill paid, much less afford everything he needed for inventions. So they made a deal—Daddy is Daedalus's patron for life, fully funding all his projects, but he and Icarus can never work for anyone else. Like my sisters, they can leave the island for shows or projects, but only for a limited time, and always with minders. For example, he's been in Athens for over a month producing the qualifications shows and training.

I've asked Icarus if he ever wonders what his life would be like if he had grown up in Athens, but he says it's a pointless question. "My dad made the choice he did; what's the point of talking about it?" One time, I asked him if he remembered his mom. "How could I? I was a baby when we left," he said. His voice was expressionless, so I couldn't tell how he felt about it.

He took over producing *The Cretan Paradoxes* two years ago, and he just started as showrunner for *The Labyrinth Contest* because his dad wanted to go back to making inventions. Because Icarus is my best friend, I can tell he's nervous about this meeting—his first with Daddy since he became the showrunner—but I'm not sure anyone else can see it.

Daddy is holding his cold martini in his hand while his dinner waits under chafing dishes on the sideboard. This will be a quick meeting. Daddy cannot stand waiting for his food.

"There's my girl," he says, standing up to give me a hug when I come to the table. With his arm around me, I can smell the wool of his suit, the cigars he smokes, gin, his cologne. The whole complex of things that say Daddy. Safety. Home.

Daddy sits back down, and I take the chair across from Icarus, giving him a little wave.

Icarus has a tablet with the data from this afternoon—it shows the minute-by-minute ratings, comparisons to the year-over-year numbers, and our engagement stats. The trend line is clear. *The Labyrinth Contest* is pulling the lowest first-day numbers in its history. Not that the opening parade is normally a giant draw or anything, but it's generally better than these dismal numbers.

"You know our problem, Icarus," Daddy says. "If people don't believe that the Minotaur can be beaten, there's no reason for them to watch. No one puts up a camera at a slaughterhouse. Nobody wants to watch an execution. They want a fight. You've seen the same numbers I have. Our best ratings come when the competitors have a fighting chance. Like that one girl, two years ago, the one who used the rope off the wall—what was her name?"

"Lydia," I say. She was a runner, skilled at throwing knives, long and lean, with her hair in a braid down her back. She survived the maze for three hours, the ratings growing with every minute, every obstacle beaten, every desperate stratagem. I wasn't watching at the time, but I've seen the replays. She stripped a rope from one of the obstacles off the wall and used it to set a trap for the Minotaur, tangling and tying him down.

Our audience had tripled by the time he finally finished her off.

The next day, in the maze, I put salve on the rope burns on the Minotaur's body and comforted him from the pain. I got him ready for the next competitor.

My stomach clenches; I don't want to go through it all again. But I will.

"Yes, Lydia," Daddy says, nodding. "We need more like that. More competitors who are worthy of my Minotaur. More who can put up a fight. The gods sent this contest to me so we could show our triumph over Athens. To make up for the loss of my son . . ."

He takes another drink of his martini. Talking about my lost older brother always makes him upset.

"*The Labyrinth Contest* is on so we can show that even their best and most beautiful, their strongest and smartest, aren't enough to beat *my* Minotaur in *my* maze. However, my victory doesn't mean a thing if no one is watching."

"Yes, sir," Icarus says. "I understand."

Daddy leans in toward Icarus, his voice dropping dangerously.

"I don't need for you to understand," Daddy says, then roars, "I need for you to do something about it."

Icarus stays in place in his chair, staring at Daddy, but he blinks repeatedly. He's hiding it well, but he's intimidated. I'm sure Daddy has seen it, too.

Daddy stares at him for a silent second, making sure he has the point, then he turns to me.

"Ariadne," he says. "You want to tell me what was going on today in the VIP box? Why you were laughing instead of watching the competitors?"

I think of that boy in the box. His eyes on me. His smile. Like this isn't deadly serious.

"It was nothing, Daddy," I say. "It won't happen again."

"Better not," he says, patting my hand. "Now, tell me what you've got. Any thoughts on the competitors? Anyone we should be watching?"

"The Amazon," I say. "Hippolyta."

"Hippolyta is a star," Icarus says, pulling up a picture of her on his tablet and showing it to Daddy. It's a still from one of the qualification episodes in Athens last month, and she's just navigated some insane challenge in booty shorts and a gold sports bra.

"Do you think she's a threat in the maze?" Daddy asks me.

"Maybe," I say. "I can't tell yet. She's brave, that's for sure. The question is if she's smart enough."

"We'll see," Icarus says. "I'll assign a camera crew to follow her."

"Also the tall guy who looks like a Visigoth," I say.

"Vortigern," Icarus says, calling up a picture on his tablet. It's a video from weapons training in Athens after they qualified—Vortigern throwing a spear. One of the first things that the competitors learn in their training is to use the maze against the Minotaur. They are not allowed to go in with weapons, but they can use anything they find there.

"He's good at weapons, and built like a tank," I say. "He might be able to cause some damage."

"That's my girl," Daddy says, resting his hand over mine. "I'm sure you ask yourself why you have to do this while your sisters are off gallivanting for the cameras, with their shoes and their helicopters and those boys."

"I don't care about all that," I say. Because I don't. I don't want to be doing what my sisters are doing. That is for sure. I'd just rather not be doing this, either.

"I know," Daddy says, his eyes crinkling in a smile. "You aren't like the others. Not like other girls at all. That's why you're my favorite—but don't tell your mother; she says we're not allowed favorites."

I feel the warmth of his hand on mine and I know that I am loved. Safe. Protected. His favorite. Sometimes I think he even forgets that I'm a girl at all. Sometimes I think I might be enough to make up for his lost son.

He lets go of my hand and picks up his glass. "You kids get out of here. I've got one more meeting and then I need to eat and talk security with my team."

Icarus stands up, and I wish I could leave now and go to my room and get lost in VR for a few hours before I have to face the next two weeks, but I can't because I promised to help Acalle.

"Um, Daddy," I say, and he looks over at me.

Icarus sits back down. He hates having anything happen that he doesn't know about, so there's no way he's going to leave me alone to talk to Daddy.

"You're still here?" Daddy says, his light tone softening the words.

"Not for long," I say. "Acalle and Xenodice wanted me to ask you something."

"What do those silly girls want now?" he grumbles.

"Xenodice wants shoes," I say.

"Shoes, shoes, shoes . . . ," he says, but then he calls to his bodyguard, "Cut a blank check for Xenodice—item, shoes."

"Yes, sir," the bodyguard says.

"What else?" Daddy says.

This will be a tough one. "Acalle doesn't want you to bring Heracles in."

"What?" Icarus says too loudly, and I glare at him.

Daddy takes a sip of his martini. "Did she say why?"

"She says she's afraid of him."

Daddy makes a dismissive sound. "Afraid? What's that about? That boy wouldn't hurt a fly . . ."

I decide not to bring up that the reason Heracles had to do his labors was because he murdered his wife. Or that he nearly killed his best friend the last time he was here. The gods have forgiven him, so it's not polite to mention it. It does seem pertinent to this question, but Daddy wouldn't appreciate me saying it. He always says that if the gods have forgiven someone, it isn't our position to judge.

"She seemed very serious," I say, looking at Icarus this time. "She wants a different plotline."

"I've already storyboarded—" Icarus starts, but I interrupt him.

"She's scared, Icarus. Acalle is scared."

I let that sink in. Acalle isn't scared of anything.

"Can't you think of something else?" I say.

"What do you say, kid?" Daddy asks Icarus. "If we're taking out Heracles, I need something even better."

"Please," I mouth at Icarus.

"Okay, okay," Icarus says, the wheels turning. "I'll come up with something blockbuster."

"It had better be," Daddy says. "Now, get out of here, kids, my food is getting cold."

Icarus puts an arm around me as we walk to the door, giving me a squeeze. "Gods, it's good to see you," he says.

"How were your meetings—" I start to ask, but he interrupts me.

"Not now, Ariadne."

The bodyguard opens the door for us. "Five minutes," he says to someone standing in the hallway.

When the bodyguard closes the door behind us, I see who he was talking to. It's the boy from the VIP box, standing right there, leaning against the wall.

His stance is casual, like he isn't getting ready to go talk to the most powerful man in Crete. The most powerful man in the known world, actually. He isn't as relaxed as he seems, though, because I can see a tightness to his face. A nervousness.

Who is this kid? Why is he waiting to see Daddy?

Then he sees me, and everything in his face changes. It's like the sun comes out.

He takes two steps forward.

"Well, hello," he says, holding his hand out to me.

I let him shake my hand. His hand is much larger than mine, and the calluses brush lightly against my palm. It doesn't feel like any other handshake I've ever had before. There is nothing businesslike or impersonal about his hand on mine.

"Ariadne," he says, not letting go of my hand. "I'm so glad to see you in person. You're my favorite Paradox."

The hair stands up on my arms. "I'm not a Paradox."

I pull my hand back from his.

"Yes, you are," the boy says, looking at me with undisguised interest. "You most definitely are . . ."

"No," I say, shaking my head and fighting disappointment. "I'm not on *The Cretan Paradoxes*. You have me confused with my sisters."

"I promise that I don't. You're there; you have to know where to look—in the background. You're the one to watch. Not Acalle and Xenodice."

One of my sisters' favorite things to do is to try to trick me into appearing on *The Cretan Paradoxes*. They attempt, so far without success, to draw me into their plotlines. I've never had a full appearance on their show, but it's true that I'm sometimes seen walking through a room or slamming my door or flipping off the cameras.

"Whatever," I say, attempting a withering look. It is compromised by the fact that I'm blushing the color of a pomegranate.

The dining room door opens, and the bodyguard says, "He's ready to see you now."

"I'll find you later," the boy says, then goes into the dining room.

I don't answer, my mouth dry.

"Well, well, well," Icarus says once we are in the elevator.

"What?" I say, daring a look at him in the mirrored wall.

He's smirking. "Aren't you going to ask me who that was?"

"Why?" I say. "You're going to tell me anyway."

"That, my dear, was the prince of Athens."

I laugh. "That's impossible. The prince of Athens is my second cousin and he's about five years old."

"Not that one," Icarus says. "This is the new prince of Athens, Theseus."

"The new prince of Athens?" I say. "Did he spring out of his father's head? Rise from the sea?"

"Don't you watch anything?" Icarus says, disgusted. "It's everywhere on the gossip feeds."

I roll my eyes. He knows I hate that stuff. It's bad enough living in the middle of a gossip feed; I don't want to watch them, too.

"Apparently he was the product of some fling that the king had years ago," Icarus says. "The king has made him the prince. The queen is pissed."

"I bet she is." The queen of Athens is a witch named Medea, my mother's cousin. "If he's taking the place of Medea's kid, I'm surprised he's still alive. I wonder why he's seeing Daddy."

"Probably some diplomatic business," Icarus says, then leans in close to me. "The real question is how long it's going to take for him to get into *your* diplomatic business?"

I punch him in the arm. "Shut up. Whatever."

"I saw how he looked at you, and don't tell me that you didn't look right back, because I know you, sister, and you did."

"Nope, nope, not going to happen," I say, telling myself the same thing.

"Because you have *so* much else going on right now," he says.

"I do," I say.

"Ariadne, video games do not count."

I don't dignify that with a response.

When we hit the lobby, Icarus is met by a crowd of production staffers, all demanding his attention, and I leave him to his work. He'll be busy for hours.

Not me. I don't have anywhere to be until lunchtime tomorrow. Unless I'm needed in the maze.

I make it back to my room and eat the dinner that is waiting for me on a tray. Then I change into my favorite pajamas, flannel ones with cherries on them, my ball of silver thread in the hip pocket.

I prop myself up on the idiotic throw pillows my mother insists on installing on my bed, then put on my VR headset. Finally. Now I can get back to playing *First Blood*.

I'm hoping the game will make me not think about that boy. Theseus. The gods-be-cursed prince of Athens. The first boy who has ever looked at me with interest would turn out to be from our greatest enemy. There is not one thing in my life that can be easy.

The techno music from the party my mother and sisters are throwing for our guests and the media is loud enough that I can hear it over the game's audio, even with my headset on. I turn up the volume. I need to concentrate. The next boss is a pain.

A text bubble crosses my line of vision. It's Icarus, sending a screenshot from his live feed of the party. He's set up a secure channel between our phones so he can share the things that no one else in the world will ever get to see.

This is one of those.

It's a picture of Xenodice dancing on a tabletop, but it's an outtake, not one he'll send to the magazines, because her eyes are half-closed and she looks weird. Also, one of her boobs has fallen out of the side of her shirt. I pause my game and reply— *Nothing I haven't seen before.*

I restart the game. I'm playing as Atalanta, and I have to get past Achelous, an old man river god. I've had this game for weeks and still have not been able to get past this one stinking river god. Icarus sends me another picture of Xenodice, still up on the table, but she's dealt with the shirt problem by taking it off. I ignore it.

When you play as Atalanta, you can't defeat Achelous by wrestling him, which is too bad. It stinks to fight a river god with weapons. I pull out my sword. It's worth a try.

More near-pornographic pictures of my sisters cross my view. Icarus thinks they're hilarious. I find them awful and embarrassing, but I seem to be the only one. Icarus will pick the two or three best ones and release those to the media. He'll save the video for the *Paradoxes*. The trick with Acalle and Xenodice is showing enough, without showing too much. They aren't porn stars. Although, based on the look in Xenodice's eyes, there might be a sex tape from tonight. The sex tapes are a whole other business line. They are released separately, through surrogates who pay millions for them. It's been a few months since one surfaced. She's due.

Do they like it? I wonder.

I would hate it, but I'm not sure about my sisters. I know they love the modeling shoots. Love the clothes. Love the drama. Love the boys. I don't even think they mind the sex tapes, as long as they like who they are with.

My phone rings. Icarus isn't giving up.

"Aren't you at work?" I say, battering Achelous with my sword, beating at his watery form. I fail, epically. He takes my sword from me, then rips my shirt off and carries me underwater. It's the downside of playing as Atalanta. If you're Meleager you get to keep your shirt on when you drown.

"I am at work, at the party. Come down with me," Icarus says in his most charming voice. "It will be fun."

"No, I guarantee you, it won't." What about fire arrows? Will they work on Achelous?

"There's a super-cute boy in a satyr costume. I'll text you his picture."

"Don't," I say, knowing exactly what the guy in the satyr costume will look like. Icarus has one type—ripped and blond, like the barbarian hordes in *Romans v. Germans*.

"The prince of Athens is here, looking hot."

"Perfect," I say. "I'm sure he'll love my flannel pj's."

"He might," Icarus says. "How can you tell if you don't try?"

"I'm not showing Theseus my pajamas," I say, still playing my game.

I can't get my arrows to light because my flint is wet. Achelous grabs me. This time he rips my pants off, too.

"Crap," I say.

"Ariadne, are you in VR? Pause it and listen to me. Or I won't be your best friend anymore."

I roll my eyes, but I pause the game. "Fine, I'll talk to you, but I'm still not going to your party." Atalanta has been reborn and is standing there, waiting for me to play again.

"I get dumb around cute boys," Icarus says. "I won't be able to introduce myself. I'll look stupid or say the wrong thing."

"Then get Acalle to introduce you."

"Oh Hades no," he says emphatically. "The last time I got Acalle to introduce me to someone, they ended up making out in the banquette right next to me the whole night. Not what I was going for. You can't trust Acalle not to jump on someone."

"If he's gay . . ."

"He might be bi—I didn't send a questionnaire. Besides, Acalle never worries about that particular roadblock. But you . . . You can introduce me to someone and not outshine me."

"Thanks," I say, trying not to let his words sting. I don't want to go to the party. I don't want people looking at me. However, that doesn't mean I want my undesirability announced to me, either.

Icarus knows me too well. His voice is conciliatory. "I didn't mean it bad, Ariadne. Come on, please? This one time?"

I imagine it. Seeing Theseus. Talking with Theseus. Dancing with Theseus. Being normal. That's not my life.

Achelous is shaking his fist at me from the river. There has to be some way I can beat him.

"I have to go now, Icarus. You're on your own with the satyr. You'll figure it out. You always do." I hang up the phone and go back to my game.

I finally manage to defeat Achelous using a weighted net, which seems like it goes against all physical laws, but okay. Then I defeat a bunch of mini-bosses and finally, I'm standing there with the rest of the heroes, facing the Caledonian Boar in an open clearing in the middle of a forest. The boar is huge, with bristling red fur and tusks longer than my arm. Its deep-set eyes are dark red, like dried blood.

An idiot NPC runs forward, only to be gored by those tusks and tossed into the nearest tree, where he hangs grotesquely. The spear is heavy in my hand, even though it's only pixels. I can do this. Atalanta *will* draw first blood. I throw my spear and it hits the boar's shoulder, bringing it to the ground. A rush of triumph fills me. I did it.

I am the hero.

Then the boar cries out in rage and confusion, an animal in pain, before it is surrounded and chopped to pieces by my fellow heroes. I hate myself a little, and the game makers, and the gods. Here was this miraculous creature, giant, chthonic, and I've thrown my sharpened stick at it, bringing it down. Pixels, I know. Still.

My phone rings again. It's Daddy. I take off the headset and answer.

"Hi, Daddy," I say.

The party is still bumping downstairs, but that isn't the reason why when I put my feet on the floor, it rumbles beneath me. Far down, in the maze under the city, the Minotaur is making an earthquake.

"I need your help," Daddy says.

"Sure," I say, standing up, pushing away my tiredness, thinking of everything I need to bring with me.

"I'm so sorry to ask you to do this, sweetheart," Daddy says. "The fourth time this month, too."

Fifth, I think, but don't say. What would be the point of saying? Daddy doesn't make the earthquakes. It isn't his fault.

So I say, "No, no, it's fine." I hang up the phone. I put on my rainboots. I say a quick prayer.

Then I leave my room, headed to the maze.

THREE

WHEN I GET IN THE HALLWAY, I HEAR ACALLE AND Xenodice before I see them. They are each being supported by a different guy, trailed by a crowd of burly guys with shoulder-mounted cameras, lights, and boom mics. My sisters stumble, giggling, when the floor shakes.

Xenodice did, at some point, put her shirt back on. However, given the way she is hanging all over the dude who is holding her up, I have to guess it won't be on for long.

I stuff my hands in my pockets. I would go back in my room, but it's not worth it. It's unlikely that they will even notice me anyway.

Acalle stops, letting Xenodice and the camera crew go on down the hallway past her.

"Ariadne," she drawls, stepping away from the guy. The floor rumbles slightly, and it is too much for Acalle's balance. She tips toward me and I grab her to keep her from falling on the floor.

"Hey," she says, her words slurred. "You did me a solid today, with Daddy. Icarus told me they changed my storyline. I'm getting a competitor."

I realize the guy she's with is Vortigern, the competitor who looks like a Visigoth.

"No problem," I say. I hate seeing her like this, but I don't have a leg to stand on when it comes to judging people for what they do.

"Ariadne . . . ," she says, like she's going to ask me something.

"I have to go," I say, passing her back to Vortigern, who takes her on down the long private family hallway toward her suite, and I turn away.

My boots sink into the thick pile carpeting as I walk by the doorways—my parents'; the fifty guest rooms, because sometimes people need to host a party with fifty close friends and family members who are too important to stay in the high-rise hotel Daddy built a few years ago.

Along the walls, giant pictures of my family hang in gilded frames. Acalle and Xenodice on horseback when they used to compete in dressage. Pictures of them skiing. Before they were the Paradoxes. Before they were famous. My brother who is dead, the one we went to war with the Athenians over. Even me in a pink dress, identical to the ones my older sisters are wearing.

It's another life.

There is one picture missing from the walls. My younger brother, Asterion, who no one ever talks about.

I pass a few of the uniformed workers, but they turn their faces to the wall. They aren't allowed to put their eyes on us. No matter what happens. The security cameras are watching, but they don't bother me much. If there's one thing you get used to in Crete, it's cameras.

I arrive at the elevator at the end of the long hallway. This elevator doesn't have openings on most floors of the palace— only this floor, the lobby, and the maze. This is the family entrance to the maze, although I'm the only one who uses it. The elevator doors are white and gilded, like the others, but this one requires a retinal scan.

The elevator car is the last taste of the palace before I drop into the other world of the maze. When I first started taking this elevator, I was eye level with the golden buttons on the white leather–upholstered walls. Now my head nearly touches the dangling pendants of the crystal chandelier. I always wonder why Daedalus continued the decorative theme of the family hall into this elevator. Did he think my parents would take this ride into the maze? That my mother would visit the Minotaur?

Laughable. My mother never mentions the Minotaur. I wonder if she even remembers his connection to her.

After a long, silent drop, the elevator glides open and I step into the maze. It's dim and damp, like a cave, and the poured concrete wall is cool as I run my fingers along it. On the walls, mounted cameras record my every move.

Daedalus could have designed anything he wanted. He could have put in rubber floors or glass rooms or hung marble on the walls. He could have made it look ancient, with stone walls and grottoes, like catacombs.

He chose concrete. The brutalist maze.

He says it made it easy to design the obstacles. Easy to expand. It also hoses off for cleaning.

Here I'm in the safe part of the maze, where the cleaning staff sweep and handymen tackle their punch lists. This part of the maze is where the competitors are housed during *The Labyrinth Contest*. Where there is a heavy metal door that leads to a loading dock where I bring the cows for the Minotaur to eat on Sundays.

From here, though, it's only a few steps to the dangerous part of the maze, the winding, twisting prison where Crete keeps its monster. The Minotaur.

The maze is enormous, at least fifty acres, underground, spreading under the palace, under Temple Row, under the stadium. During *The Labyrinth Contest*, the competitors will enter through the large and fabulously decorated gate in the stadium, but that's not necessary for the things I do in a normal week. My entrance is an unadorned titanium door with a retinal scanner beside it.

I endure the scan. I know what's coming for me once the door opens, but there are some things you can't prepare for, no matter how many times you face them. I hold my breath against the smell as the door slides open.

I have exactly five seconds to go through before the alarms start going off. Nobody wants to take any chances on the Minotaur breaking out. Once I step through, the door slides closed behind me, and I am plunged into darkness. Water drips. The floor vibrates under my feet. I feel, more than hear, the rumbling growl rising from deep in the maze.

He's out there, somewhere, raging. On a normal day, he would run the maze, making the obstacles look easy. Not now. He's not playing. He's destroying.

I take the ball of silver thread out of my pocket. I'm the only person who has one. It lets me navigate the maze. After Daddy told me about the gods' plan for me, Daedalus gave me the thread, cool and metallic.

Daedalus doesn't go into the maze with the Minotaur. If he needs to fix an obstacle or make repairs or expand anything, he manages it from the control panel upstairs. He isolates the portion that needs work using retractable titanium-alloy doors that descend from the ceiling. But I'm the only person who ever goes *into* the maze. The only person the Minotaur won't attack.

It's why the gods chose me to be the Keeper of the Maze.

I attach the thread to the hook in the wall, the one that tells the maze it's me. It turns off the obstacles. The greenish-yellow track lighting along the floor turns on with a hum, and I make my way down. The concrete under my feet is textured slightly, so it isn't too slick. Cow bones cluster in the corners, like rocks that gather in the bends of a river. I make my pattern, a right and two lefts, a right and two lefts, while my thread spools out behind me, a sparkling tether to the world above.

The cameras record my picture. Even here, the cameras are on me.

As I walk, I sing. So he will know it is me.

The smell of a slaughterhouse surrounds me; the hundreds of gallons of water that Daedalus runs through the maze can't completely obliterate the smell. The Minotaur is roaring, wailing, bellowing with the call of a maddened bull; the walls shudder with his rage.

When I get near the last turn, I rest my hand against the coolness of the concrete, letting it steady me, as I prepare for what I'm going to see. It trembles under my hand.

I can already tell it's going to be bad. But there's nothing else for me to do. I hang my ball of thread from the final hook and move out of the dimness of the corridor and into the bright light of the room at the center of the maze, where the cameras don't go.

It is only now that I can say his name. My voice is barely audible under his roaring, but shouting would only make him worse. I do what I've always done, calling to him like I always have, bringing him back from the edge. I close my eyes, preparing myself for what I'll see in his room.

Preparing myself to help my brother.

"Asterion, Asterion," I say, walking forward.

FOUR

ASTERION RUNS AT FULL SPEED AND SMASHES HIS massive, furry head into the wall, tearing at the tattered padding with his horns.

He throws himself into it, battering the walls with his fists. His hands and arms are bloodied from the times he's made contact with the concrete under the torn upholstery. His bare back is riddled with scars, both the ones he's given himself and the ones the competitors have given him.

"Asterion," I say.

He turns and looks at me, his eyes blood red with his rage. His mouth foaming.

He is terrifying. Or he would be, if I didn't know him so well. If he wasn't my baby brother. I'm not afraid of him, just sad.

"Hey, buddy," I say, keeping my voice light, like he's been throwing a tantrum instead of making Crete tremble. "What's going on?"

He shudders, like he's waking up from a dream, and the red fades from his eyes. They return to their sweet dark brown, and I know my brother is back. He's overcome the bull, at least for now.

Asterion hangs his head. He doesn't know why this happens. He doesn't know how to stop it. I know this for sure, because if he did know, it wouldn't happen.

"Let's get you cleaned up," I say, and I unlock the dented and beaten metal cabinet of medical supplies in the corner of his room, taking out a towel and gauze and tape, then locking it up again. I sit on the edge of his bed, a poured concrete platform in the middle of the room, and call him over to me. The edges of the bed are cracked from the times he's kicked it. When he first moved down here, there was a mattress, but he ripped it to shreds years ago. Now there's only his pile of blankets. Mostly the new ones I brought down in January, but I can see his soft blue blanket, the one he had when he was a baby. Somehow, he's managed to keep it whole, even when the others have been torn to pieces in his rages.

He sits down next to me, and I wipe the blood off him with the towel.

He is subdued. Embarrassed. His gaze focused on the floor. He can't talk to me with words, but we have the sign language we made when he was little.

He signs, *I'm sorry.*

"What happened?" I ask.

He shrugs. He can't tell me. He can never tell me.

I put my hand on his knee. "I love you," I say.

He touches his heart, then points at me. It's his way of saying he loves me, too.

"I know," I say. I wonder for the millionth time what he would be like if things were different. He's thirteen. Would his voice be changing? Would he have crushes on girls?

I stop myself. I'm chasing ghosts. I have to focus on the present. The person he is. Not the one I wish he was.

"Let's fix those cuts and bruises, and I'll tell you about what's been going on upstairs." While I bandage him up, I keep a steady stream of talk, leaving out anything upsetting.

I tell him about Xenodice's request for shoes. A failed soufflé that had Mother in a state. I don't tell him about meeting Theseus, because what is there to say, really? I met a boy from Athens and I can't get him out of my head?

"The contest has started," I say, making my voice bright. "They'll draw their numbers day after tomorrow, and then I'll start bringing them down."

I say this as though it is a treat, not something I hate. It would bother Asterion if he knew how much I dread leading the competitors down, and he has enough to worry about without thinking of me.

I spread antibiotic cream on his knuckles and wrap a bandage around each finger.

44

"Maybe this will be the last year we have to do this," I say, keeping my voice bright and hopeful. Daddy says the gods answer our prayers, but on their timescale, not ours. "Maybe by the end of next week, you'll be in a room upstairs."

He does have a room on the family hallway. A baby's nursery, with a crib and changing table that was never used. My mother won't let anyone alter anything in the room except for cleaning it, in the same way that nothing changes in Androgeous's room. The shrines to her two lost sons—one murdered in Athens, and one who was lost on the day he was born.

"What color would you want it to be?"

He signs, *Blue*.

"I'm sure Mother would be happy to get it decorated however you'd want it."

Although I'm not actually sure about that. My room does have those stupid throw pillows. She's very opinionated about decorating. We will figure it out.

This has to be the year. He's been suffering for so long.

His head sags on his shoulders. He's exhausted.

"Let's get you to bed," I say.

He shakes his head and makes the sign he always makes before I leave, the sign he's made since he was a toddler. Two hands together, open in front of him. It's the sign for book. So I go over to the shelf in the corner, the only area of the room that hasn't been destroyed. His treasures. There's the painted pottery bull I made for him when I took that pottery class. I was thirteen, the same age he is now. A feather. A seashell. The book of myths.

He settles on the bed, and I tuck his blanket around him. I ask him to point at the story he wants, and he chooses the Caledonian Boar. Perfect. So I read him the story of how Atalanta and the others slaughtered the monster that the gods had sent to punish Calydon. The story I played in *First Blood*, the boar I slaughtered earlier tonight.

He makes the sign for *Why?* at each important part of the story.

He loves to ask this about the myths. I try to answer. But *why* is the hardest question. Why did the gods send the boar? Because the king was a bad king. Why did the boar have to die? Because he was destroying too much. Why, why, why? At the end of the day, the only answer I have—the only answer for either of us—is the gods.

Because the gods wanted it that way.

There are no more *why*s after that.

When I finish reading the story, Asterion is nearly asleep, but he raises up and manages two more signs. He shakes his head, then pushes his fist out from his chest. *No go.* He repeats it. *No go.*

"No," I say, settling him back down. "I won't go. I'll wait till you're asleep."

I rest my hand on his back, feeling it rise and fall with his breath. I watch him drop into an exhausted sleep, and I don't let go until I'm sure he won't wake up.

When he's asleep, I find it easier to remember how he used to be. A baby with the head of a calf.

He wasn't what my parents were expecting. They had the nursery decorated, and his name picked out. They were sure that he would be a boy to replace Androgeous—a prince.

That's not what happened. He had a baby's body, but short horns, ears that stuck out, a pink nose, and soft brown fur on his face.

When he was born, my mother freaked out. She wouldn't hold him. She wouldn't even look at him. Even though it wasn't his fault he was born that way. If it was anyone's fault, it was hers. Or the gods'.

She wouldn't leave her room for a month, seeing only my sisters and her stylist. When she came out, she never mentioned the baby. Never said his name. The only sign that she remembers him is that untouched nursery. My sisters followed her lead, pretending it had never happened. Pretending he had never been born.

At first, they didn't know where to put him. They tried a room on the family hallway, as far from my mother as possible. Daddy brought in people to take care of him after they'd signed extensive NDAs, but no one knew what to do with him—was he a baby or a calf?

I knew.

From the first time I heard him crying with no one to comfort him. He was my baby brother, and I wouldn't let anyone tell me different. He doesn't have a cow's eyes. He has a boy's eyes.

I loved Asterion so much that I thought that I could make him be okay. When his toddler's body changed into a man's, much too quickly, and they moved him down here, under-ground, his eyes didn't change. I knew he was still my brother, and I kept loving him.

I kept loving Asterion, even when his rages started. I had taken him on a walk into the fields for some fresh air. I thought he might like seeing the cows.

I was wrong. With a bellow of rage, he ripped the leash from my hands, leapt the fence, and fell upon the herd. No matter how I screamed, he didn't stop. He tore them to pieces with his teeth and hands and horns. He feasted on their flesh. When he was done, not one of the hundred head of cattle was left alive. When he came back to me, slick with gore, he butted me gently with the top of his furry head, carefully keeping his horns away from me. They found us in the pasture, me near catatonic in shock; him curled up next to me, asleep.

Just like he is now.

After that, Daddy decided it wasn't safe for him to ever leave the maze.

For a long time, I didn't know about the wooden cow. It was only when I was twelve that I finally asked Icarus what the whispered moos that follow my mother meant. He pointed me toward the paparazzi footage. It didn't change anything.

I wait another half hour for Asterion to be well and truly asleep, then I make my way back out of the maze, rolling up my ball of thread as I go.

I buzz with tiredness.

When I take my thread off the hook, a soft click tells me the obstacles have been re-engaged. The emergency track lighting drops out, and the only thing visible is the glowing red light from the retinal scanner next to the door. I lean into it and let the gliding red light cross my eye, and with a swoosh of air, the sealed door unlocks and slides open. I step through and take a deep breath of the sweet air.

The poured concrete hallway is dim, the only light is the bluish glow of the light strip that runs along the base of the poured concrete wall, more atmospheric than illuminating. Since the overhead lights are off, it must be lights-out in the competitors' accommodations. The block of fourteen bedrooms and a common room that we only use once a year. Cameras watching their every move, recording the drama that fourteen teenagers can generate when they are fighting for their lives.

They're asleep now. Or maybe not sleeping. But at least in their rooms.

I'm almost to the elevator when something catches my foot, and I stumble.

"What the . . . ," I say, falling forward, throwing my hands out to catch myself.

A dumb idea, I think, as my legs are tangled in whatever I fell over and my hands scrape across the poured concrete floor.

"Are you okay?" someone asks.

Laid out on the floor, I close my eyes, because I know that voice, even though I've only heard it once. Even in the shadowy half-light, I can tell it's him. Theseus. I fell over Theseus. For some reason he was sitting on the floor across from the elevator, legs stretched out in front of him, and I tripped over him. This is not how I wanted to see him again.

"Here, let me help you," he says, coming forward. He smells like soap, and peppermint gum, with a hint of sweaty dancing and alcohol.

I don't want him to see me like this. Don't want him to catch the lingering scent that inundates anything I wear into the maze.

"No, no, I'm fine," I say, shaking off his hand, scrambling to pull myself up and limp to the elevator.

In trying to stand, I push my bloody knee and ragged hands against the concrete floor again, and the pain pulls me up short. It isn't a terrible pain, only the throbbing of a bruise and the burning sting of torn skin, but it is enough.

On top of everything else, it is too much.

I take a breath, then lean back against the concrete wall, bringing my knees up toward my chest. In the dim half-light, the gaping hole in the knee of my pajamas is a black emptiness. I tore them. I press my fingers into my stinging, bleeding palms.

"Are you okay?" Theseus asks again.

"I told you, I'm fine."

"You don't look fine," he says, scooting over so he's sitting next to me, pulling his knees up to the same angle as mine.

"You tore your pajamas." He gently touches my leg, right above the tear. "Flannel, right? That sucks."

In the half-light, it is hard to see his face, but he says it like someone who appreciates good pajamas and understands why it would be upsetting to have ruined them.

He slides his fingers into the hole and rubs the torn fabric between his fingers and thumb. "These are exactly the right kind of soft."

The backs of his fingers barely graze the top of my knee and my pulse pounds hard in my neck. My mouth is dry. It's my knee. A knee. Nothing sexy about a knee, you would think. However, I'm glad that I'm sitting down, because if I was standing, I would be shaking.

"How are your hands?" he asks.

"It's nothing," I say again, repeating myself like an idiot, clutching my hands to my sides. I don't want him to see my skinned-up hands, like I'm a kid who fell off her bike. I don't want him to treat me like I'm a child.

He doesn't stop touching my knee; instead, he lightly runs his fingers across the skin. Not saying anything. Not asking anymore about my hands. I don't move his hand away. Even though I know I should. He is touching me, gently, and I don't know what to do about it.

Somehow being with Theseus makes me feel different, like the edges of me are fuzzy. Like the distance that I keep between myself and other people, the distance I have to keep, is collapsed.

I don't understand the feeling. All I know is that I don't want it to go away.

I look at him more carefully, taking him in after the shock of tripping over him. Of falling.

In the semidarkness, he is stripped of color. Just dark tousled hair, his eyes and brows shadows in his face. I want to run my fingers across the stubble on his cheeks. I want to touch his white open-collared shirt under his dark jacket.

I don't, of course.

"What brings you down to the maze in the middle of the night?" he asks me.

"The earthquake," I say, then stop myself. What am I doing? I can't tell him that. No one other than my family, Icarus and Daedalus, and a few of our closest staff members, all of whom have iron-clad NDAs, know that I'm the Keeper of the Maze.

"Why would you come down here because of an earthquake?" Theseus asks.

"Never mind," I say.

Everything about what I do in the maze is completely restricted information. And that is not even considering the fact that he is an Athenian, one of our enemies. I can't tell him anything.

Which makes me think, why is he here? Random people don't end up on this floor. Even VIPs. In fact, there is a big RE-STRICTED sign right over our heads. You can't even get on this floor without a retinal scan. There's no way an Athenian should be sitting out here unsupervised.

Or asking me questions. Or touching my leg.

"What are *you* doing here?" I ask, moving his hand off me.

"I didn't mean to be, believe me," he says. "I went to the

party upstairs." Then he cocks his head to the side. "You weren't there . . ."

"I don't go to parties," I say.

"You should," he says. "It wasn't half bad. They had some of those little quiches, and the DJ was pretty good."

"I don't . . ." I'm about to say I don't like parties, they're too loud, et cetera, but then I stop; none of this has anything to do with my questions.

"Why are you here, Theseus?" I ask.

"I went to the party upstairs, and then when the competitors came down here for the after-party, I came with them."

"Icarus let you?" I ask. The competitors have an after-party every night of the contest. It is the source of a large amount of must-see viewing. Drunken hookups and such, but it is generally a competitor-only event.

He nods. "Yeah, he said it was fine if I came. It sounded better than watching pay-per-view in my room."

"So why aren't you in the accommodations now?" I ask.

He runs his hand through his hair. "There were complications . . ."

"Complications? What kind of complications?"

He hesitates. "It turns out that one of the competitor's intentions were not limited to friendship . . ."

"Oh," I say, understanding instantly. One of the competitors wanted to hook up with him. I blush, irritatingly, images of what that would be like rushing into my mind before I can push them away.

"Who was it?" I ask, but then I answer my own question. "Hippolyta. It was Hippolyta."

Of course it was. She went through the guys in the qualifications in Athens like the tissues in a box. Of course she was shooting for Theseus.

He nods.

Then I am mad at myself. I have been letting him touch me when he was making out with Hippolyta.

"So, how'd it go?" I ask, letting my voice drip with sarcasm. "Your first taste of Amazon—"

"No, no," he says, stopping me. "You don't understand. I didn't mess around with her."

"What do you mean?" I ask. "You're telling me that you could have had Hippolyta, the most beautiful woman on *The Labyrinth Contest*, and you didn't?"

Hippolyta is as beautiful as my sisters are, and I've never seen anyone say no to my sisters when they were truly determined. Never. While I don't like thinking about him hooking up with Hippolyta, I find that I can't really believe that he'd had the chance to, and he didn't.

Or if he did, there has to be a reason. Everyone has reasons. Everyone has an agenda.

"I wasn't feeling it," he says, his voice light. Like he's saying vanilla isn't his favorite flavor of ice cream.

"You weren't feeling it?" I ask. "Seriously?"

"Seriously," he says. "Why don't you believe me?"

"Because I've seen Hippolyta. She's gorgeous."

"I know she's gorgeous," he says, and then he shrugs. "I don't like being forced into things. It's not my style."

Without even knowing they're going to, the words leave my mouth, "It's not my style, either, but it's generally seemed that I'm the only person on the whole planet who feels that way."

"Ariadne, I . . . ," he says, and there is something about the intensity of his voice. I have goose bumps. His eyes are bright, and he's a little nervous. Like he's telling me the most important thing in the world.

I remember, in a flash, the one time Icarus kissed me, five years ago. He only did it to check and see if he was really gay. His lips were soft, and after about a second, he pulled back, saying with a brisk laugh, "Nothing. You?"

I laughed, too, back then, even though it hurt.

I haven't gotten close to kissing anyone since then.

I know, all of a sudden, that Theseus is going to kiss me. I have no idea what I'm going to do about it, other than to say for certain that I will kiss him back.

Before he can kiss me, he leans toward me and grabs my right hand. My scraped, bruised, and burning right hand.

My stifled cry of pain kills the mood with amazing effectiveness.

"Oh Hades, Ariadne, you did hurt your hand." He holds it into the dim light, and the scrape is a dark stain on my palm.

"Why didn't you tell me?" he asks.

"It didn't seem important," I say softly.

"Come on, let's get you upstairs so you can get that cleaned up. You're going to get an infection."

Nothing like medical talk to make me feel like an idiot.

"Fine," I say, standing up and facing the elevator that will take us back up into the lighted world above. I lean into the retinal scanner, then press the UP button.

As soon as we step on the elevator car, he will see me. Torn, bloodied, and messy. He will be full of questions that I'm not allowed to answer.

Without really deciding to do it, I turn toward him. I go up on tiptoe and press my lips to his. They are exactly as soft as I have been imagining. He tastes like he smells. Clean, minty. Fresh.

It's an instant, a moment, a flash, before the elevator dings and the doors slide open.

I pull back quickly and step into the elevator, seeing myself in the mirrored interior.

Messy ponytail. Torn pajamas. Rubber boots.

He, on the other hand, looks very cute, and surprised as he follows me onto the elevator.

I push the button for the lobby.

I'm not surprised when he asks me, "Why do you have rain-boots on?"

I don't answer. I can't answer.

"Do you go into the maze?" he asks.

I look away, not wanting to see his face. "I can't talk about this."

"Ariadne," he says. "Look at me."

When I do, all I see is concern. Empathy. It stabs through my heart.

His voice drops down a level. "What do they make you do?"

The words rise up in me. My secrets. I could tell him. The things I've never told anyone, not even Icarus. The terror of the cows when the doors open and they can smell the Minotaur. The competitors. My brother's pain.

I look up at the cameras on the ceiling. "Stop asking me questions."

"I'm trying to help you," he says, his voice quiet.

"You can't," I say. The elevator stops and the doors glide open.

I walk out of the elevator into the empty lobby, and he follows me.

"You should be able to find your way back from here," I say, pointing across the expanse of marble and gold to the walkway that leads to the hotel.

"Ariadne," he says, holding my wrist, right below the torn skin on my palm. It felt so intimate and private to have him touch me underground, but here, in the wide-open expanse of marble and gold that is the lobby, anyone could walk out of one of these elevators; cameras watch us from every corner. I feel exposed.

Is my face showing everything that I am feeling and thinking? How much I want him to keep touching me? If I'm not careful, I will reveal everything to him.

"When can I see you again?" he whispers. Then he lifts my hand and gently kisses my wrist, right at the place where my blue veins show through my skin. A shiver runs through me.

Oh gods.

I pull my hand out of his.

"I don't know," I say, getting back onto the elevator. "I don't know."

FIVE

I WAKE UP WITH A JOLT. IN MY DREAMS, I HAVE BEEN running the maze. There is nothing novel in that—it's basically my recurring dream. What's weird is who I'm chasing. Every other night that I've had this dream, I've been chasing my brother, the Minotaur. Last night, I was chasing Theseus.

Oh gods. Theseus.

Did I dream everything that happened last night, seeing him in the hallway? Him touching me? Me kissing him?

Oh gods. I kissed him. Did that really happen?

I look down at my scraped palm, then at the spot on my wrist above it, where he kissed me. Yes. It happened. I can still feel the imprint of his lips on my wrist like a brand.

What am I going to do?

I want to see him again, but I can't. Because apparently, I can't trust myself to think clearly when I'm with him.

How can I have gotten myself in this situation? I came so close to telling him everything, and I don't know anything about him. I don't even know what he was doing down there last night, waiting for me to trip on him. I mostly believe that he didn't hook up with Hippolyta, but, still, why was he down there? He never told me.

I jump in the shower, carefully scrubbing my hands and my knee. Then I pull on jeans and a hooded sweatshirt. I have five hours until I have to put on the pressed chiton, hanging off the back of my closet door. Five hours until I have to put on my mask.

Like every other morning, toast and orange juice are waiting for me on a tray when I get out of the bathroom. Dependably, it appears, ten minutes after I get out of bed. They time it so that I never see the person who delivers food.

I take a small piece of my toast and throw it into the fireplace, with its gas log that burns constantly, day or night. An offering for the gods. I say the same prayer I always do—*Please remove the curse from my brother*—then I grab my ball of silver thread and my phone and leave my room. I take the elevator up to the 161st floor at the top of Daedalus's tower. It was 158 floors, but last year we added a few more because some Persians built a 160-story tower.

At the center of the top floor, there is a room without

windows. The control room. It takes a retinal scan to get in. A Klaxon sounds and lights flash while the door is open, to warn anyone inside that they are no longer secure. As soon as the door closes, the sound stops.

Screens cover almost every surface—LCD monitors for editing, the control panel for the maze, a bank of monitors for the security feeds. The only thing that isn't electronic is Icarus's big inspiration board. He's got drawings he's done for his ideas for projects—movies, TV, multimedia games. My favorite is a self-portrait wearing a full set of wings. The feathers are in every color of the rainbow, a striking contrast to his monochrome clothes.

As I expected, Icarus is sitting in his favorite chair, peering at one of the screens through his thick-rimmed black glasses, headphones covering his ears.

He is wearing his uniform—black jeans, white shirt, black moto jacket, black sneakers. I remember when he adopted it, five years ago—he told me that the greatest artists had a uniform, so they could put their energy into their art, not their clothes. I miss when he actually picked out his own clothes. There was this one pair of orange corduroys that I dearly loved. Not that he would admit to wearing them now.

He doesn't look up when I come in, he's so absorbed in what he's doing, so I have to tap his shoulder.

He jumps out of his chair.

"Hades, Ariadne, give a guy a warning, would you?"

"Didn't you notice the horns and flashing lights?"

He looks harassed, running his fingers through his already aggressively tousled hair. "Look, Ariadne, I've got a hundred hours of video that have to be edited down to ten minutes of film. I've got fourteen stultifying competitors who I have to turn into stars, and my dad is off, somewhere, dealing with"—he glances at his phone, which dings—"centerpieces. Apparently. Why in the world your mother can't deal with the centerpieces, I don't know . . . Why the raw footage is stored in a place that requires top secret clearances, so most of my staff isn't allowed up here, that is another question . . . Why I agreed to run a show that has had its ratings drop for the last ten years . . . So basically, yeah, it would be fair to say that I'm too busy for horns and flashing lights."

He glances at his watch.

"Wait, aren't you supposed to be on set for the makeovers?" He looks at a printed-out schedule on a sheet of eleven-by-seventeen paper, which is marked up in highlighter and sitting on the desk next to him. He points at it. "Look, here you are, in orange, makeover episode."

I can see that everything involving me has been highlighted in orange. There's a lot of orange on his printout.

"Hours away, Icarus; it's hours away."

"Don't you have to get ready?" he asks.

I cock my head to the side.

"Right, right. You're you, so no." He narrows his eyes at me. "One of these days, sister, one of these days. I'm getting you into hair and makeup if it kills me."

"No, you aren't," I say, "because if you do, I will be the one to kill you. Best friend or no best friend."

He sighs. "You would have fun if you let yourself relax. You don't have to take everything so seriously, Ariadne. Why can't you be a girl for once?"

"That is an incredibly sexist thing to say. Being female doesn't make me like makeup. Do I give you crap about what you like? Do I ask you when you are going to start throwing the discus? Or marathoning? Or any other guy stuff?"

"No, you don't, but the question is, Ariadne, what do you like? How do you know? Because you never try anything. Maybe hair and makeup isn't your thing, but what *is* your thing?"

We've had this conversation so many times, and I'm definitely not interested in having it now. "I'm not talking about this, Icarus."

"For the muses' sake, Ariadne, take a class or something . . ."

"You're one to talk—did you actually set up any meetings when you were on the mainland? Did you talk to anyone about your projects?"

I point at his inspiration board.

"That's not the same, Ariadne," he says, irritated. "I didn't have a moment of free time while I was in Athens. Running this show is going to be my stepping stone to bigger and better things, but that means I actually have to step on the stone. If I can't run this well, no one will give me anything else to do. You, on the other hand, have nothing but free time."

"This is not why I'm here, Icarus."

He gives me a knowing look. "I know why you're here. You're here to say thank you."

"Why would I be saying thank you?"

"A certain boy, name starts with *T*, ends with *s*, waiting for you along a long hallway . . ."

"Icarus, you conniving snake, what did you do?"

He throws up his hands. "Hold it right there. I didn't *make* Theseus go down to the maze level. I told him that if he went to the accommodations there would be some chance he would see you, thus leaving him there for you to find. You should be thanking me. Not complaining."

I sigh. "I don't need your interference, Icarus."

"Yes, you do," he says. "I'm trying to add some excitement to your boring life, and if you had a shred of loving-kindness in that raisin-dry heart of yours, you would say thank you. You kissed him, too, although that was barely enough to count, but when he kissed your wrist, it was hot."

I am blushing red hot right now. Icarus left him down there so I would trip on him?

"How could you be so sure that he wanted to see me?" I ask. "Maybe he wanted Hippolyta?"

"No, he isn't interested in Hippolyta, he's interested in you, and I can show you proof."

Icarus pushes a few buttons, unplugs his headphones, and on the big screen in front of him, I can see a crowd of sweaty bodies and flashing lights, the electronic dance music thumping underneath everything.

The camera pans the whole room—my mother's creation. Topless girls painted gold dance on platforms suspended from the ceiling, occasionally tossing gold dust down on the crowd so that the gold sticks to sweaty shoulders and bare backs, glitters in hair, and sits like dandruff on the shoulders of the men's suit jackets. Waiters walk the room with gold-rimmed fluted glasses and canapés balanced on golden trays.

The camera finds Theseus standing next to Vortigern, who is clearly going for a barbarian thing: bare chest, tight leather pants. Theseus looks great, of course—blue suit jacket, open-collared white shirt. Hair just messy enough.

Vortigern hands Theseus a shot glass and Theseus downs it.

Then the camera turns, and five of the female competitors make their way through the crowd. It looks like the people on the dance floor are moving to make way for the girls, but of course there is a big, bulky old guy holding a giant camera and trailed by two or three other guys with lights and microphones pushing through the crowd. We keep that hidden from the audience.

The competitors haven't been made over yet, so they are still wearing the clothes they brought from home. Their Athens-appropriate party wear is hopelessly behind the times here in Crete. The competitors are sparkled out in their polyester department-store finery—glitter and sequins and artificial bling.

Except for the girl at the center. Hippolyta. The Amazon. She is dressed for battle. A backless golden Amazon breastplate. Held up by what, exactly? It's unclear. Her leather fighting kilt barely covers her behind. Her thighs are solid, incredibly strong. She looks like a sculpture of a goddess.

She's gorgeous. Not that I'm jealous. Okay, I'm a tiny bit jealous.

The camera turns back to Theseus and Vortigern, and Vortigern steps toward her. "Hey, Hippolyta, you want to dance?"

She raises her eyebrow. "No."

"But last night . . . ," he says.

"Last night was last night, and today is today, and I don't want to dance with you." She steps closer to Theseus. Very close. "You, on the other hand," she says, looking him up and down. "You're looking fine, Your Majesty, very fine indeed."

"Thank you," Theseus says. "Hey, don't worry about the *Your Majesty* stuff. Like I said on the way over, *Theseus* is good."

She takes another step closer, the camera following her in, and Theseus's face is impossible to read.

"How do I look, Theseus?" She almost whispers his name.

"Nice, very nice," he says, smiling, but there is none of the sparkle I see when he's looking at me. I catch myself feeling happy about that, and then I'm irritated at myself.

"Did you get the memo about the gold?" Theseus asks, waving at the décor, and to me it sounds like he's teasing.

If he is, Hippolyta doesn't notice.

"This?" she says, running her hands down her body, drawing attention to every bit of her. "I thought it might come in handy."

She leans in closer. "Come see me later, if you'd like to help me get out of it."

Theseus gives nothing away. "I'll keep it in mind," he says.

The music changes and Hippolyta turns away. "Come on, girls," she announces, raising her arms in the air. "This is my song."

"Bye, Hippolyta," Vortigern says, his voice breaking a little.

She leads the other girls away, but the cameras stay with Theseus and Vortigern.

"What a woman," Vortigern says.

"More than I can handle," Theseus says, shaking his head. "More than I can handle."

Icarus stops the film.

"See, he wasn't interested in the Amazon. He came down there because I told him that you would be there if he waited for you, and I'm not the only one who sees it. Watch."

Icarus cues up another clip.

Vortigern and Theseus are still together, standing against the wall in another part of the room. Theseus is slightly disheveled, eyes a little bleary. He's looking around, but it's not clear who he is looking for, and I'm not sure whose POV the camera is coming from.

Then I hear a breathy voice, and everything is clear.

Acalle.

The camera pulls back to show her marching toward Theseus with her model's stride.

"Gods," Vortigern says loudly. "It's Acalle."

"I know that, you idiot," Theseus whispers. Then he holds out his hand, "Princess Acalle, so nice to meet you."

"Yeah, yeah, yeah," she says, shaking out her hair and ignoring his hand. "She isn't here, by the way."

"I'm sorry, what?" he asks.

"I've seen you the whole night, looking around. My sister Ariadne isn't here. She's not coming. She doesn't come to these."

"I wasn't looking for . . . ," he says.

"Sure," she says. "Look, you seem like a nice guy, but I'm not stupid, no matter what you may have heard. I can see you are interested in her. Don't mess with her, okay? Don't say anything you don't mean."

I blush, not able to decide if I'm embarrassed that Acalle is talking to Theseus about me, or if I'm glad that she cares enough to say something.

She turns to Vortigern. "You, on the other hand, can tell *me* anything you like, as long as I get to keep looking at you." She runs a manicured hand down his bare chest and he groans. "You are really amazing," she says. "Did anyone ever tell you that?"

"You're. So. Beautiful," he manages.

"That's more like it." She grabs his hand. "Dance with me?"

She leads him out to the dance floor. Thus is Hippolyta forgotten under the spell of Acalle.

Icarus stops the tape. "Acalle can see it, so why can't you?"

I feel like growling at both of them. "I don't need your help, Icarus. And I don't have time for this. Gods, this is going to get me in so much trouble. What if he starts asking me questions?"

Icarus stands and puts his hands on my shoulders. "You *do* need my help, because you are hopeless. You need to relax and enjoy yourself. You've met a guy, you like him, he likes you. Go with the flow for a while. You don't have to tell him your life story, you know. Now, get out of here and let me get back to work. I've got a show to make."

My sneakers squeak on the polished marble floors as I walk out of the elevator into the lobby, and the people in front of me waiting for the elevator step backward, like I'm an ambulance and they're the cars on the road.

I know what I'm supposed to be doing—getting ready for my part of the makeovers. The competitors will be getting facials and waxing and wardrobe by now, but the only thing I want to do is find Theseus.

I hear my name shouted across the lobby, echoing off the marble and gold surfaces.

I turn, and Theseus is jogging toward me.

I tell my heart to slow down. It doesn't listen. I guess he's looking for me, too.

Before he can get to me, my security detail is in motion.

In theory, I know that my bodyguards are keeping track of me whenever I go into the public areas of the palace, but it's surprising how fast they can move out of the shadows. They are tall, dark-haired, nearly interchangeable, and terribly discreet guys in suits. They have him surrounded before I take a step in his direction.

All around us in the lobby, people scatter. Nobody wants to be in the way if there's an incident.

"Stop, stop," I shout, before they have a chance to Taser him. "It's okay."

In the center, Theseus is holding his hands out, looking charming, trying to defuse the situation. "Sorry, sorry, I was hoping to talk to the lady," he says.

My bodyguards are not charmed.

"Guys, guys," I say, "he's my friend."

Okay, maybe that isn't exactly what he is, but my bodyguards aren't the type for nuance.

They take a step back, giving Theseus some personal space, and I reach through the circle of them, holding my hand out to him.

He takes my hand, and where we are touching, it is like I have an electrical pulse coursing through me. Theseus is in sharp focus, while everyone milling around watching us—the bodyguards, workers, and tourists—is an annoying distraction.

"Let's get out of here," I say, pulling him across the lobby, down one of the hallways where we aren't so exposed.

As we walk, Theseus lifts my hand up and looks at it, the pink skin and abraded flesh from my fall last night. "That cleaned up well," he says.

"Yeah," I say, not sure what else to say now. Not sure what happens next.

"You wanted to talk to me?" I ask finally.

"Do you know where we can find some breakfast?" he asks.

I stop walking and look at him, taking my hand back. "You chased me across the lobby for breakfast? You know, there are many, many people here who can help you find something to eat. Legions of staff. No need to find me."

He laughs, then looks at me seriously. "Okay, it's not breakfast."

He runs his hand across his eyes, dark-rimmed from lack of sleep. "I wanted to see you."

Me too, I don't say.

"Is there anywhere we can talk . . . privately?"

"Privately?" I manage, my mouth dry.

He glances up at the ceiling to where a security camera is mounted, a microphone beside it. "Not filmed . . ."

"Why?" I whisper.

"I have some questions," he says. "About you. About *The Labyrinth Contest*. About everything."

I'm not disappointed. What did I think he was going to say? I'm planning to kiss you? What would I even do if he said that? Okay, that's a lie. I'm super-disappointed. Questions about me? About *The Labyrinth Contest*?

I turn away. "I can't talk about everything. Have a great day."

"Wait, wait, Ariadne," he says. "I said that wrong. Can't I talk to you, please?"

He leans in toward me. My gaze drops to his mouth, full lips a little chapped. I have a flash of what they felt like last night, for that instant. What they felt like on my wrist.

I find that I have questions of my own. What if he kissed me again? What if he did it for real? Like someone who actually knows how to kiss? Why is he so interested in me? Why does he affect me this way?

Not that I'd ask him those.

I look around nervously. What would it hurt for me to spend a tiny bit more time with him?

I think hard, trying to come up with somewhere private. Somewhere in the palace where things are not filmed. There are only two places where the cameras aren't running—the control room and the center of the maze—and there's no way I'm taking Theseus to either of those places.

I have one idea. "Do you have any running shoes?" I ask.

He nods. "Sure."

"Meet me back here in ten minutes."

"What about breakfast?" he asks.

"You are a resourceful person, I'm sure you can figure it out."

In my room, I change into exercise clothes, moving my ball of thread and my phone to the pocket of my shorts. I don't remember the last time I shaved my legs. I consider running a razor over them, then change my mind, because number one, that would suggest that I care what Theseus thinks about my legs, and number two, it would give me a rash.

Theseus meets me in the lobby. I spot him quickly in the crowd of elderly sightseers, middle-aged people coming to work, and my sisters' rabid tween fans. Sleeveless T-shirt, biceps. Really good legs. I mean great legs. Gods.

"Ready?" I ask, and together we start jogging, our feet hammering the marble floors.

My bodyguards join up with us as soon as we leave the golden doors of the palace. Somehow they are always wearing the right clothes for whatever activity I'm up to. It's like they know what I'm doing before I do.

"I thought you said we'd be alone," Theseus says, in step beside me.

I laugh at that. "I don't get to be alone."

I put on a burst of speed, wondering if he will be able to keep up with me. Running is the only way that I can ever pretend to be free. My bodyguards are in good shape, and they can always catch me eventually, but it is possible to get out ahead of them, if I work at it. In reality, I know I'm a fish on a line and I can never truly get away, but the wind comes up off the harbor, and it blows my hair back from my face, and my feet are fleet on the ground, and I feel alive, like I'm flying, and that's something.

For the first time in my life, there is someone running with me, matching me step for step.

I take Theseus on my longest approved route, the farthest I'm allowed to go. We fly down the long staircases, away from the palace compound. We pass the tourists with their cameras taking pictures of the sights. They look at us once they see my bodyguards and take their pictures of our backs, in case we're anyone important. It's early, though, so they are there in ones and twos, and it's easy to weave around them. Not like it will be this afternoon, when the crowds will make it impossible to move at a speed any faster than a tourist holding a camera phone up to the skyline.

We're running at a nice pace, fast enough to be breathing hard, but slow enough to talk.

"You have questions?" I ask.

"Here? Now?" he asks.

"You wanted no cameras," I say, "and this is the best I've got." I wave at the sky. "Out here, there is no one to hear us but the birds and the gods, as long as we are faster than my bodyguards."

I look back at the four of them, jogging in lockstep, their eyes hidden behind their sunglasses.

"So talk," I say as we reach the bottom of the stairs and turn right, onto Temple Row.

"Okay," he says. "Why did you go into the maze last night?"

Gods, first question and we're already in dangerous territory.

"You don't know that I went into the maze," I say.

"You were wearing rainboots last night," he says. "The maze is the only logical place that you might have been."

I imagine telling him about my brother's rage. Telling him

about the earthquakes, but I can't. "Sometimes I have to go down there."

"In your pajamas?"

"In my pajamas."

We get to the temples, tall white marble, with their gilded domes, and in front of each temple there is a statue of a god watching us with lidless eyes.

"Why are you asking me these questions, Theseus?" I ask. "What do you want from me? What do you want me to say?"

"I want to know what you have to do with this. I want to know what you think about it. On the glimpses I've had of you on the *Paradoxes*, you have always seemed like a nice person. Yet you are part of this atrocity. Why?"

"Your competitors don't think it's an atrocity," I say. "They're jumping for their chance to go into the maze, ready for their shot at the Minotaur."

"Yeah, I know what they think—every one of them is convinced that they're the hero who's going to single-handedly kill the Minotaur, end the dominion of Crete over Athens, and get their name in the stars and an energy drink sponsorship. I'm not asking you that. I'm asking what you think about it."

We run past the Temple of Zeus and the stadium is sitting there, directly ahead of us, colossal and imposing. You can't see them, but the tunnels of the maze are under our feet.

"Theseus, I can't talk about *The Labyrinth Contest*," I say. What would be the good of talking about it? "I can't talk about any of it."

"It doesn't seem right that you would need to be in the maze," Theseus says. "That they would send you in there. That's not normal."

We turn away from the stadium, onto the harbor road. We reach a high point, looking out at the whole waterfront stretched out below us. The tall buildings and the casinos, the cruise ships pulled up to the wharf.

I wave my hand, indicating the whole city. "What about this looks normal to you?"

Far out, at the narrow harbor mouth, a giant bronze head lays on its side, the light glinting off his bronze hair. I point at him. "Like him, he's super-normal. Everyone's got one, I hear."

"What *is* that?" Theseus says, laughing.

"Giant bronze automaton head," I say. "Talos. Daedalus built him. He used to be a hundred feet tall, but his body was destroyed. The head still sits there, watching the ships that come in and out. Keeping an eye on everything for Daddy. If you're lucky, while you're here, we'll get to go down to the harbor to watch him incinerate something as a demonstration. We don't get any unauthorized coming and going in Crete. You're lucky we let you in, prince of Athens."

He looks at me. "You people are crazy . . . Who destroyed him?"

"My mom's cousin, a woman named Medea. Oh wait, you know her, right? She's married to your dad."

"Medea?" he asks, incredulous. "Do I know Medea? She's

only tried to kill me about fifteen times. Lucky I'm not a bronze automaton."

"She tried to kill you?" I ask, pulling up short. When I first heard that Theseus was the new prince of Athens, I made a joke to Icarus that I thought it was surprising that he was still alive, but I wasn't being serious. However, now that I think about it, Medea is famous for the many murders she's gotten away with: She's killed her own brother, her ex-husband's uncle, her ex-husband's new wife, and worst of all, her own kids. Yet somehow, she always lands on her feet—she gets the gods to forgive her and then finds a new hero to hitch her wagon to.

"Gods, she's a horrible person," I say.

"You're telling me," he says.

"What did she do?" I ask.

"First she got my dad to make me fight a bunch of dangerous beasts to prove that I was *worthy*, and finally, right before I left on this trip, she tried to get him to give me a toast with poisoned wine."

"Gods," I say again. "Is she still married to your dad?"

"As far as I know," he says.

"And you're okay with that?"

"It's complicated. My dad has a younger brother, and he and his sons, the Pallantides, have tried to overthrow my dad a few times, but they're afraid of Medea."

"As they should be," I say.

"Definitely. Anyway, my dad is worried that he won't be strong enough to fight off the Pallantides without Medea."

"So it's okay that she tried to kill you, because she's protecting your dad?"

"Something like that," he says. "Also, they've tried to assassinate me twice, and he wants to keep having Medea around because their son, Medus, would still be the prince if the Pallantides succeed in offing me."

"That's messed up," I say.

Theseus shrugs. "You're telling me."

"So it sounds to me like all you've gotten from this prince thing is a bunch of people trying to murder you," I say.

"Yes."

"So why are you still doing it?"

He shrugs. "Think of it this way—if I was still a nobody kid from nowhere, I wouldn't be racing you to the decapitated automaton." He tags me. "You're it."

He takes off, and I am in step right with him.

We are headed down toward the harbor, and the screaming gulls and smell of salt surround us. We turn toward the wharves and shipyards, leaving my bodyguards in the dust.

He slows to a walk and together we go down the jetty, where one long ship is moored. A slim black hull with black sails furled and tied to its tall masts. It is the *Parthenos*, the sailing yacht that Theseus and the Athenians took to get here. It is customary to pretend that it is waiting to take home whatever Athenian defeats the Minotaur. The black sails tell a different story. It is a funeral ship, waiting to carry fourteen bodies back across the sea. If they can even find a body.

My bodyguards stay back, keeping their distance from a ship of ill omen.

Theseus looks at me. His face is deadly serious.

"Look," he says, "I'm new here. I'm new to Crete, and new to being a prince. My dad's wife has tried to kill me. Other people have, too. I don't have anyone on my side, and there's so much that I don't understand. Ariadne, you're the first person I've met since I left my hometown who seems like you are yourself. You're the first person who feels true. I want to talk to you."

Gods, I want to believe him. That this could be all it is—a boy without friends talking to a girl. But there's more here. I'm sure of it. He's a prince of Athens, even if he has only been one for a little while. He's the last person I should trust.

"What about you, Theseus?" I ask. "How true are you?"

"Pretty true, I'd say," he says.

"Really? Then why did you come to Crete? I feel like there has to be an ulterior motive, but I don't know what it could be. Are you trying to help the competitors? Find out about the maze? Something else? I don't know. We've never had any Athenian officials come for *The Labyrinth Contest* before. No princes."

"Technically, there haven't been any Athenian princes before now," he says, "unless you count Medus, and he's a kid. Not an official."

He is deflecting, but I won't let him get away with it. I look at him.

We are almost at the end of my route. It's now or never.

"Why are you here, Theseus?"

He wipes his sweaty hair off his forehead. "The truth?" he asks.

I nod.

"I couldn't deal with these kids coming here year after year to die, and no one from Athens, from the royal family, recognizing it. No one trying to do something about it. I came here because I'm trying to stop it, Ariadne. It's time for *The Labyrinth Contest* to end. Enough people have died."

His face is intense and utterly sincere. No joke. No smile.

I imagine him traveling back to Athens in that ship with its crew, alone because the fourteen teenagers were devoured by the Minotaur. My brother.

I shudder.

He grabs my hand, looking at me intently, his eyes dark and serious. "I need someone to help me. I'm looking for a friend. I need to understand what is happening here."

The unspoken message of his hand holding mine is clear, too. He runs his fingers across my knuckles, and the feeling ricochets through my whole body.

He wants more than that. I do, too.

The magnetic pull between us is so strong that I lean in toward him. Toward those lips. He's sweaty, but so am I. The cool breeze blows across both of us, carrying away our stench.

Theseus draws me closer, his hand moving down to my hip, and when it passes over my pocket, my ball of thread presses against my leg. And with it, the weight of my responsibilities. Of every reason why I can't tell him anything.

What would it mean to tell him everything? It would mean defying my father. Defying the gods. It would mean giving Athens knowledge they can't have. Knowledge that Theseus could give to one of the competitors to help them in the maze.

I can't do it.

I have a pang of regret, because in another universe, another world, with another monster, I would tell him everything. I would be a friend. I would be more than a friend.

I pull away from him. "No," I say, shaking my head. "I'm sorry, Theseus, I can't."

"Are you going to tell me what you were doing in the maze last night?" he asks.

"No, I can't tell you that, either."

I set off up the hill as fast as I can go. Pumping my arms and legs, forcing the air into my lungs. Making my body hurt so much that I can't feel what I'm pushing away, and Theseus is in step with me the whole way.

We don't talk as we run up the hill together, putting one foot in front of the other. My four shadows trail behind us.

Back in my room, I'm dripping with sweat. My heart rate has returned to normal, but my body still hums with the exertion of the run. My hands tremble as I take off my shoes. I can barely manage to untie the laces.

I lie down on the marble bathroom floor, unable to say if I

feel this way because of having run harder than I have in months or because of Prince Theseus.

My shoulders press against the cold stone of the floor, and I force myself to breathe, still feeling Theseus's hand on mine, his words in my head—*I'm looking for a friend.*

I had something so big, so real, and I pushed it away.

He doesn't understand the situation. I don't get to have friends. Not real ones, except for Icarus.

I stand up from the cold floor, strip off my running clothes, putting my phone and thread on the counter to keep them safe, and then step into the shower.

Once I've washed off from the run, I blow-dry my hair stick-straight, making sure to get it completely dry. The things I do to keep my mother from sending a stylist to me.

Now it's time for the costume.

I take the chiton down off its hanger, the linen fabric scratchy on my hands.

It's been almost a year since I've had to wear one of these. My stomach twists with nausea. I don't want to do this. I don't want to put this thing on. It's bad enough that I have to wear it for the fourteen days of *The Labyrinth Contest*, but every year, the extra time for a photo shoot feels irritating. Like why couldn't they Photoshop me in from last year?

As I pull the chiton on over my head, I remember the first time I put one on. My mother was there then, to pin the shoulders and drape everything correctly.

"You look like you belong in another world," she had said, smiling. "Like you should go right up to Mount Olympus."

"Good girl," Daddy had said, before he gave me my mask.

It continued the same way for a long time: my mother coming to the room to pin me and make sure everything was fitting correctly, and Daddy giving me the mask.

When I was thirteen, it all changed, in the seventh season of *The Labyrinth Contest*. Mother brought Mathilde, her head stylist, and they were trying to pin and change the chiton, pulling it tight over my new breasts, adding a slit to show my legs, and I lost it. The first season of the *Paradoxes* had wrapped, and they needed material—drama, storylines, characters. I had done everything I could to hide my changing body from my mother, but she was not fooled by baggy sweatshirts. Even at thirteen, I wasn't stupid. I knew what my mother was trying to do. I knew what she was trying to make me into.

I broke every one of the porcelain dolls on my keepsake shelf by throwing them at my mother and Mathilde, and then at the door once they fled from the room.

My mother said that I needed to be punished, that I needed to do a penance. But Daddy made her leave me alone. He got someone to make the chitons the old way and to add a zipper so that I could get into them by myself. After that, I haven't needed any help to get ready.

My first penance came later that year for something else, and it is my plan to have it be the only one I ever have to do.

The white fabric hangs down to my ankles and I slip on the sandals. I put my phone and the ball of silver thread in the concealed pocket.

I take my mask out of its wooden box.

It is white, featureless, with holes for the eyes. I wonder what has happened to the ones I've worn the years before. A line of ten masks, steadily growing in size. Blank faces. Empty eyes.

The person I must become to do what I do.

I tie it on and look at myself in the long mirror on the back of my door. I look like a phantom. Like a ghost come up from Hades to take the souls of the living. Which I am.

I leave my room, whispering my prayer as I go—*Please remove the curse from my brother.*

My bodyguards are waiting for me at the doors to the ballroom, where the makeover festivities are happening, and they flank me as I enter.

The ballroom is transformed—the vast open space with its gilded walls and parquet floors is now a stage set for transformation. The fourteen competitors have been here since early this morning for buffing and waxing, styling and dressing. Open-fronted tents have been built from billowing white fabric, and inside each one, there is a gilded chair upholstered in white, and racks and piles of clothes, a riot of colors and fabrics. It creates a vision of luxury and abundance.

However, one step beyond the view of the cameras, there are

bright klieg lights, electrical cords taped to the floor, and people shouting at the production assistants, who are everywhere. There are at least a hundred people buzzing around this room— grips and camera operators, stylists of all varieties, producers with duties that Icarus has tried to explain to me but I can never manage to keep straight.

I'm two minutes late, and usually, Icarus would be waiting for me at the door. But he isn't, which is weird.

The action swirls around me. Through the holes in my mask I scan the room, looking for Icarus. For whatever reason, he isn't here. Thankfully, I know what to do.

This is hardly my first makeover.

I'm here as a prop. Set dressing.

Over on one wall, I see the setup for the photo shoot and I head in that direction.

The fourteen competitors are gathered there, waiting for their pictures. They have their backs to me, facing the photographer. They are in their official uniforms—this year they are black leather, riveted with gold. As is typical for the past few years, the producers have gone with the bridesmaid approach— different styles to suit different body types. In the beginning, it was more of a cheerleader thing with everyone dressed the same, but it looked pretty ridiculous, because the bravest and most beautiful have widely varying body types and what suits a six-foot-tall warrior can look absurd on a five-foot gymnast.

Even from behind, they look so different from yesterday. It's amazing what money can do, even for people who were already beautiful. And they know it. They toss their hair, now falling down their backs in smooth waterfalls; they run their hands over their skin, buffed to a shine. Their outfits have been selected for each of the next fourteen days, clothes that are more expensive than the average person's car. They are world-famous now. This transformation will be broadcast worldwide. The pictures they are taking today will be on the cover of every magazine tomorrow.

"It's the Keeper of the Maze," someone says, and I brace myself as, one by one, they turn to look at me.

I am thankful for my mask, because the looks they are sending my way are deadly.

These competitors believe that they will win. As the ads say, *The Minotaur is not immortal. Someday, someone will win.* However, showing up here in my mask and chiton, I represent the chance that they might not.

"There you are," Acalle says as she breaks through the crowd of competitors, Xenodice, the photographer, and an irritated-looking producer following behind her.

Acalle is wearing a midriff-baring halter top, a tight pencil skirt, and high-heeled sandals that lace up to right below her knees. Her hair and makeup are flawless, and she is holding a clipboard.

"Acalle," I say. "Why do you have a clipboard?"

"Icarus left me in charge of this photo shoot because he got called out," she says. "Isn't it great? He says I grasp his vision better than anyone else in this place."

The producer does not look like she thinks it is great and Xenodice whines, "Why didn't he ask me? I'm older . . . I've been on the show longer . . ."

"Xenodice, you don't know what side of the camera to look out of," Acalle says. "You are eye candy. Isn't that enough?"

"Whatever," Xenodice says, but she waggles her derriere, as though she's taking it out for a test drive. Sure enough, many of the competitors swivel their gazes to her. She shimmies her shoulders in satisfaction.

Acalle and the photographer move the competitors around, grouping them and setting them up, then bringing me in at the last minute.

"Where is Icarus, exactly?" I ask Acalle as she lifts my right arm. This is taking far longer than it should, and I'm hot under the lights.

"How do I know?" she says. "Icarus said there was a new plotline that would push Heracles right off the radar. Thanks again for that, by the way. I really owe you."

"A plotline?" I ask.

Our world runs on storyboards, each one carefully laid out by Icarus in the months before the show started and tweaked as he saw who made it through the qualifications in Athens. That's why the makeovers are so important, they set everything up. The whole thing depends on people rooting for competitors, wanting to follow the competitors. The competitors have roles to play. The good girl. The hero. The bad girl. The villain. The troublemaker. The sidekick. As they go into the maze, the plotlines will be built around them. Hours of viewing. Who will the hero be hooking up with the night before his turn in the maze? What are the new obstacles? Who thinks they will win? Who thinks they won't? How much drama can fourteen fame-hungry teenagers with too much time and too much money and death in their future generate?

"Today?" I ask. "Isn't it pretty late to be adding a plotline?"

Why am *I* not in the meeting? Generally, I would be there for anything having to do with plotlines for *The Labyrinth Contest* by this stage. I tune out for the sex-and-drama parts of the planning, but I pay attention to everything having to do with the maze.

"I don't know," Acalle says, clearly annoyed. "He grabbed that new prince of Athens and left to see Daddy."

My heart starts to beat faster.

Theseus?

I do not like the sound of that.

"Wait, where are you going?" Acalle asks as I turn and walk away from the photo shoot.

SIX

IN NO TIME, I'M ON THE ELEVATOR THAT LEADS TO Daddy's office on the forty-ninth floor.

His secretary is sitting at her desk out in front of his door, filing her nails.

"Oh gods," she says, standing up and dropping her nail file. "I wasn't expecting . . ."

I hate the quickly stifled look of panic on her face. I hate the way her hand slips into the pocket of her jacket. I'm sure she is touching a piece of iron that she keeps there. To ward against bad luck.

Against me and my mask, although in her defense, she doesn't actually know it's me, but still.

She forces her face into a rictus of a smile, pulling herself together. "Can I help you?"

"I need to speak with the king," I say.

"He's in a meeting," she says, her tone apologetic. She's about to tell me to come back in a few minutes, but I'm not having it. I should be in this meeting. If it's about the contest, it's related to the Minotaur, and if it's related to the Minotaur, I need to know about it.

"I need to talk to him," I say, letting no hint of niceness into my voice.

She stares at the mask, touches her pocket again, then presses the button to call Daddy. "Sir, you have a visitor," she says.

"I get a lot of visitors," Daddy says. "Who is it?"

"The Keeper of the Maze," she tells him, her voice squeaking.

There is silence for a few seconds, and then Daddy's voice comes back over the line. "Send her in. We're wrapping up here."

I brush past her desk and she flinches away from me. I hold my head higher.

Daddy is sitting at his large wooden desk, and Theseus and Icarus sit in the chairs in front of the desk. They both stand as I come in.

Icarus is wearing his uniform, and Theseus has on another suit, this one charcoal gray. It's a good color for him. Again, no tie.

Icarus is annoyed at my interruption, and he's not even trying to hide it.

Theseus doesn't show me anything. His dark eyes are blank. It hurts my feelings, but then I remember, I'm wearing the mask. He doesn't even know it is me.

"What is it?" Daddy asks.

"Acalle said Icarus was talking about a new story," I say. "I want to know what it is."

Icarus touches his watch. "Aren't you supposed to be at make-over photos?"

"Yes," I say, my tone annoyed. "That's where I talked to Acalle. And yes, I already took my pictures. What's going on, Icarus? If there are changes, I need to be in the loop."

Icarus looks away, shiftily, I think. Theseus watches me.

Daddy comes out from around his desk and puts his hand on my shoulder, placating me.

"I know you want to be involved with everything, but you have bigger fish to fry. You are supposed to be thinking about the maze." He squeezes my arm. "You haven't forgotten why we're here, have you? You haven't forgotten the gods?"

"Praise the gods," the priests in the corner say, and we chorus, "Praise the gods."

"Now, you boys get out of here," Daddy says. "You too," he adds, gesturing at the priests and at his bodyguards. "Give us a few minutes alone."

Everyone leaves, and as soon as the door closes, Daddy takes off my mask, setting it on his desk.

"Now, do you want to tell me why you have been wandering around the palace in your Keeper of the Maze getup? That's not how we do things around here."

I start to feel very lame that I came tearing upstairs to find out what Theseus and Icarus were up to. I could have waited an hour and called Icarus to ask him. Although I'm not sure he would have told me what's really going on. He was looking very shifty.

"Is it about this boy Theseus? I heard you took him running with you. Is this something I should be worried about?"

"No, no," I say too quickly, my cheeks on fire.

"Good," Daddy says, clearly deciding to ignore my red face. "Don't forget, Ariadne, he's an Athenian. We can never trust them."

"Yes, Daddy," I say.

"Whatever happens, you can't let him distract you from the reason that we're here."

I nod.

"I understand," I say.

"You say that, but I'm not sure you do," Daddy says, squeezing my shoulder. "Here's the thing, sweetheart, here's the thing—the gods don't ask us to carry any burdens we can't manage. The gods have faith in you, Ariadne. I need to know why you are having so much trouble with your faith in them."

The disappointment is clear on his face.

I hate that look. I'm failing Daddy, failing my brother. Failing the gods. I have to believe. Like Daddy.

"Daddy, no," I say. "I do have faith in them. I really do."

"It's not enough to say it, Ariadne. When you say it, it's just words. It is with your actions that you will show the gods your faith. You have work to do, but instead, you're up here, snooping? Where is your head, Ariadne?"

"Daddy," I say, "I didn't mean . . ."

He shushes me, still talking. "You're worried about plotlines instead of the job the gods gave to you and you alone?" Tears pool in his eyes. "This hurts me, Ariadne. Without our belief in the gods, without our absolute fealty to what they have commanded, who knows what will happen? To you? To the Minotaur? Have you forgotten your penance?"

"No, Daddy," I say, and the choking feeling rises in me, but I push it away. Anything to not remember that penance. It was four years ago, but still sometimes it comes at me in the night, or when I'm not expecting it, trying to suffocate me.

He pulls me in for a hug, his arms tight around me. I am surrounded by the smell of him that I love. Wool and cigars and his cologne. He holds me like he'd never let me go.

"I know you haven't, sweetheart," he says. "I know you haven't."

He lets go of me but keeps his arm over my shoulder as we look out of the window. From up here, the lines of people waiting to get into the stadium for tonight's festivities look as tiny as ants.

"Icarus and that prince"—the way he says it makes it sound like a slur—"are adding something to *The Labyrinth Contest* to replace Acalle's Heracles story. It doesn't affect you. I promise. Don't worry, Ariadne."

He pulls me in for one last squeeze. "Trust the gods. I do."

"Yes, Daddy," I say.

"That's my girl," he says. "You're the best of them."

"Thanks, Daddy," I say as I leave the room.

I go back to my room and play video games in my underwear for the hours before it's time to get ready for the night's events. It's lame, I know, but I don't know what else to do. I certainly don't want to spend any time thinking.

So I kill harpies on my VR headset for a few hours before I put on another tasteful black dress and head to the stadium.

Now I'm in our box surrounded by my family, waiting for the next episode of *The Labyrinth Contest* to begin. The sun has set outside the stadium's domed ceiling. Tonight is the official opening ceremony.

I'm in the front row with my parents and sisters. Theseus is sitting way down at the other end of the row, near the entrance to the box. I am not close enough to talk to him, but his eyes are on me, flashing with interest and humor.

I force myself to look away, remembering the conversation I had with Daddy. I'm not supposed to be thinking about an Athenian boy. I'm sure it doesn't mean anything anyway. He probably looks at everyone like that. Just because nobody has ever looked at *me* that way before doesn't mean anything to him.

Around us and below us, the stands are packed with people getting to their seats. Families are here with popcorn. Couples on first dates. Old and young and everyone in between. They look at their tickets, and try to get glimpses of my sisters, and laugh when they see themselves on the Jumbotron, while pop music plays on the speakers.

The music stops, the lights drop, and everyone gets in their seats.

Silence envelops the stadium.

A lone panpipe plays, followed by a slow, New Age electronic beat and amplified bouzouki.

A spotlight falls on a woman in a long robe walking out onto the field, holding a single lighted candle; her image is projected up onto the Jumbotron.

Everyone is quiet.

She sings a wordless song, both reverent and eerie.

Then Daedalus's voice echoes through the speakers, much slower and more deliberate than his normal speech. "To the honor of the gods, we dedicate this contest."

Spotlights find three priests in white robes who lead out a cream-colored bull; not quite as large or as white as the bull that rose from the sea years ago, but still very substantial. The altar is near our box, reminding everyone that Daddy has the gods on speed dial.

The priests get to their bloody work. The head priest pulls out his stone knife and leans over the bull, and I want to look away. I've been around enough sacrifice. But I watch. The bull bellows as the knife cuts in, and the smell of blood rises as the animal is drained, butchered, and hoisted onto the fire.

The priests march out, their white robes stained with blood, and the people in the stands mouth their words of petition and praise. I can't say whether they mean them, but I am dead serious as I whisper my own small prayer. The one I always say when the gods are invoked.

Please remove the curse from my brother.

I wonder sometimes if the gods are even listening.

The music stops, and the stadium is again plunged into darkness. The first round of fireworks explodes, reflecting off the domed ceiling. It's the largest indoor fireworks display in history, twice as big as last year, and the people gasp. Daddy's face is illuminated in the flash of phosphorescent light. He looks pleased. That's good. He's been grouchy since we got here because of the empty seats in the stadium. They've covered up three of the sections with purple fabric so it's not so obvious that there are nowhere near eighty thousand people here. I guess that after ten times, teenagers being eaten by a monster isn't the draw it once was. What really matters to Daddy is the viewing numbers worldwide, and we won't know those until later.

The fireworks finish, and the spotlights focus on Daedalus, standing in the middle of the stage. He wears a black double-breasted suit that gives him the illusion of bulk. His tie is printed with tiny images of the Minotaur. A bit of irony for the cameras.

"Ladies and gentlemen." His voice is amplified throughout

the stadium. "Welcome to the eleventh annual Battle against the Minotaur!"

The people cheer at that. But it is nothing compared to the noise they will make later this week, when I lead the Athenians to the maze.

Before the competitors are brought out, we have to be reminded why the children of Athens must die. The audience needs to be reminded of our tragedy—the death of my brother Androgeous, murdered by the Athenians. They need to be reminded that this contest isn't a mindless spectacle. It's divine punishment.

The drums play a martial beat, and a line of our soldiers, in their dress uniforms, marches out onto the field. The leader holds a torch high in the air. Daedalus's voice is solemn now, like the narrator on a war documentary.

"Let us never forget the reason we are here," he says. "We honor a lost life. A lost hope. A lost dream of the nation."

The lead soldier lights the huge chalice in the middle of the stadium, and the bowl fills with flame. On the Jumbotron, there is a memorial film—videos and stills—images of the same smiling, charismatic face, from babyhood to young manhood. My older brother, who I don't remember. Daddy's heir. In the final picture, Androgeous is crowned in laurels and wreathed in metals, the victor of the Pan-Athenian games. It was the last day of his life.

"Let us remember our lost prince, Androgeous," Daedalus says.

My mother's face would collapse in sorrow now if her frozen facial muscles permitted it. She touches the bracelet on her wrist with the image of Androgeous. Daddy glowers.

Theseus looks at his shoes, seeming a little ashamed.

Which he should be.

This happened because Athens couldn't protect my brother.

"What do we deserve?" Daedalus calls to the crowd.

Daddy starts the response. "Vengeance!"

"What do we demand?"

My mother answers this one. "Blood!"

The call rumbles, filling the stadium, back and forth, from side to side—"Blood!" "Vengeance!" "Blood!" "Vengeance!"

Theseus leans back in his chair, like he's watching some sort of exhibition. The fourteen competitors are still backstage, watching from the wings, waiting to be introduced, as tens of thousands of people call for their blood. Right now, Theseus is the only representative of Athens in a stadium full of people calling for vengeance. In his shoes, I'd be afraid.

Instead, he gives me a bemused, flirtatious look that says "Can you believe this?"

Around us the faces of the people are contorted in rage. But Theseus is looking at me like we're the only two people in the world.

I don't look away, even though I know I should.

Daedalus makes a fist and thrusts it high in the sky. The crowd falls silent.

"Who is the tool of our vengeance?" Daedalus calls.

I drop my eyes from Theseus's. I can't flirt with him now. This is too important.

The drumroll begins, and the crowd calls out the syllables "Min-o-taur! Min-o-taur!"

Daedalus spreads his arms wide. "I give you, the monster in the maze, Minos's bull, the tool of the gods' vengeance—the Minotaur."

The spotlights shift to shades of red and orange, and the music changes to a steady beat, deep and ominous. The rhythm echoes off the dome. Hundreds of dancers fill the stadium floor, pulling yards and yards of fabric between them, drawing out the shape of the maze in the center of the field, a map.

The question is always, how will they represent the Minotaur in a way that is adequately terrifying? Every year, we have this problem. It can't be a man in a bull mask, because that's silly. It obviously can't be the Minotaur himself. There's no telling what he might do if you brought him out here. Eat the dancers, for one thing.

A low bellow sounds from every speaker, shaking the ground. People look around, apprehensive. Wondering what is coming for them. Everyone here knows about the Minotaur. Yet the sound of his roar triggers something elemental in most people. A reaction at the most basic level. A rush of fear from the base of the brain.

Not for me. For me, the sound is as familiar as my own breath.

From the center of the fabric maze, a column of white smoke

rises. Red and gold lights flash and a huge form is projected onto the smoke.

It is the image of the Minotaur, twenty feet tall. I shiver because this is no man in a mask, no animated figure, half man, half bull. No, it is a video image of the Minotaur himself, taken from one of the cameras in the maze, and he's enraged, rabid, his eyes red like fire and his mouth smeared with blood.

I glance at Theseus, and I see the horror and disgust on his face.

It hurts my heart.

Looking at the image on the screen, I can understand why he feels that way. If this was the only way I knew the Minotaur, I'd be disgusted, too. But this isn't how I know my baby brother.

Then a ram's horn is blown, amplified a thousand times through the stadium. The lights drop out and we are plunged into darkness.

The presentation is starting.

When the lights come back up, Theseus is gone from his seat.

The lights shift to a bright blue and white—the colors of Athens.

The music changes, no longer terrifying but stirring and patriotic.

"Now," Daedalus says, "the final fourteen, the champions of Athens. This year's competitors."

The crowd cheers raucously, but there is an ugly undercurrent in many of their cries.

In Crete, the audience wants the competitors to do well, but not too well. Many bets will be placed tonight on people's favorites. How long they will last in the maze. How they will do on the obstacles. Whether they can get a hit in on the Minotaur. How many minutes it will be before they die. No one is betting that competitors will win. In Crete, we show support for our monster. We root for the bull.

Daedalus introduces each competitor individually, like he always does. His tone is exactly right. His whole manner suggests that it will be fine. That this is a game. One of them will win. Fame and fortune are in their future, if they can face this one last challenge from the gods.

Vortigern is out first, wearing a warrior kilt, black leather with gold stitching, his upper body bare except for the shoulder plates. His chest is waxed and oiled, shining.

They show his video on the Jumbotron. I don't really pay attention.

It's always the same. We'll have pictures from his home in whatever sad village or tiny apartment he came from—his parents' tears, coupled with their pride, the certainty that he will be the one to win, bringing fame, endorsements, a way out of their hideous lives. There are highlights from competition and training in Athens.

I look around the box, wondering again where Theseus is.

One by one the competitors are introduced. Beautiful,

well-oiled, strong. Exactly like every other year. I watch them, wondering what kind of damage they could do in the maze, how long they will last.

Hippolyta, the Amazon, is thirteenth. She's wearing a short black leather dress, belted in gold. Her fists are clenched, her head high. You would never know what she is facing. Horns and teeth and death in the dark. With the whole world watching.

The music is thumping and the lights are flashing; something is building and everyone in the stadium can feel it. We're almost done.

"We present our final competitor," Daedalus intones.

Thirteen kids are lined up on the stage, in their black leather and gold. A spot is empty in the middle. We are waiting on the lowest-scoring boy of the competition. The kid with the long straggly hair. Although by the end of his makeover that hair was gone.

It is taking too long. Something is off. Even my sisters are looking around curiously.

No one comes out.

The crowd is stomping, demanding the fourteenth Athenian. The music beats in time with their feet, in time with our hearts. The spotlights swoop around the stadium, making wide circles of light on the crowd in their seats, like the last competitor might be hiding among us.

Then, the lights drop out, and a single spotlight illuminates the entrance to the field.

The music stops, and everyone leans forward in anticipation.

A lone figure comes onto the field.

My mouth goes dry.

It is Theseus.

The light follows him as he makes the long walk to the stage.

He is wearing a warrior kilt, his chest bare.

In close-up on the Jumbotron, his quizzical humor is gone. His relaxed energy has disappeared. Instead, he looks flinty and determined. One hundred percent unironically heroic. As different as he could possibly be from when I met him.

What is he doing? With a sinking feeling in my gut, I already know.

The lights come up and he stands facing Daedalus in front of the stage, where the other competitors are waiting, as dumbfounded as the rest of us.

"Why have you come forward, prince of Athens?" Daedalus asks.

"I will face the Minotaur," Theseus announces, his voice clear and strong, reverberating through the stadium. "As the prince of Athens, I have a duty to protect my people."

But he can't.

You don't volunteer to be a competitor. That isn't how it works. There are qualifications, obstacle courses, wrestling matches, a fricking swimsuit competition. The same every year. Required by the gods. Theseus hasn't done any of it.

We cut for commercial, and on the stadium floor, the dancers come back to distract the audience while we are waiting.

Theseus looks relaxed and calm in his warrior kilt.

Like he could wait all day.

My mother whispers to my sisters, "Social media blast—now." They both pull out their phones and start typing furiously. They are telling their millions of followers that something big is going on with *The Labyrinth Contest.*

Daddy will be happy about that.

The commercial break stretches on and my sisters' fingers fly on their screens. This must be why Theseus and Icarus were in the meeting with Daddy. They planned this and kept it a secret.

A red light flashes to tell us that the commercial is almost over, the dancers run off the stage, and Theseus stands in the spotlight, shoulders back, like he's being watched by the whole world. Which he is.

From the center of the arena, Daedalus speaks again. "Theseus, you are the prince of Athens. You are exempt from *The Labyrinth Contest.*"

"I am never exempt from the challenges of my people," Theseus answers. His voice sounds strange to me.

"The king will decide," Daedalus says. "Your Majesty, what is your command? Will Theseus be allowed to compete?"

A spotlight shines on Daddy and he stands, straight, tall, and broad, and he waits a second, letting the crowd suffer in anticipation. All eyes on him. Total silence in the arena.

Daddy's face is stern. "Prince of Athens, this is a bold request. You are asking me to change the rules and replace one of our competitors with you? Is that so?"

104

Theseus's voice is clear. "The gods demanded that the bravest and most beautiful would be the ones to fight the Minotaur. As the prince of Athens, I claim that right. I did not compete in Athens, but I have proven myself many times over. I must fight the Minotaur."

"What do my people say?" Daddy asks. "Should I let the prince of Athens face the Minotaur?"

The crowd roars its approval, and my heart is shouting no, no, no.

"There can be no doubt of his bravery," Daddy says.

I don't want Theseus to compete.

"Or his beauty," Acalle whispers from her seat, and Xenodice giggles.

Fear rises in me.

"Theseus will face the Minotaur," Daddy says. "May the gods help him."

The crowd erupts in cheers.

Theseus joins the competitors on the stage. He calls them into a circle around him. His arms are raised, his voice is deep and resonant. "This year, the Minotaur will be the sacrifice. This is the year the contest ends."

His face is blown up on the Jumbotron. Then he winks. A wink that will launch a million GIFs.

My heart stops. In that moment, I see it. Unless I can stop him, Theseus will either kill my brother or be killed himself.

SEVEN

I LEAVE THE BOX WITH MY FAMILY IN A DAZE.

A sick feeling of impending disaster fills me, like I'm in a car speeding toward an intersection where a puppy is standing, oblivious, and there isn't time to stop it. There isn't time to avoid the collision.

My mind whirls. Is there no way I can stop this? No way I can go back to ten minutes ago when the only boy I've ever fallen for didn't volunteer to try to kill my brother?

My family moves through the crowd of spectators with our perimeter of security guards, my sisters waving and blowing kisses at the fans who are squealing and snapping pictures. I squeeze past them to get close to Daddy. To try to talk him out of this.

I've barely reached his side when Icarus runs up next to us, holding his tablet.

"Your Majesty, King Minos," he says. "In that one commercial break, our viewing numbers doubled. The last ten minutes of tonight's show had the highest numbers since season three."

Daddy stops walking to look at the screen, and we gather around.

He slaps Icarus on the back, "Nice work, son."

Icarus is practically glowing. Daddy is a praise-miser, so it's pretty amazing to get a compliment out of him. Icarus has gotten so wrapped up in getting *The Labyrinth Contest* ratings up, I wonder if he's even thinking about making his own stuff anymore.

Daddy points at the engagement stats. "The social media push right there, during the commercial break, that's really something. Great job thinking on your feet," he says to my mother, who nods graciously, accepting his praise.

He turns to look at me. "How do you like our big surprise?" he asks. "That was the plotline Icarus was working on. That idiot Theseus asked us to put him in there."

My stomach clenches, seeing how proud he is of this. Oh gods. This is going to be even harder than I thought.

"It was definitely a surprise," I say.

"It was a gift from the gods, that's what it was," he says.

"Praise the gods," we say.

We start walking again, and I pull Daddy's sleeve. "Daddy,

I'm not sure this is a good idea. What if he has some secret plan? What if he actually hurts the Minotaur?"

Daddy starts to laugh, his chuckle building to a full guffaw. "Ariadne, this is the Minotaur we're talking about. He's killed a hundred and forty Athenians with no trouble—their strongest and best. I'm sure they all had a plan to defeat him, and you see where it got them. You think this one boy might hurt him?"

"I don't know, maybe?" I say.

"I think you're worried because you have gotten a crush on our Athenian. As I told you, they're nothing but trouble." He pats my hand. "Make sure you get enough sleep tonight, and I don't want to hear one more word from you about getting Theseus out of *The Labyrinth Contest*."

He gives my arm a quick squeeze, then climbs into his limousine after my mother.

I look around urgently, fighting off panic. There is no reason to panic. There must be some way to solve this problem.

Icarus. I have to talk to Icarus. He can help me.

He's absentmindedly getting into his own car, looking at his tablet, and I jump in after him.

"Oh hey, Ariadne," he says, looking up from the screen.

I hit him in the arm.

"Ow," he says. He has forced his face into a look of innocence, but it's not fooling me. "What was that for?"

"Don't give me that, Icarus. How could you?"

"How could I what?"

I run my hand through my hair distractedly. "Did it enter

your mind that I might not want Theseus to be on *The Labyrinth Contest*?"

"Why not, Ariadne? Because you think he's cute? I mean, I think he's cute, too, but that doesn't mean he shouldn't face the Minotaur if he wants to."

"Icarus—" I start.

"I didn't force him into it. He's the one who asked me—begged me, actually, if you want the truth about it."

"You didn't have to let him. You didn't have to tell my dad about it. Admit it, this is about you getting sucked into the ratings game. This is about you being selfish."

"*I'm* being selfish?" he says. "You're the one who is attempting to hold back the biggest thing that has happened to *The Labyrinth Contest* in years because you've got a crush on somebody."

"You didn't have to do this," I say.

He turns toward me and grabs my shoulders. "Ariadne, this thing that you are thinking of having is a fling. Gods know you deserve one, but that's what this is. Summer loving. You do not get to have a future with the prince of Athens. He's not going to be your boyfriend. I hate to be your tough-love friend here, but that's the truth."

"I don't want him to be my boyfriend!" I say.

Icarus raises his eyebrow.

"I don't, but I *do* like him. You know that. Why did you let him volunteer?" I ask.

He squeezes my shoulders.

"You misunderstand things, Ariadne. He was going to ask

your dad to volunteer no matter what I did. He was getting on the show. If you think about it, I'm helping you. I was able to use him to swap out the Acalle/Heracles plotline that *you* asked me to leave out. We had a whole narrative thread to replace— their meeting, fighting, Heracles coaching, sneaking around— and this fills all those holes."

"I don't care about the Acalle/Heracles plotline," I shout.

The car pulls to a stop.

"If you didn't care about it, why did you ask to end it?"

"I was trying to be nice," I say through gritted teeth, following him out of the car.

"Well, that is your problem in a nutshell," he says.

"Icarus, what have you agreed to? What is Theseus going to do?"

He shrugs. "Follow me up to the control room and I'll show you. I have to look over the footage anyway."

Together we ride the elevator up to the 161st floor, Icarus's foot tapping with impatience the whole way, while I force myself not to visualize every bad thing that could come of this. Theseus dead in the maze. My brother dead in the maze. Both of them, dead in the maze.

Once we both get through the retinal scanner, Icarus calls up the video from earlier today.

Daddy is sitting at his desk chair in his office on the forty-ninth floor, looking at some papers.

"Your Majesty, Icarus and Theseus here to see you," Daddy's secretary's voice comes in over the intercom.

"Send them in," Daddy says.

Icarus and Theseus come in.

"Have a seat," Daddy says.

Icarus and Theseus sit down in the two chairs in front of Daddy's desk.

They are smaller than Daddy's chair, so the boys look diminished across from Daddy.

Daddy turns to Theseus. "Icarus tells me you have an idea."

"Sure, sure," Theseus says, rubbing his palms on his pant legs like he's nervous, like he's drying off the sweat. "I want to go into the maze. I want to have a chance against the Minotaur."

"Really?" Daddy says, leaning forward. He's interested. "Then why didn't you go through qualifications and training in Athens?"

"I wanted to enter, but my dad wouldn't let me." Theseus sounds like an aggrieved teenager. "It wasn't fair. I mean, I was the one to kill the Crommyonian Sow. I am the slayer of the Cretan Bull. I'm the person who single-handedly cleared the pirates from our coast."

I cannot get over how much he doesn't sound like himself.

He sounds cocky. Callow. Why?

"I want to be the Hero of Athens," and the capitalization of that title is clear in his words. "How can I be the hero if someone else is the one to kill the Minotaur?"

Daddy turns to Icarus. "What about the sponsors, Icarus, what would they have to say about this?"

Icarus laughs. "The sponsors? They'd be in Elysium. I mean, seriously, sir, we've been dying for something to add zing to our ratings. That's why we were talking about that Heracles/Acalle business, but this, this would be huge. The bump in ratings will be . . . We'd be talking seasons four or five kind of numbers, I think."

"I don't want four or five numbers, Icarus, I want season one numbers," Daddy growls.

"Sure, sure," Icarus says, "depending on what number Theseus draws, how much engagement we can get, whatever happens with other competitors, we could maybe see something in that general area."

Daddy turns back to Theseus.

"What about your father? What will he have to say about this?"

Theseus looks stubborn. "He won't like it," he says. "He won't like it at all, but it will be fine."

Daddy's gloating smirk is hidden, but I know it is there. He loves that Aegeus won't like this. It will be another chance for Daddy to punish the king of Athens for Androgeous's death.

"What about the extra kid?" Daddy asks. "The one you would be replacing? Have you talked about this with the competitors?"

Theseus shifts in his chair. "I haven't mentioned this to anyone but Icarus. I had to keep it secret."

Was he about to tell me when we were running? When he

asked me to help him? Or was he going to tell me something else?

"So they couldn't talk you out of it?" Daddy asks.

Theseus grimaces. "A little," he says. "Plus, I didn't want to embarrass myself if you said no."

"I was thinking that Theseus could replace the lowest-scoring competitor," Icarus says.

"Have you looked at him?" Theseus says. "He's terrified. I don't think he's going to mind hanging out and eating the catering instead of going into the maze."

"It's a good idea," Daddy says. He glances at the priests in the corner. "What would the gods say, do you think?"

The older priest looks thoughtful. "It is a valid question for debate. The gods demanded only that the competitors be the bravest and most beautiful of Athens. It is up to you to determine who those are through the qualifications. If you were to try to substitute someone cowardly or unattractive, I would fear the wrath of the gods . . ."

"Clearly, that is not true of Theseus," Icarus says, the annoyance clear in his voice. "Look at him."

Theseus looks embarrassed.

"There is no denying that the prince of Athens is a hero, and quite attractive," the priest intones. "The gods would have no problems with this plan."

"We have to keep it as secret as possible," Theseus says. "That way my dad can't forbid it. I would never want to disobey a direct order from my father."

"Of course not, of course not," Daddy says. "No one but those of us in this room will know the plan until it is about to begin. Is that possible, Icarus?"

"Totally," Icarus says. "I'm running the staging. That won't be a problem."

The buzzer goes off on Daddy's desk.

"Sir, you have a visitor," his secretary says.

Daddy looks annoyed.

"I get a lot of visitors," Daddy says. "Who is it?"

"The Keeper of the Maze," she says, and I see a guilty look on Icarus's face. Theseus's face shows nothing.

"Send her in," Daddy says to the intercom. "We're wrapping up here."

As the door to the office opens, Daddy says, "Yes, let's do this. Icarus, you handle the logistics."

They shake hands.

I feel sick to my stomach.

Icarus pauses the video feed. "You know the rest," he says. "You can't stop this, Ariadne. Theseus is moving into his room in the accommodations as we speak."

"Why are you doing this to me?" I ask quietly.

I walk over to his inspiration board on the wall, where he's added another self-portrait with wings on, but this time, the color has been leached from the feathers, now they are only silver.

He follows me to the board, lightly touching the picture. "When the prince of Athens lands in my lap and gives me the chance to beat my dad's season one numbers, I'd be crazy not to take that opportunity."

"Since when do you let ratings control your decisions?" I ask.

"Ariadne, if ratings are high, it means people are watching, and if people are watching, I'm doing my job right. If I do my job right, I'll have the chance to have other jobs in the future. That's how this goes. It's business." He turns back to his monitor. "Can I get back to work now?"

"Fine," I say, leaving the room.

As I take the long elevator ride down, I decide to head to my own room. To put my VR headset on and get back to killing harpies.

Therefore, I surprise myself by walking past my own door, down the long hallway, to the elevator that only goes to the maze level.

I am going to talk to Theseus. I am going to find out what he is up to.

I get out of the elevator on the lowest level and go to the frosted-glass door to the accommodations.

I have never been in this hallway before. Never explored where the competitors stay when they are here. I've never had a reason to visit a competitor during filming, and it's the last thing I want to think about on the fifty weeks of the year when *The Labyrinth Contest* isn't on.

I go through the retinal scanner and the door slides open.

The common room is empty and dark, the doors to the individual rooms closed. The competitors are upstairs, at the party my mother and sisters are throwing, showing off their new clothes and shining skin. Icarus said that Theseus was down here moving into his room.

I look at the nameplates outside each of the doors until I find Theseus's. His name is on a piece of paper taped over the nameplate of the boy he replaced.

I press the button to open the door before I can change my mind. The door slides open soundlessly.

Theseus kneels on the floor in front of the large open fireplace that has been built into the concrete wall. In profile, his expression is bleak, empty. Like he's been staring into the abyss. I feel a tug of connection. It is the look of someone who has been pulled into a whirlpool and knows, with absolute certainty, that there is no escaping. That you are going to drown. It is the look I wear on my heart.

Who is this boy?

He stares into the flames, and on the seventy-inch flatscreen mounted over the fireplace, a video image of my mother in a bikini enthuses about the islands' lovely beaches and casinos. As though the competitors will have a chance to visit the casinos before their final gamble against the Minotaur in the dark.

House always wins.

Theseus jumps to his feet as the door glides closed behind me. He runs his fingers through his hair, then gives me a friendly smile, his emptiness stowed away like he's closing a pop-up window on his browser. He steps toward me, and he's truly looking at me. Appraising. Curious. Interested. Nobody looks at me this way.

"Are you here for my last request?" he says, his tone flirtatious. I'm off-balance. I don't know what I was expecting, but it wasn't this. I don't say anything. I just stare at him.

"A joke," he says. "That's a joke."

"Well, it wasn't funny," I say.

"Not even a little bit amusing?" he asks. "Because I am hoping to get another laugh out of you at some point."

I remember him making me laugh yesterday in the VIP box. Before this whole mess.

"I need to talk to you," I say.

"Come in, come in, sit down," he says. "Welcome to my bomb shelter."

It does look like a bomb shelter. A very glam one. His room is built in the same concrete as the maze. It has an industrial luxury, with leather and unfinished wood and stainless steel. Other than a black leather beanbag on the floor in front of the flatscreen, the only place to sit is the bed, cantilevered, standing out from the wall, the black leather–upholstered mattress piled with furs.

It is artfully rumpled, but it doesn't look like Theseus has slept in it.

In the four corners of the ceiling, the cameras sit like spiders spinning their webs, waiting for something to happen. The set dressers were here this morning, getting everything ready, making the beds enticingly comfortable. Outside of lights-out, the competitors have the run of this hallway, visiting each other's rooms as much as they like.

It's crazy what people will do when their days are numbered.

Impending death sells.

I sit down carefully on the edge of the bed, keeping both of my feet on the floor. I'm trying to be businesslike.

It's hard to be professional sitting on someone's bed, but I'm doing my best.

Theseus looks at me expectantly. "Why are you here?" he asks, softly, and it isn't a question, it's an invitation.

"Because you aren't telling the truth, somehow," I say. "You're up to something—You're hiding something."

"Funny," he says, "I could say the same thing about you."

I press my temples in frustration. "Why are you doing this? Why did you volunteer?"

"It's what I said in the stadium," he says. "I can't let these people die and not do something to stop it. I'm the prince of Athens."

"I'm the last person in the world who is impressed by that, right? You've been prince for what, two weeks?"

"Six months," he says.

"Fine, six months. And you're going to immediately get yourself killed? I don't see how that helps your people."

"It helps my people to have a prince of Athens who cares about them. Who would actually *do* something to stop this. Besides, I'm not going to be killed."

"How can you be so sure?" I ask, getting to the heart of my question. "Why do you believe you can do this? Why are you the one who can end this when none of the others could? Don't tell me it's because you're the Hero of Athens. Because that's not a thing. If it was a thing, every city would have one. A Hero of Corinth. A Hero of Sparta. Don't tell my dad, or else next thing you know he'll say we need to get one of our own, and how will they decide which of my sisters gets to take possession?"

He laughs, and I'm irritated at myself for smiling in return.

"I did kill the Cretan Bull at Marathon," he says.

That's our bull. The one that was my mother's lover, the one that went insane.

"How old was that bull anyway?" I ask. "It seems to me he must have been getting pretty elderly by now. I'm not sure about a bull's lifespan, but it can't be too much longer than fifteen years."

"It wasn't easy," he says.

"Sure, sure," I say. "But the Minotaur is not some elderly bull who has been put out to pasture . . ."

"I fought every bandit along the Mediterranean coast," he says. "I killed the Crommyonian Sow."

"The what?"

"The Crommyonian Sow . . . it was this super-dangerous wild pig."

"Okay, okay," I say, "I believe you. But what I'm telling you is that none of those would prepare you for the Minotaur. And I think you know it. I've seen the film. If you were the person you were pretending to be in the meeting with my dad, maybe you would believe that, but you aren't."

"What do you mean, pretending?" he asks.

"You weren't yourself with my father. Don't tell me you don't know it. All that stuff about the Cretan Bull—"

"I told you, it did happen," he interrupts.

"That's not it," I say. "You didn't even sound like yourself."

He shrugs. "Over the course of my life, I've found it's helpful to be what people expect you to be. *The Labyrinth Contest* needs a big, dumb princely volunteer, and I am happy to comply. Now that I've answered your questions"—he leans in a little closer to me—"I have a few of my own."

He picks up my hand and runs his thumb across the backs of my fingers, drops his eyes to my mouth. My throat is dry; I don't say anything.

"I want to know why you pretended you'd never seen me before when you walked into your dad's office. I know you're the Keeper of the Maze, Ariadne, a mask isn't enough to keep me from recognizing the rest of you."

I jump to my feet. "Gods, Theseus, I can't talk about that. You're making this more difficult."

He holds up his hands in apology.

"Making what more difficult?" he says. "Come on, I promise I'll keep my hands to myself. Why are you here?"

I sit back down, pushing away the hollowness I have now that his hand isn't on mine. We do not belong together. We don't.

"I want to know what you are planning. I want to know why you are so sure of yourself. I want to know why you aren't afraid."

He shrugs.

"It's my destiny to be here. To do this. If I'm meant to kill the Minotaur, it will happen. I will do it."

His steely determination is right there on his face. His utter certainty. I feel a great sadness, hiding behind my eyes, waiting to overwhelm me.

He grabs my hand, staring hard at me. "You don't want me to kill the Minotaur," he says with dawning understanding.

"Can't you tell my dad and Icarus that you don't want to volunteer anymore?" I manage.

He laughs. "I don't think that's an option."

He's so close that his breath tickles my cheek. He smells like soap and salt water.

"I've been watching you," Theseus says, still holding my hand. "For years. I've watched the glimpses of you on the *Paradoxes*, and I realized today that I've been watching you without knowing it on *The Labyrinth Contest* when you were the Keeper of the Maze. There's no way you want to be doing this. Our deaths don't make you happy. You don't get off on it. I can tell."

"How can you know that?" I whisper, pulling my hand back.

"I trust you. I know you wring your hands when you are nervous," he says, and clasps his hands around my twisting fingers. "I know you like to wear flannel pajamas with cherries on them. I know that there's no one here who appreciates you.

I know that there's no way you enjoy your job, leading the competitors. You hate the cameras."

He leans in close to me, moving my hair away from the side of my face and putting his mouth next to my ear. "I know you don't want me to die."

I shiver at the whisper of his breath on my skin. I have been wandering dark corridors for too long. Turning and turning and turning in upon myself. He's right. I don't want him to die. He's offering me a tiny crack of light in the darkness.

"Am I right?" he whispers.

I nod.

"Then why aren't you happy about me ending it?"

I look up, and on the wall across from us, the video of my mother continues. Now she is sunbathing on her stomach, her bikini top untied to better bronze her back. The camera pulls out, showing the island, the white sand beach, and the endless wine-dark sea beyond.

For a moment there, I was a girl, talking to a boy. I had forgotten my mother. I almost forgot the maze.

"I have to protect the Minotaur," I say.

"Why?" he asks.

"I can't tell you," I whisper.

"Can you tell anyone?" he asks.

"No."

He laughs. "We're quite a pair, aren't we? I don't know if there are two lonelier people on the island of Crete, or the whole world." His voice is light, but his face has the same look it had when I came in the room, of hopelessness. I want to howl in kinship.

We are sitting so close together.

My pulse is racing.

Then we are leaning toward each other, and it's hard for me to say who touches who first. I am kissing Theseus, and I forget everything else.

I am lost to everything but soft lips and breath and his arms wrapping around me. It doesn't stop, until I have to pull away because it is too much.

Theseus gently touches my lower lip. "I've been wanting to do that since I met you."

"Me too," I hear myself saying. "Me too."

He leans in and kisses my neck gently, barely tickling my skin. His voice is so soft the microphones might not catch it. "Ariadne, I know you don't want me to die. Please help me in the maze, and after I win, I'll take you to Athens with me."

I want to be angry with him, but I can't be. He doesn't know why it's so important that the Minotaur stay alive. I don't doubt that he is telling me the truth. He would take me with him. Take me away from the cameras and *The Labyrinth Contest* and everything that I hate. But he's asked me for the one thing I can never, ever do.

"I can't," I say, shaking my head. "I can't."

That's when the walls start shaking.

"I have to go," I say, jumping up, unconsciously pulling the ball of thread out of my pocket.

"What's this?" Theseus asks. He turns my hand over and looks at the glint of silver in between my fingers.

"Nothing important," I say, slipping the thread back into my pocket, pretending it isn't the most important thing in my life.

"I have to go, Theseus. Good night."

"When will I see you again?" he asks, following me to the door.

"I don't know," I say. "I don't know."

As I leave the room, he says in a low voice, "You are going to help me. I know it."

It's the last thing I hear as the door slides closed behind me.

I run to the entrance to the maze. Quickly, I get my retinal scan. Hook my thread into its place and wait for the emergency lighting to go on.

I'm irritated at myself for not having rainboots. My flats are thin and the floor of the maze is wet. The whole time, Asterion's breathing echoes off the walls around me, making my song small and insignificant against the noise.

Finally, I hang my silver thread on the last hook, the one that tells the maze I've made it through.

Asterion isn't here. He's out in the maze somewhere. He has never not been here by the time I get to his room.

"Asterion," I call, fighting to keep the apprehension out of my voice. "Asterion."

He is breathing somewhere close, but I can't tell where he is, and I am frozen.

My heart beats fast. "Asterion?" I say, and my voice is quiet, frightened.

When he enters the room, his eyes are red and angry, and he swings his head from side to side.

I fight to keep myself calm, but I feel like prey.

"Asterion," I say. "Asterion, look at me."

After a scary second, his eyes clear, back to their own sweet brown color, so sad. He signs, *I'm sorry. I'm sorry.*

He makes the signs again and again, and I wrap my arms around him, petting the fur on the back of his giant head. I hold him as we sit together on the floor, and I wish I could cry. I want to cry for the boy he should be. For the girl I was. For everything. But I can't.

We are like that for a very long time. Then I stand up. I have to be strong, for Asterion.

He is bloodied and cut from whatever he's done in the maze.

I go to the cabinet and get the towel and the bandages.

I try to raise his spirits and mine. "The drawing is tomorrow," I say. "They will get their numbers . . ."

I can't go on. Now that I know that Theseus will be one of them.

My voice trails off.

There's nothing to say.

When he's finally calm, sitting on his bed, he sets the pottery bull beside him and looks up at me, searching and sad. *Why?* he signs, and then points at himself.

"I don't understand," I say.

He makes the sign again, then points at himself.

"Why you?" I ask.

He nods, making the signs again and again. *Why me? Why me?*

"I don't know, buddy," I say. "I don't know."

Asterion finally lays down on his bed. *Don't go*, he signs.

"No," I say, "I'll wait till you're asleep."

As his breathing settles, I ask myself the same question over and over—is there anything that I can do to help him? Anything to end this?

EIGHT

THE NEXT MORNING, I WAKE UP STARVING. I AM STILL
in my clothes from the night before, and I can barely remember coming upstairs, making my way down the hall, and stumbling into my bed.

Checking my phone, I see that I have about twenty missed
texts from Icarus. Must be something about the party last night.
I'll read them after I've washed off the grime of the maze.

I look at Icarus's messages while I eat the toast that arrived
while I was in the shower.

Call me—the first one says, from 9:15 pm, which must have
been a few minutes after I went down to see Theseus. The party
would have barely started.

I wouldn't have thought my sisters had much time to get into too much trouble.

Seriously, call me—9:30.

Oh my gods, Ariadne, call me—9:45.

It goes on from there in escalating levels of excitement and profanity.

I dial Icarus. He picks up after half a ring.

"Oh my gods, Ariadne, where have you been?" he shouts.

"Good morning to you, too, Icarus, did you have a good time at the party last night? Something exciting happen?"

"I don't want to talk to you about it on the phone. You have to see it," he says.

"When?" I ask.

"Now. Right now. Seriously."

"Okay," I say. "Let me get some shoes on."

I pull on jeans, a T-shirt, and some sneakers, then throw a bit of my breakfast toast into the fireplace as an offering and utter my usual prayer: *Please remove the curse from my brother.*

I say it to the ceiling as I close my door. Maybe today someone is listening.

I ride up to the 161st floor distracted. There are so many things on my mind—Theseus volunteering, Asterion's suffering, Theseus's lips on mine.

I go through the retinal scan and then open the door to the control room, where I am met with a truly horrifying scene.

The walls of the darkened room are covered in screens, and

they all show the same scene. Me and Theseus. From every angle.

Icarus is in his rolling chair, and he looks like he got exactly what he wanted for his birthday.

Walking into a room with twenty big-screen televisions showing pictures of me? Not my favorite thing. And that's in a normal situation—one that doesn't involve a hot guy and whatever happened between us. Or didn't.

Icarus spins toward me and stands up. He's shaking his head, holding his arms wide in amazement.

"Why didn't you tell me you were going down to see Theseus?" he says, throwing his arms around me. He's so happy. "If you'd told me, I could have sent a style team. I could have gotten you some better clothes. Some lip gloss . . ."

I duck free from his hug. "It was an accident. It's not what you think."

"An accident? An accident? A freaking gold mine, Ariadne, that's what this is!"

He runs to the keyboard, pushing his hair off his forehead. "Look here." He points to a screen to his left, where he pulls in on a tight close-up. It's when Theseus whispered in my ear. He kissed me there, right before he asked me to help him in the maze, and my neck tingles now, remembering his lips. I'm ashamed of myself, because he was asking me to betray my brother, and what I remember is that his lips felt nice on my neck.

Stupid neck.

"And this!" Icarus says, running over to another screen where you have a clear look at Theseus's face when he was holding my hands, telling me that he knew me. Yeah, it's intense.

Icarus pulls up the same view from the other camera, where you can see me. He pauses the tape. "Look at your face," he says. "Your face . . ."

I do look at myself, and I have to look away because it's embarrassing. How into him I am is as clear as can be, readable by any audience.

"Girl," Icarus says, "I didn't even know you could look like that. I mean, that . . . That's sexy—distill it, bottle it, and sell it, and you'd be a billionaire. Wait, you already are . . ." He holds out his arms in wonderment. "I mean, seriously, you get done talking to me and immediately go down to make out with him? Why didn't you tell me?"

"I didn't *plan* to go down to see him," I say. "Also, I wasn't making out with him. It was one kiss."

"One really intense, long kiss—" Icarus starts.

I interrupt. "If you watched the video, you can see I went down there to ask him some questions, to see what he's up to. Why he's pretending."

"Yeah, yeah, yeah," Icarus says. "Sure. That's definitely why you went down there." He rolls his eyes. "I should have guessed when I saw the first shots from day before yesterday . . . Look at these."

He pushes a few buttons and calls up video of me and Theseus in the VIP box.

Theseus and I are having some pretty serious eye sex.

"It's going to take some careful editing, let me tell you," Icarus says. "I'll have to add some makeup to your face in post, but it will work for a setup. I could have done a much better job with the coverage if you'd told me."

I'm so confused. "If I'd told you what?"

"That you wanted to be a plotline."

Oh no. This is not where I was going. I cross my arms over my chest. "Icarus, I don't want to be a plotline. I went down to find out if I could change Theseus's mind."

He sinks down into his chair, the happiness draining from his face. "You meant that?" His voice is matter-of-fact.

"Yes, of course I meant it. What did you think I meant?"

"I thought it was an excuse for you to go and see him. You must have wanted to be in a plotline."

"No," I say. "I hate plotlines. You know that. That's something my sisters do. Not me. They're on the *Paradoxes*. Not me."

He stands and starts to pace. "You're telling me that you thought you could waltz down to the accommodations and have a flirt-off with a competitor and not have that be turned into must-see viewing? You thought you could avoid the show? Because you don't *want* to be on it?"

"Icarus, you have to delete these," I say.

"Delete them? Delete them?" He's shouting now. "I can't delete them. We don't delete video."

I have my hands on my hips. I'm not giving up.

Icarus is still pacing and shouting. "There is one place, one place, in this whole Panopticon of a city, where you don't have cameras on you. Do you know where that is? It's right here, in this room."

There are not cameras at the center of the maze, either, but there's no reason to mention that.

"You have to listen to me—this is serious," he says. "Anything you do that is interesting in this palace will be made into a show. The only reason that hasn't happened to you before is that you've never done anything interesting before now. You went to see the prince of Athens, who volunteered to be a competitor. You two have stellar sexual chemistry, and he asked for your help on *The Labyrinth Contest*."

"You heard that?" I thought maybe he was quiet enough the microphones might have missed it.

"Yes, yes, I heard that," he says. "Of course I heard that."

He sits back into his chair, then presses a button on one of his screens, and there's Theseus's voice, whisper-soft. "Help me in the maze, and after I win, I'll take you to Athens with me."

"I mean, what a great story!" Icarus says, spinning in his chair.

The consequences are cascading through my head. The most basic rule of life on Crete is that we don't betray Daddy. Not ever. That's why Daedalus signed a lifetime contract. He has as much money as he ever needs for his projects and inventions, but he and Icarus can never not work here. When Icarus's mother didn't want to come to Crete, they left her behind.

"Does Daddy think I'm going to help Theseus?" I ask. "That I'll help our enemy?"

Now Icarus is laughing. "You're worried about your father? He's over the moon. He knows you'll never betray him. He thinks you're a genius. He thinks you did this to build ratings. *The Labyrinth Contest* has been losing viewers. You know the problem as well as anybody. After ten years, people have stopped believing that it's possible to beat the Minotaur. They've stopped believing that the competitors can win. But now? You've fixed it! People will believe . . ."

"Because they think I'm helping Theseus," I say.

"Exactly! Forbidden love? The Keeper of the Maze unmasked? The chance the Minotaur will be beaten? Our ratings are going to be through the roof! By the time Theseus manages to get in your pants, the whole world is going to be talking about you two."

I can envision the storyboard Icarus is planning, and where it heads. I've seen this movie before, but it stars my sisters.

"No," I say, shaking my head. "He's not getting in my pants! I don't even want him there."

Icarus spins and looks at me hard. "Don't give me that. I saw your face. You want this as much as he does."

Icarus and I have been friends for years. We've made fun of my sisters since *The Cretan Paradoxes* premiered. How can he believe that this is what I want? "Being attracted to someone and wanting to hook up with them on camera are not the same thing, don't you know that? Stop, Icarus . . . Just stop. I can't do this."

"Oh, you can, and you will. This is happening, Ariadne. So you'd better get ready. The advertisers are already lining up to increase their sponsorships for tonight's show."

"For tonight?" I'm shouting now. "For the drawing? How do they know? You told them? Without asking me?"

He stands up, putting his hands on my shoulders. "You're wigging out," he says, keeping his voice calm, "and you're probably going to break a blood vessel in your eye, which makeup cannot cover, and looks like crap, so calm down."

He grins at me, turning on his charm, but I fight it, standing straight as a statue.

"How could you?" I say through gritted teeth.

His laugh is brittle. "You think I make these decisions. Adorable. Ariadne, I'm not in any position to say no. If you cared so much about your privacy, you shouldn't have gone down there."

"What are they going to do to me?" I ask him quietly.

"Turn you into a story."

I make it back to my room in a daze. I don't know how to get out of this. I am buzzing with anger. I want to smash the walls, I want to knock everything down. I wish I could cause an earthquake like the Minotaur, but I can't do that. It wouldn't help me anyway. A plotline?

I can't be in a plotline. That's not a thing I do.

I have to clear my head. For that, I need to move.

I head out for a run, taking a different route than yesterday, avoiding everywhere I went with Theseus.

I put on my headphones, turning the beats up loud enough that they can block out the voices in my head. Unfortunately, the volume dial doesn't reach infinity.

Back in my room after my run, I stand under the stream of water in the shower, washing off the sweat and dirt of the road. I don't know how long I've been in here. The steam fills the space around me, hiding me from myself. My eyelids droop. I was up way too late last night.

A sharp rap on the shower door snaps me out of my daze.

"I'm here!" My mother. She opens the shower door and turns the water off, like I'm a child.

This isn't normal for us.

"Okay . . . ," I say, reaching out of the shower for the hook where my towel hangs. She holds it out of my grasp. She is smiling, which is not generally the expression her face wears when she is looking at me.

"I've been waiting for this day for *years!*" She is ebullient.

She still has my towel. I'm dripping wet and naked.

"Can you explain everything after you give me my towel?"

"Not until I have a look at you." She looks me up and down, frowning. "Gods, Ariadne, you look like a satyr. When was the last time you depilated your legs?" She leans in closer. "Or your eyebrows?"

"Mother . . . ," I say, working to keep my voice calm and grabbing my towel from her hand. I tuck it around myself, trying to regain some dignity.

"Don't be sullen, Ariadne, it doesn't become you." She stands next to me, looking at us both in the mirror, and tucks my wet hair back behind my ear. "I have longed for this day—the moment in a young girl's life when she is ready to become a woman. I'm so pleased that I can be here to help you."

I turn to look at her, my foreboding growing. "What are we talking about?"

She's still talking to the face in the mirror, patting her own hair. "I've seen the video of you with our young prince—he is a specimen, isn't he?"

"What, exactly, are you helping me with?" I ask carefully.

Her triumph is terrifying. "Becoming a star, of course. Daddy says the ratings are on a scale we haven't seen in years. Won't your sisters be jealous?"

"I don't want to be a star."

She lets out a low laugh. "Don't be ridiculous. Every girl wants her time in the spotlight."

My panic is rising, and I can hear it in my voice. "I don't want that. I promise I don't."

My mother stands silent for a long moment, looking at me. "You might as well decide that you do, darling, because I am telling you now, you do not have any choice . . ."

"Why not?" I say, and my voice is frantic.

My mother turns toward the mirror, and her own face. She touches her cheek. Her voice sounds far away and dreamy.

"Because the gods demand it."

She stares into her own face, like she's curious about what she might find in there.

"When the gods demand something, you must do it."

She doesn't wait for me to answer but looks at me, taking me in.

"Aegeus's son has come to Crete," she says. "He has volunteered, against his father's wishes, to fight my Minotaur. Not only that, Eros has struck him with an arrow, making him fall in love, or perhaps lust, with one of my daughters—"

"He didn't . . . ," I interrupt. "He hasn't . . . He was pretending . . ."

She laughs at me. "You are a child. I can see the mark of Eros on him, as bright as a brand. It is on you, too, for that matter."

She touches my face gently, and I can see a strange hunger in her eyes. It terrifies me.

"This is being planned by the gods, Ariadne. For my revenge. Now the king of Athens will have to suffer the loss of his son, and the Athenian people will lose the boy who should have been their king. They will suffer as I have suffered and you will draw out their suffering, so I can savor it. What better gift could you offer your mother? What better gift for the brother you lost? Because when the people see this mark upon you, they will believe the ridiculous idea that you could ever possibly help him slay the Minotaur. It's a perfect circle of vengeance. You *will* play your part. As I have."

I stare at her face in the mirror, and I shiver in the cold, pulling the towel tighter around me.

"Now for you." She puts her hands on either side of my face, looking at me with a knowing smirk. I don't like this look. "You tell me you don't want this, and yet, the stink of Eros covers you. I can see it, even now. You are a different girl today than you were yesterday. You will be yet another one tomorrow. Trust in Eros, darling. He may make life difficult, challenging, painful at times, but there is always pleasure there."

She wraps her arm around me. "Now, let's get you ready for your debut. It's time to prepare you for tonight."

I see that light in her eyes. She is planning a makeover.

"No, no, I'm not doing it," I say.

For years, I have successfully resisted my mother's attempts to groom me to her specifications. Despite her comments about everything from the thickness of my ankles to the length of my nose, I have managed to keep her at bay. I have stayed true to myself.

"You aren't in charge of my prep," I say, tightening my towel around myself. She hasn't been for years.

"I am now. After your little trip to the accommodations last night, the mask is coming off. You're mine."

"I'm calling Daddy," I say, finding my phone on the bathroom counter.

She puts her hands on her hips. "Call him. See what he says."

She looks supremely confident, but I'm not worried. As long as he picks up, Daddy will take my side in this. He always does. He has since I was thirteen.

"What's up, buttercup?" he says, picking up on the first ring. "You've got five seconds."

Five seconds. Gods. "Daddy, Mother is trying to make me over. Would you tell her to leave me alone? I can get ready on my own."

"Let her do her thing, sweetheart," he says. "It'll make her happy. I'll see you tonight before you go on. Don't call again."

He hangs up.

I hold the phone loosely in my hand, looking at her. She's triumphant. She knew what he would say before I called. Why would Daddy let her do this? I want to fight, to kick and scream and pitch a fit like a little baby. Like I did when I was thirteen, the first time she tried this. That time, I had Daddy to back me up.

"Now we'll get you ready for the spotlight," my mother says. "Won't it be fun?"

No. It won't be fun, but I don't say it. What would be the point?

"First the waxing!" she calls, like she's hosting a slumber party and it's time for pedicures. She pulls me out of the bathroom.

Standing in the middle of my bedroom is Mathilde, the ancient crone who oversees every aspect of my mother's beauty rituals, forbidding and silent in her black dress. She has my mother's makeup case, as big as a suitcase.

This never happens. Mother and Mathilde never pay attention to what I am wearing or doing, other than to complain about it. Even though Acalle and Xenodice have their own hair and makeup people, they can expect a long visit before any big event.

Why should they bother with me?

I have the mask, so there is no need for makeup. I wear the long chiton. On a normal Sunday, when I'm leading the cows down, I wear jeans and a T-shirt. With the cameras off, there's no reason to dress up.

Mathilde stirs a pot of hot wax. I remember when this happened to Acalle. She has a lot of hair. She's famous for it. What everyone doesn't know is that her lustrous locks are accompanied by black hair on her arms and legs, even a downy fuzz on her upper lip. Her first waxing was a major project. She had barely turned twelve when Mother first came for her, and I heard her screams from my room.

When it was over, she was smooth, hairless—like she came from another species. She never was the same after that.

Mother holds me down on top of the white sheet that Mathilde has spread over my bed.

"Let's look nice for the cameras!" Mother says cheerfully.

"The cameras aren't going to be looking there!" I shriek as Mathilde drips hot wax on a particularly sensitive area.

"I wouldn't bet on that, darling," Mother says, holding me while Mathilde pushes down on the cloth.

What does she think I'm going to be doing? In a flash, I have an image of my sisters and their lovers, artfully lit and posed, in videos that get millions of views, that show everything, while showing nothing. Okay, not nothing. They show a lot.

"No," I say, and I am saying no to her implication, and no to Mathilde ripping the cloth off, and no to the cameras, no to everything.

Mathilde keeps methodically ripping the cloth off my skin.

I scream, but they don't stop.

Until finally, it's over.

My mother slaps my behind, the charm from her bracelet hitting my skin. "That's the last of it, darling; you're smooth as a dolphin now."

She's right. There's not a hair left on my body. I look like a statue. Hairless and smooth. Like my sisters.

"Now, let's get you dressed," Mother says.

In a daze, I look at the back of my closet door, where my chiton usually hangs. The gauzy white dress on the hanger doesn't look like a bedsheet. I can tell it's going to be too low and exposed even without trying it on. And the back? The back is open, with two cords pretending to hold it up.

It's barely a dress. Hades, it's barely a bathing suit.

"I can't wear that," I say, keeping my voice calm. "There's nowhere to put my thread."

My mother pulls out a small silver handbag. "We've thought of that."

Mother and Mathilde are not taking no for an answer. After presenting me with some truly embarrassing underwear, they manhandle me into the dress, double-sided taping and tightening. After the fluffing and draping, they get to work on my makeup.

It's not that I've never put makeup on before—I did grow up in this family—but I've never had my makeup done by Mathilde. She barely speaks, other than brusque orders—open my eyes, close my eyes, don't fidget. Meanwhile, Mother picks colors and palettes and directs the whole business. Eyelashes are glued to my lids, and foundation is spread over my face.

When she lines the inside of my bottom eyelid and my tears well up, my mother's voice is harsh. "No tears," she says. "You'll ruin everything."

As Mathilde starts packing up the makeup, my mother blow-dries my hair.

"Such a nice color," she says when she finishes, letting it fall from her hands. "Thank the gods, because there's hardly time to dye it."

With a firm hand, she ties my hair back in a chignon, away from my face. "So you can't hide behind it," she says. I didn't know she'd noticed.

My mother spins my chair, so I'm facing myself in the mirror. I blink. I can barely believe it's me. Everything about me is emphasized, enlarged, highlighted. Mother stands behind me.

Her face is so beautiful, radiant. Mine is beautiful, too. But strange to me, not like my own. I look like my sisters.

"Tonight is the night the world will finally see your face," my mother says. "Then they will see you, seeing Theseus's face. If all goes well, we'll break the Internet." My mother smiles at me. A real, genuine one. Not something I'm used to. "We're so proud of you," she says. "I was starting to wonder if it would ever happen to you. Your first time."

My first time?

My eyes get wide in the mirror. "No," I say, "it's not what you think. Theseus and I . . . We're not. I'm not doing this. Daddy won't make me."

She rests her hand on the top of my head.

"Oh, darling. Eros has touched you. Daddy and I won't be *making* you do anything. I've seen the footage of you with him in the accommodations. You'll do whatever Eros wants you to. Daddy and I couldn't keep you out of Theseus's bed if we tried."

"I won't do it." My voice is firm. I don't want her to be confused. Even though the thought of Theseus makes me ache. I'm not letting this happen.

"Of course you will, and you'll love it. Nobody refuses the gods."

Her face gets a faraway, dreamy look. "For years, I wasn't sure if it would ever happen to me—not that I didn't love your father, I did and do—but ecstasy? I wasn't sure if the gods would ever grant me that."

It hits me like a lightning bolt. She's talking about the pasture. About the wooden cow.

"The bull?" I say, my voice louder than I'd intended.

The familiar tight, cruel expression falls across her face. Then she laughs. "You disapprove? I ask you, Ariadne, how could I have been wrong when the gods made it so?"

NINE

I NORMALLY MAKE THE TRIP FROM THE PALACE TO THE
stadium by myself (if you don't count my bodyguards) in my own
SUV, playing games on my phone.

Not tonight. Tonight, my mother is managing transporta-
tion.

It's an hour and a half before showtime, and she leads me
through the lobby, the few people who aren't down at the stadium yet looking at us curiously. From beyond the massive
doors, there is a buzz of noise. Voices. The clicking of cameras.
The *whoomp, whoomp, whoomp* of a helicopter's rotors. A scrum.

When the golden doors slide open, I see my mother's shining black SUV pulled up in the valet lane. The doors of the car

are open and waiting, like we're doing a getaway from a bank robbery.

Then my bodyguards whip off their suit coats and hold them up, blocking anyone from seeing me. As they push me toward the SUV, I see nothing but the flashes of cameras held high in the air trying to get a shot of me over the top of the curtain of menswear. I make an undignified leap into the car and then settle back into the seat. How do my sisters make this look easy?

Once we're in the car, the driver peels out, nearly sideswiping one of the photographers, who was pressing his camera to my window, trying to get a shot of me.

I look at my mother in shock. "What happened? Why were they here?"

"To see you, darling. I tipped them off, of course," she says, looking at herself in a small mirror as she applies her lipstick.

"Why?" I ask.

She shrugs. "We have to get the buzz going. So that when you and Theseus get down to business, the whole world will be watching."

"I'm not doing what you think I'm doing," I say.

"Maybe so, darling, but I'm pretty sure they got a picture of your ta-tas when you were getting into the car, so I suspect you're going to be doing a lot of things that you aren't used to tonight."

I look down and see that the leap into the car has made my dress precariously low. I pull it up.

The SUV drives through the stadium gate, where a golf cart and a driver are waiting. My mother comes with me in the golf cart, which doesn't really seem necessary, and we drive to the greenroom in the bowels of the building, where Icarus is waiting for us. My mother hands me off to him, like I'm a baton in a relay race. Like I'm a six-year-old girl again. Like she's afraid I might bolt.

Which I have considered.

She gives me a quick air kiss, taking one last look at me. "I'm so proud of you, darling." Then she's back in the golf cart, riding away toward her spot in the VIP box with my sisters.

Meanwhile, Icarus is giving me a full up-and-down. "You look amazing, a-maz-ing. I told you that you would."

"Shut up," I say, walking into the room, where a spread of snacks, a widescreen, and a big comfortable sofa are waiting for me.

Icarus shifts to business. "We need to talk about the plan for tonight."

"I'm assuming I'll be doing the same thing I always do. Handing out cards, guiding competitors. Only this time, in double-sided tape."

"Not quite," he says. "Watch."

He points at the widescreen mounted on the wall. It's a live feed of the pre-drawing show. The sound is muted, but I don't need the sound on to know what they are saying. It's a tradition, like the rest of *The Labyrinth Contest*. An hour-long wrap-up of everything that has happened up to now. You could watch it this year or the first year and nothing would change but the faces of the Athenians who will die.

Of course, this year *is* different. Theseus volunteered. My stomach twists as I see the image of Theseus walking out onto the field from yesterday. Icarus turns the sound on.

Daedalus's practiced announcer voice comes through the speakers. "Tonight, we have something new in the history of *The Labyrinth Contest*."

Theseus's face is back on the screen, but this time, he's looking at me. It's video from last night, in the accommodations. The video is taken from over my shoulder, so you have my view of Theseus's face. Full of desire.

I have a rush of my own feelings, answering, an echo of last night. Can it really have even happened? How can we have both been so naked, even though we were fully clothed?

Then Theseus's voice, full of secrets, over a black screen. "Ariadne, I know you don't want me to die."

"Betrayal," Daedalus intones. "Forbidden love. An untold story. All will be revealed tonight. After the drawing, we have a very special episode—*The Princess, Unmasked*."

At the cut to commercial, Icarus mutes the widescreen.

I'm speechless for a full ten seconds, opening and closing my mouth like a fish on land. Finally, I croak out, "You're making me into a very special episode, Icarus? No, no."

"It's going to be epic," he says. Like this is a normal show. Like he is telling me about a new plotline with my sisters and

148

Spartan identical twin brothers and mistaken identities. Like this isn't *me* we're talking about. I don't do this.

Not anymore.

"Watch this," he says, linking his phone into the widescreen.

"Do I have to?" I say.

"Yes, you do," he says. "You've got to see what we're doing. The first half is everything that has happened before—watch."

The title sequence and theme music for *The Labyrinth Contest* plays, the same as every year, except VERY SPECIAL EPISODE is written in curving script over the show's logo. Then, after the fade to black, we see something different from every other year. Instead of opening with the stadium and the drawing, the video shows the *Parthenos*, the Athenians' ship, sailing, with a hero shot of Theseus standing at the bow.

Then Daedalus speaks: "*When the competitors came from Athens this year, little did we know that young love would awaken.*"

I make a gagging noise.

"Shut up, Ariadne," Icarus says. "Watch. You need to see what you have to do."

"*Their connection was obvious to any who were watching. Attraction at first sight.*"

The video cuts to the scene of Theseus and me together in the hallway outside Daddy's office. Theseus trying to talk with me. "You're the Paradox that *I* want to watch."

"Oh gods, it's so cheesy," I say.

"Yeah, that's *totally* what you were thinking at the time," Icarus says, his tone dry.

When the camera cuts to me, I'm blushing, but I don't look like I think he's cheesy.

"I'm not a Paradox," I say, there in the hallway.

"Yes, you are," he says, "you most definitely are . . ."

"We'll go to commercial here," Icarus says, "and then, when we get back, we'll have this . . ."

Icarus has put together a truly embarrassing sequence, a solid minute of me walking the hallways of the palace looking mopey, with a heartbreaking pop song in the background, interposed with film of Theseus staring into his fireplace.

"Icarus!" I say. "A music video, really?"

"Listen," he says, irritated.

Daedalus's voice is a near-whisper. *"Who would have guessed that attraction would be enough to draw the most private of princesses down to see Theseus in the wee hours of the night?"*

I watch myself on the surveillance feed, rounding the corner of the hallway that leads to the accommodations. Then I'm opening Theseus's door. Once we're in his room, it's high-quality video, reminding me that the rooms are designed as stages, always ready for action. The video that Icarus has made doesn't show Theseus kneeling on the floor; it doesn't show the bleak look in his eyes. That must not be the look they're going for.

Instead, Theseus runs his fingers through his hair and I say, "I need to talk to you."

"We'll go to commercial here," Icarus says.

When the video resumes, Theseus and I are sitting together on the bed. We are not touching, but when Theseus says, "Why are you here?" and I look at his mouth, the tension between us is palpable. When he touches my hand, leaning in toward me, the camera is on him, not me, and his soulful look is basically designed to make young girls swoon. Icarus has taken out everything I told Theseus. There's nothing about my suspicions of him. Nothing about his conversation with Daddy. Nothing about my secrets.

Instead, Icarus has one shot of me looking lovestruck, and then he jumps right to Theseus saying, "I trust you . . ."

Then Theseus asks for my help, and next we are kissing.

I look away from the kissing, not wanting to watch myself. "The kissing happened first," I say. "He kissed me and then he asked for my help."

"If you look at it honestly, Ariadne, it's more that you kissed him," Icarus says.

"I didn't!"

"Would you like to rewind it and watch again?"

"No. No I wouldn't."

"We moved the order because it's better this way. It makes more sense."

Back on the video, there is no mention of the earthquake, just me saying, "I have to go," and walking away.

The camera stays on my back as Theseus whispers, "You are going to help me. I know it."

I can see that the viewers of the world will be mad at me for not telling him I'm going to help him. How could I let someone that cute die?

"What have you storyboarded next?" I ask, my voice dull.

"We'll show you and Theseus's reaction to whatever number he draws," Icarus says.

"And then?" I ask, dread building in me.

"You aren't going to like it," he says.

"Seriously, Icarus? You're just now figuring this out? I don't like *any* of this. In fact, I hate it. I want my mask back."

"Well, that isn't happening," Icarus says. "This is your own fault, Ariadne. Nobody made you go down there to see him. Nobody made this happen but you."

"Stop saying that. What are you planning, Icarus? Tell me!" I shout, banging my fist down on the table of snacks.

"Calm down, calm down, sister," he says. "Let me show you."

He takes out a drawing pad where he has storyboarded the second half of his very special episode.

A girl in very high heels is walking across a crowded dance floor. "Who is that supposed to be?"

"You," he says.

"I don't have shoes like that, Icarus. I can't walk in those."

"Your footwear is the least of our worries, Ariadne," he says. He flips the pages of the drawing pad, and I walk across the crowded dance floor, looking for someone, and then I find Theseus.

Icarus points at the picture of Theseus and me together. "This is where you'll tell him that you want to talk to him alone."

He flips the page, showing Theseus and me walking down

the long hallways of the palace. At least he has me carrying my shoes.

Then we are in a strange crooked room together, sitting on a chaise longue.

"Where is that?" I ask.

"A new room that your mother made," Icarus says. "This is where you are going to tell Theseus that you will help him in the maze. That you will help him kill the Minotaur."

The blood drains from my face.

This is an impossible situation.

I can't even explain the things that Theseus makes me feel. Like I'm bound to him by an invisible rope. Like I've been asleep my whole life, and I finally woke up. Like I am on fire.

But then there is the Minotaur in the maze, alone. If I don't protect him, no one will.

"I can't help him, Icarus."

"No one wants you to actually help him. You're only going to tell him that you will."

"I'm going to *lie* to him?"

Icarus looks at me, incredulous. "Yes, you're going to be lying. This is about ratings. The people will *believe* that Theseus has a chance in the maze, which will make it way better when he is finally defeated."

"Won't it occur to everyone that Daddy will stop me, since it's on TV?"

"Willing suspension of disbelief is an amazing thing, Ariadne."

"I can't," I say.

I'm so angry. But that's not enough. Sad? That, too. I could have guessed what they were going to do. He told me they were going to. My mother told me. I guess I didn't really believe them.

"This isn't me," I say. "I'm not doing this."

His voice is placating, but dead serious. "Oh yes. You are. Look, Ariadne, I'm sorry, but this is happening."

A loud knock sounds on the greenroom door. It swings open, and Daddy walks in, followed by his bodyguards and the priests with their doves in a cage.

"Daddy!" I cry, letting myself be wrapped in one of his big hugs.

"Sweetheart," Daddy says, patting me twice, then pushing me away. "Don't rumple the suit."

I have a sinking feeling in my stomach.

He looks me up and down and whistles. "Your mother did her magic, I see. You look beautiful."

He isn't going to help me.

Then he looks at Icarus. "Beat it, kid. I need to have some words with my girl."

Icarus nearly trips over his feet getting out the door.

Daddy looks at the taller of his bodyguards. "Mix me a drink, would you? Make it a stiff one."

The other bodyguard stays by the door.

Any room where Daddy might be coming is stocked with a locked bar cabinet, his favorite gin and vermouth, a jar of olives, and a martini shaker. Cold glasses. New ice on the hour.

"One for my girl, too," Daddy says, "now that I think about it."

This is a first.

"Sit," he says, pointing at the sofa. I lower myself down carefully, pulling my dress down over my thighs. Daddy takes the spot beside me and watches his bodyguard mix our drinks. When I get mine, it's so full I have to hold it carefully to not have any splash out.

"To new beginnings," Daddy says, clinking my glass.

He watches me take a small sip. I splutter, it burns.

Daddy pats my knee, then takes a long pull from his own glass. "Don't worry, sweetheart, you'll get used to it."

I hope not.

"Let me ask you something," he says. "Why did you go see that Athenian in his room?"

His voice is calm, conversational.

"I went to see Theseus because I thought he was lying." It feels so long ago now. "I thought he was planning something. That he might hurt the Minotaur . . ."

"Hmm," Daddy says, taking a sip from his drink. "That's not what your mother thinks."

"No," I say, and my voice breaks a little, and I'm stumbling, because I'm not used to justifying myself. "Mother thinks I went down there because of Theseus. But that's not it . . ."

"Is this that thing you were asking me about yesterday when we were leaving the stadium?" he says, and there is an edge to his voice. He's mad at me.

I nod.

"What did I say?" he asks, leaning closer.

"Not to worry about it," I whisper.

"So you went to see that boy anyway?"

"Daddy," I say, looking at him, searching for some sign that he is listening to me. "I thought if Theseus was up to something, I should find out what it was. I was only trying to help—"

He holds his hand up, stopping my explanation. "What do you think this is, Ariadne? A game?"

His voice has none of its normal soft tone. It is hard, cold. His disapproval radiates off him.

His bodyguard is making another martini. The ice clinks in the shaker, the only sound in the silence of the room.

My eyes are on the floor. He's never looked at me like this. I think of the times I've stood by when Daddy has looked at my sisters in exactly this way. The many times that their selfishness had dishonored the gods. With shame, I remember my own righteous feeling, that I was the one the gods were smiling at, because I was doing what they wanted, what Daddy wanted, with no separation between the two things.

"You're being selfish, Ariadne. Six months ago, when Aegeus had an heir show up, out of nowhere, killing monsters left and right, a regular fricking hero, I prayed to the gods." He stands up and starts pacing, like he can't bear to be next to me anymore. "I prayed that they would do something about it. How is my vengeance complete if Aegeus has a son?" He stands in front of me, while I look at my shoes.

"Look at me, Ariadne," he says.

I look up, and Daddy looms over me, his finger in my face, his breathing heavy. "Then look what happened. The kid showed up here, and he volunteered to fight against *my* Minotaur. In *my* maze, and there's not a thing Aegeus can do about it. And now you . . . You . . . My daughter . . . The only sensible one of my children, I thought, before today . . . You start making trouble? Interfering? Worrying? Making kissy-faces with an Athenian in *my* palace?"

He's so angry. I've never had him this angry at me before. He never shouts at me like this. He always listens to what I have to say. With my sisters, it's a different story, but he's always been different with me.

"Daddy, I didn't mean—"

"Hades take you! You are my child. You are interfering with things you don't understand."

He takes a deep breath, bringing himself back under control. His face shifts from anger to disappointment.

"This is my fault," he says, shaking his head. "I have always involved you in decision making. I have let you fight above your weight class. I forget that you are still a child. I forget that you are a girl."

I'm thinking, *No, no, no.* No, I'm not a child. I'm not a girl. No, this isn't your fault. No to everything.

He sits back down beside me heavily, and his bodyguard takes his glass from his hands, then gives him a new one.

Daddy's face is tired and sad, but full of compassion for me. He puts his arm around me again. "Drink up, baby girl, and listen to your old man," he says.

Obediently, I take another sip of the drink, and my head spins.

"You are a good girl, but I have given you too much freedom. This is the gods' way of telling me that. Icarus told you about the storyline he has planned? I have to teach you obedience. The gods require it."

I look at my shoes. These ridiculous high-heeled platform shoes that my mother chose. My painted toes. The very special episode. I nod at Daddy. "Yes, Icarus told me."

"It is your penance," Daddy says. "You tried to interfere with the gods' plans, and this is the penance they demand."

The priests in the corner say, "Praise the gods."

The last time I had to do penance, I was thirteen.

I had stopped taking the cows down to the maze for sacrifice. It wasn't a decision. More like, I woke up one morning and I couldn't do it. I couldn't suffer through their bellowing fear one more time. I refused. For three weeks I held out. Mother threatened me. Daddy wouldn't let me leave my room. They wouldn't let me go down to comfort my brother. The Minotaur would not take the cows from anyone else. For three weeks, the buildings rumbled under our feet as the Minotaur's rage—and hunger—grew.

After a month, the Minotaur finally caused a big earthquake, magnitude seven. In the old city, a thousand people died. Because I didn't do my job.

People died, and it was my fault. The Minotaur suffered, and it was my fault. The gods knew that I was a selfish girl who cared more about herself than her brother and her people.

I paid my penance to Poseidon—god of the sea, god of earthquakes, god of horses, our patron god. The god who sent the white bull.

There is a concrete block with an iron ring in it placed on a sacred beach at the low-tide line. It is where they tie the horses that are sacrificed to Poseidon. The ones that are swallowed by the waves. They bound my leg to the ring with a long length of chain, and we waited.

From the boardwalk, my parents watched to make sure the penance was correctly observed. To make sure that no one took it easy on me because I was young, or because I was their daughter. Only through suffering could I be cleaned of my fault.

I thought I would drown many times that day, when the water held me down, and I struggled to get to the surface. Each time, I would barely grab a breath before the next wave smashed me under. By the time the tide receded, I was so weak I could not stand. I lay there, shivering in the sand until the waves hit the low-tide mark, and the priestess came and unchained me. If the chain had been a little shorter, I would have drowned.

I look up at Daddy. "Daddy, penance? For this? I wasn't interfering. I didn't mean to kiss Theseus, it happened—"

I stop myself, seeing his face.

"Are you questioning my judgment?" Daddy asks.

"No, Daddy, no, I'm not."

He holds up his hand. "Priests, let us see if the gods agree. Let's do an augury."

The priests in the corner jump to attention, and the doves in the cage coo nervously.

"No, Daddy," I say. I hate the auguries. "You don't have to do that. I'll do it."

"Oh no," Daddy says. "We must follow the rules—if the king's judgment is questioned, we must refer the matter to the gods."

"All honor to the gods," the priests intone in unison, beginning the recitation that will lead up to the augury. I stand without even deciding to, because I have been through the words and ritual so many times that it is inscribed into my body. The priests' words are a blur to me, because my attention is on the cage of doves. There are three in there, and they cluster at the back of the cage when the priest reaches in for one of them.

He gets one, and he holds it, tight in his fist, while the other priest closes the cage. My own heart is beating as fast as that small, frightened bird. Everything I do, it seems, leads to the death of innocents.

The priests stand at the small altar at the back of the room. Another fixture of any place Daddy might be coming.

The bird's cooing is silenced by the knife the priest keeps at his belt, and red blood stains the white feathers. The dove's small body rests on the granite top of the altar.

Quickly and expertly, the priest opens its chest cavity and pulls out the viscera. The liver and intestines, where the gods' messages to us are written. While one priest spreads out the bloody organs, the other consults a small book he has taken from his pocket, then announces what it means.

His voice is deep and resonant. "I see the signs of first love, and death. Putting on a false face. A child's obedience to the father."

"The gods have spoken," the two priests intone together.

"Amen," Daddy says.

I whisper "amen" too, because it's what you say, and because my fate is sealed, and to honor that small bird, now an unrecognizable pile of bloody flesh and feathers on the altar, left behind for the silent cleaning women who will come in after we leave. Amen for the two other doves, safe in their cage for now. Amen for me.

I still want to argue. I want to fight. How can I fight against the gods?

"I need for you to tell me that you will obey," Daddy says. "You will obey the gods."

"Yes, Daddy," I say, choking it out. "I'll do what you say. I'll do what they want."

He gives my arm a squeeze. He points at my drink, his voice gentle. "Finish it."

I down the alcohol, feeling the burning reaching down to my heart.

"Now, promise that you will betray me," he says. "It won't be too hard for you."

"What? I would never betray you," I say.

Daddy starts laughing. He laughs so hard tears run down his cheeks. "Of course you are going to betray me. You're turning into a woman and that's what women do. They fall for pieces of crap and betray their fathers. It's the way of the world. However, for today, I merely need for you to pretend."

He gestures to my outfit, my hair, the whole awful thing. "Your mother and Icarus must have given you the general idea. Go up for the drawing and look pretty for the cameras. Go to the godawful dance party your mother has planned, look pretty for the cameras. Dance with the idiot. Go wherever Icarus has you set up and tell Theseus that you will help him. Be convincing. Make the best very special episode in the history of Crete."

"Daddy," I say. "I can't lie like that. I can't promise to do this."

"Don't interrupt me." His voice is steel. "You can. You will. The gods demand it. The gods want this to happen. That's why they've put the mark of Eros on you. Anyone can see it. Theseus wants your help in the maze. You pretend to help him. For the time that he's alive, you can plot and scheme with him in front of the cameras. If the gods are truly favoring me, he'll draw number fourteen tonight, and we'll get to stretch it out over two full weeks. We'll put it on *The Labyrinth Contest*, and Aegeus will have to watch it, like everyone else. His hopes will be raised. My vengeance will be even sweeter when Aegeus thinks there's some way out for his son. Don't forget, the gods want me to succeed. Everything we have in Crete is because of the gods. When they ask us to do things, we do them. And they reward us."

"But, Daddy—" I say.

"No pouting, baby. It'll make your face ugly for the cameras."

Then he stands up, and he and the priests and the bodyguards leave. With him goes my last chance of escape.

How could the gods ask this of me? How could they make me? Then I remember, these are the same gods who created an infant monster and turned a six-year-old into a murderess. They can make me a liar, too.

"Yes, Daddy," I say to the door where he has gone.

TEN

THE DOOR OPENS AND ICARUS COMES BACK INTO THE room carefully, like someone who has barely survived a tornado. He straightens his glasses. He doesn't ask me what happened with Daddy. He doesn't have to. I'm sure the greenroom cameras feed directly to his phone.

"Told you," he says, and pulls me in for a quick hug. There is so much we both leave unsaid.

A makeup artist follows him into the greenroom and quickly repairs my makeup.

When she leaves, Icarus pulls out the microphone and power pack that he'll pin to the inside of my dress and the earpiece I'll wear so I can get the stage directions during the drawing.

"Let's get you wired up," he says.

I can't hide the hurt in my eyes, and I don't try.

"Don't look at me like that, Ariadne," he says as he expertly clips the microphone to the inside of the front of my dress, hiding it in my cleavage so the cameras won't see it. A gesture both intimate and businesslike. "You're going to be okay."

His walkie-talkie screeches. "Ten minutes to airtime."

"All right," he says, closing his black bag. "Let's get this show on the road."

I pull myself together. I've done this so many times, I'll be on autopilot.

"Ready," I say, grabbing the burlap bag that holds the cards the competitors will draw, the pieces of light-colored wood, thin and strong, exactly the size and shape of a credit card. Each with a number branded into the wood. The number that will determine the order in which the competitors will face the Minotaur. The order they will die in.

"Wait," I say, looking at the silver bag that is hanging from my wrist, holding my phone and my thread. "I can't carry this up there. It will look ridiculous."

"Leave it in the greenroom," Icarus says.

"You want me to leave my thread behind?" I say, my voice full of sarcasm. Because I'm never supposed to leave the thread anywhere. If Daddy and Daedalus could have figured out a way to implant it into my skin, I don't doubt they would have done it.

"Fine," Icarus says. "Put it in the bag with the cards."

"I'm sure one of the competitors would love to get their hands on the key to navigating the maze."

"So don't give it to them," Icarus says. "Duh."

As we walk out of the greenroom, the chill of the air-conditioning raises goose bumps on my bare shoulders and back. I miss my chiton. I miss my pockets. I miss the mask.

I climb into the golf cart next to Icarus and let him drive me to a spot under the center of the stadium floor. The maze is farther down, below us, under our feet. We're nowhere near where I'm supposed to be. I'm supposed to be hiding in a small room, waiting for the dimming of the lights and my long, slow walk across the field. Not tonight.

Icarus brings me under the stage, into the large open area that holds the stored scaffolding and lights for events at the stadium. Right in the center of the floor, directly under the stage, there's something new. They have placed a mechanical lift like you'd see at a construction site. On top of the lift is a circular platform barely big enough for someone to stand on. Surrounding it, they have a metal cage that runs from the floor to the ceiling, twenty feet up. For safety?

Far above, in the ceiling, there is a round hole, exactly the same size as the circular platform on the lift. I raise my eyebrow. "Who is going to be riding that?"

"You." Icarus makes the ta-da motion with his hands. "Isn't it cool? It was my idea. Don't worry, we tested it, you'll be fine!"

He opens the door to the cage and I step up and in. Before I can ask him what in the world I'm supposed to do now that I'm here, or how the thing is going to operate, or anything, really, his walkie-talkie starts squawking with panicked voices. "Icarus, Icarus, the hologram is down, we need you right away."

Icarus spins away from me, his mind already on the next emergency. "Wait there and listen for your cue," he says as he runs to his golf cart. "It's automated. You don't need to do anything but look pretty."

Great, because I'm so good at that.

His golf cart speeds away, and I'm alone in a cage in the vast open space under the stage. Listening to the hum of the fluorescent lights. I could be the only person in the world. I try not to think about my mother. Daddy. Theseus. I load the coverage of *The Labyrinth Contest* on my phone.

The camera pans the stadium. The stands are full now. No more purple fabric to cover empty seats. The word must have gotten out. The mechanism on the platform clicks on with a hum. On my phone, I can see giant red numbers counting down. It's about to start. The red numbers go to zero. My platform starts to rise, slowly. The cheering crowd is tinny coming out of the speaker in my phone, but it is a muffled roar from the stadium above me. Then the screen goes black and silent. The crowd above me stills.

I know the same velvety blackness is being projected on the Jumbotron in the stadium above. It is not the emptiness of the cameras being off. Not the blank screen of technical difficulties. This is the blackness of filmed darkness. The cameras are taking us somewhere. Somewhere dark. It is familiar to me.

The silence stretches, and I can imagine the audience fidgeting in their seats, wondering what is happening. Then we hear it. Breathing. Animal breathing. Daedalus's voice is velvet. "From the darkness . . ."

The blackness shades to gray as the camera starts moving. It glides through the tunnels of the maze, down toward the center. It is not a view anyone here has seen before. The only people who walk the maze are me, the competitors, and the Minotaur. No cameraman would ever dare go down there. No cameraman would survive.

Daedalus must be using a remote-control drone camera for the shots. It travels down, down, deeper into the maze. Closer to the Minotaur's room. Where the light is always on a little.

From his breathing, I can tell he's sleeping. I picture him as I see him after I sing him to sleep. Curled up on his concrete bed. His knees pulled into his chest. Each of his vertebra standing out on his back. His human arm thrown over his hairy bull's face. His blue blanket beside him. A boy. A lonely boy.

That is the last thing Icarus wants people to see. A drum sounds, thumping, echoing off the walls of the maze. The drone must be equipped with speakers.

Daedalus speaks again. "Up from the darkness rises . . ."

A bright red light flashes, highlighting the concrete walls, the bones on the floor. The people start to cheer. This is why they are here.

"A monster," Daedalus says.

The Minotaur's roar begins before the camera makes the

final turn. The camera shows a giant shape looming over it, and then it is smashed.

The feed cuts to the stadium above, the people stomping, the lights flashing, the torches and smoke on the field. My cage rattles with the tremors. A small earthquake as the Minotaur rocks the foundations in his rage.

I watch the video of the people cheering, excited. Thrilled. Their own private, personal monster. I grab the bars that hold me in the lift. The bars of my cage.

On the small screen of my phone, I have the uncanny experience of seeing myself make the long walk between the rows of torches across the field. I'm wearing the long chiton. The mask. Holding the burlap bag that carries the fate of the Athenians. But of course it isn't me. Because I'm down here, under the stage. Yet it is me, too, because it moves like me, looks like me. It's a hologram. It's me from last year, making the same walk I've always made. The same way I've always made it.

"Tonight," Daedalus intones, "you will see things never seen before. Secrets will be revealed. And tomorrow, death in the dark."

"Get ready," Icarus says in the small speaker in my ear, and the contraption I'm standing on shudders awake. As my holographic image makes the long walk to the stage, my platform begins rising, slowly. At the same time, the fourteen competitors in their black leather and gold make their procession onto the stage. Looking at this silent, masked, cloaked version of me.

It is solemn and strange and mysterious. Slowly I rise, and

as I rise, I watch myself above. Watch smoke swirl around my own masked and cloaked figure. The spot where the hologram of me was standing is now a cloud of smoke and light, opaque to the crowd. And to the video on my phone.

Right when my head is about to come up through the floor, I turn my phone off and drop it into the burlap bag with the competitors' cards and my thread. I let myself be raised up through an image of myself.

When a mechanical breeze blows away the fog, I am standing there, in front of the cameras. No mask. No chiton. In a backless dress and double-sided tape. Revealed to the world. For the first time in my life.

The gasp from the crowd is audible.

The competitors gasp, too, their faces pale. It's like they've seen a ghost.

Not Theseus. He lights up as soon as the fog clears.

There are millions of eyes on me—the competitors, the people in the stadium, the cameras beaming me to millions of viewers worldwide—but right now, none of them matter. The only person I care about seeing me is Theseus. It's like we two are the only things in focus, and everything else is a blur.

The stylists have done their work, brushing his hair back and smoothing his skin. His muscular legs are bare in the warrior kilt. My hands itch to touch him.

How did this happen? I just met the guy.

Gods. Is this the mark of Eros that my parents were talking about? Did the gods do this to me? If so, I hate them even more for it. It was one thing when they made me do things I didn't want to do—but so much worse if they are making me want things, too.

I stare at Theseus.

What is he thinking? The last time I saw him, I told him I could not help him. But he looks at me like none of it happened. Or not like that, exactly. More like it happened, but it isn't over. Like we're playing a game where he needs another turn. I have an involuntary shiver thinking about one more round. I want that, too.

The stadium lights drop, plunging us into darkness. The constellations are projected onto the ceiling of the dome, reminding us that the gods are watching. The amplified drums beat their slow, inexorable rhythm, like the heart of some giant subterranean creature. The stage vibrates under my feet. The ritual takes over, pushing away thoughts of Theseus.

The lights flash on, shining spotlights on me and the competitors, and the cameras track forward on their cables.

I don't have to think anymore. I do what I've always done. I walk to Hippolyta. As the highest-scoring competitor, she is first. She is beautiful, in full makeup, her hair elaborately curled, like this is the final round of a beauty contest, not an execution.

I'm not wearing the mask, of course, but I have the same constriction of my vision that the mask always brings. The tight focus on each competitor. I hold out the burlap sack, and she draws her card. She doesn't look at it yet. No one does. No one wants to risk the bad luck that would come from peeking out of turn. Then I pass to the next. Down the line I go. Finally, I get to Theseus. He stands relaxed, his feet spread wide, like he's getting ready to run a race that he's sure he'll win.

I hold the burlap bag out to him. I feel lighter from being around him.

There is only one card left, next to my phone and ball of thread, heavy in the bottom of the bag.

Theseus asked me about it last night.

He puts his hand on it, and I wonder what in the world I am going to do if Theseus takes my thread. If he had my thread, he could navigate the maze. If he had my thread, it would be that much easier for him to kill the Minotaur.

I have this connection to Theseus, but I have to remember that I can't trust him. He would kill my brother if given the chance.

His hand closes around my ball of thread, and I tell him with every ounce of me not to take it.

He drops the thread and draws out his card instead.

The trumpet sounds and I turn, and when I walk away from him, making my way back to my mark on the stage, I slip back into my role. Facing the audience, the cameras, and the millions watching, I say my lines. The same as they have always been.

"The cards have been drawn. The fates have spoken. The gods must be appeased." My voice echoes back at me, amplified beyond recognition.

I turn back to the competitors. "Reveal your fates."

One by one, they turn their cards over and read the number on it, starting with Hippolyta.

"Four," Hippolyta calls out in a voice of disappointment. No doubt she was hoping to go first.

She hands her card to me, and I drop it back into my bag, ready for next season.

"Two," the next boy calls. He is the one with the crew cut, whose fear I could see the first day.

"Twelve," the following girl in line says, her voice full of relief. Twelve days. She has eleven chances that someone else will kill the Minotaur for her. Eleven chances that she can go home. Eleven people to die before she gets her turn.

The numbers dwindle. Three left, now two. The nervousness grows in my stomach. Two numbers left. Fourteen or one. How long does Theseus have? Vortigern flips his card. "One," he calls out, his voice full of triumph. He will be the first to face the Minotaur.

That means Theseus has number fourteen. He will be last. Theseus stares at his card, looking mystified.

The silence stretches. The crowd is uncomfortable, not sure what to do now.

"Tell him to read his number," Icarus says into my earpiece.

"Read your number," I say, and I'm supposed to use that slow, priestly voice, but I don't. Because it is Theseus, I say it like myself.

He looks up at me like everyone else is gone.

"It isn't right," he says, and his voice is anguished.

"What is your number?" I say, even though we all know it's fourteen. I'm surprised when my voice echoes back at me, amplified. I, too, had forgotten we were here, in front of the crowd.

"Fourteen," Theseus says, his voice dull.

He hands the card to me, and I hold the small wooden rectangle in my hand.

I walk back out to the spot on the floor that I rose up from.

The audience roars. They are delighted that they will have thirteen appetizers before they get to the main event. The music starts again, pounding, and the smoke rises around me. I watch as Theseus disappears from my vision as I'm swallowed by the smoke.

I remember what Theseus told me, down in his room—how he couldn't let innocent people die when he had the chance to save them. Wasn't this always a danger, that he would go last?

I look down at the card in my hand. A simple piece of wood.

The machine lowers me under the stage. Icarus is waiting for me at the bottom of the cage, with a golf cart. He takes the card from my hand, drops it into the burlap bag, and then fishes out my phone and ball of thread and hands them back to me along with my silver handbag.

"Let's get you something to eat," he says. "Your mother says you have to be ready for the party in two hours. Plus, I still need to show you your lines."

* * *

We take the golf cart back to the stadium entrance, then ride in my SUV back to the palace.

A production assistant is waiting inside the doors with sandwiches for both of us. We eat while Icarus leads me to the area on the first level where my mother's dance party will be hosted. It is an enormous U-shaped room, surrounding an outdoor plaza with a giant lighted stage and a swimming pool. Inside, there are bars along every wall, banquette seating, dance floors, an elevated DJ booth. Disco balls hang from the ceiling, ironically. Maybe.

The party is only an hour or so away, so right now, the room is a blur of activity as everyone makes sure that the setting is exactly right.

"You'll be starting here," Icarus says.

"At the party?" I say. "Do I have to?"

"Yes, yes, you do," he says. "This is the path you will need to take. That way we won't have to make a camera crew follow you."

"Okay," I say.

We go to the ninetieth floor. Not a floor I've spent any time on.

Our feet are silent on the thick pile carpet.

"Here we are," Icarus says as we come into a three-story-high atrium with a wall of windows. Unlike most of the palace, this space is not cream and gold. Instead, the walls are black, only

175

the accents are in gold. A flight of floating black Lucite stairs climbs along the back wall of the atrium. We take the stairs to a black door, and when I open it, we are in another room I've never seen.

I can tell it's new from the smell of fresh paint. They probably took the tags off the furniture this morning. Which isn't surprising. I swear sometimes my mother's decorating gets more hits on the Internet than Xenodice's behind.

The room is strange. My mother really let some architect show off in here. The walls are sloped, twice as tall on the outside as at the entrance, and the large, eight-paned windows are set at the same cockeyed angle as the walls. They are covered in mosaic tile in an abstract design of swirls and whorls, done in black and dove gray. The only furniture is a very long, ultra-streamlined red chaise longue; a black midcentury-modern cube end table with a planter full of wheatgrass on top; and a black onyx obelisk on a pedestal in the middle of the room. The chaise longue looks like a comic-book drawing of a sofa—the place where the villain's girlfriend would be lazing in evening wear, drinking cocktails and watching him hatch his evil plans.

Icarus stands behind me and puts his hands on my shoulders. "I was thinking you wouldn't feel comfortable with a cameraman in here with you and Theseus yet—"

"*Yet?*" I say, glancing back at him. "Icarus, this isn't going to be a regular thing."

He squeezes my shoulders. "I'm trying to make it better

for you." He lets go of me and moves to the wall. "Since I didn't want to send in a cameraman, you're going to have to watch your position in the room. Cameras and microphones are installed here." He points at the center of a distinctive whorl in the mosaic. "Make sure you keep that in mind. We've positioned the chaise longue where we'll get plenty of good angles and great light as long as you stay there. Think of it as your red zone. If you mess this up, I can promise you that after the first cut to commercial, your dad will have me send a cameraman in here pronto."

"I can't do this, Icarus," I say, turning back toward the door.

"Yes, you can," he says, his voice professional. "This isn't a decision, Ariadne. It's happening." He pulls me in close, putting his arm around me. "It'll be like ripping off a Band-Aid, popping your reality cherry. It doesn't even hurt that much your first time. Or so I've been told."

He's practically begging me to laugh, to take some of the awkwardness away. But I can't.

"How can you ask me to do this?" I say.

He looks at me so seriously, the same as he has always been—a lonely boy, sad and true—my only friend. "Ariadne, I don't have any choice—and neither do you. This"—he gestures at the room, my dress, everything—"this is our life, yours and mine. The best we can do is make it as beautiful as possible. We have to make *you* as beautiful as we can."

"How can that be enough?"

"It has to be," he says. "Beautiful or ugly, those are the only choices we have. Unless you'd like another kind of penance? A kind of penance that doesn't involve soft cushions and a cute boy?"

I shiver, remembering the chain on my ankle and the waves pulling me under.

Icarus hands me a piece of paper. "Your lines," he says. "Memorize them."

I look down at them—three sentences: *I can't stop thinking about you. I can't stand the thought of you dying. I'll help you . . .*

"Not much dialogue," I say.

"Yeah, people are not staying up late for this very special episode because they want to watch you *talk* to Theseus. You need to convince Theseus, and the viewing public, that you have fallen for him, that you are betraying your family, and the gods, for him. By the end of this very special episode, we need to see some skin."

"I can't . . . ," I say.

"You can."

All this time, I thought the deaths of the Athenians were the only sacrifice the gods demanded. I was wrong. The gods were asking something of me, too. More than my childhood, which they stole so long ago I barely remember it. They have to take my soul, too.

Icarus kisses me lightly on the forehead. "You can do this."

I whisper, "Don't make me."

He leans in close to my ear. "This isn't me. Don't ever think I'd do this to you. Neither of us has any choice."

Together we leave that crooked room, as he goes back to showrunning, and I return to my own room and whatever new outfit my mother has planned for me to wear.

Guess you can't risk being underdressed for betrayal.

ELEVEN

FOR THE FIRST TIME IN MY LIFE, I'M ATTENDING ONE OF my mother's dance parties. It's exactly as horrible as I'd feared. The flashing red lights, the hanging smoke, the music so loud and rhythmic that it pushes out coherent thought.

It is a crush of beautiful people, posing for one another and the cameras. The Athenians are here, too. Traditionally, the night of the drawing brings some real drama on *The Labyrinth Contest*. A fight. Drunken confessions. Hookups galore. Someone will get pushed into that pool fully clothed before the evening is over.

People do crazy things when their days are numbered.

I stand at the corner of the room, unsure about what I'm even supposed to do. The cameras are here. My bodyguards are behind me. I spot two of the Athenians making out on the dance floor. There's no sign of Theseus.

I understand my blocking for tonight.

Now I have to survive it.

My mother breezes past, arm in arm with Xenodice. She pauses to take a hard look at me, appraising, pleased with her handiwork. "Dance, darling," she says before she is off.

I escape to the bathroom instead. In the ladies' room, the music descends from deafening to mind-numbing.

I look at my face in the mirror. I don't even look like myself. My makeup was reapplied when I went back to my room, and they've put me into a different dress. This one is very pale blue, signaling my ingénue status, but it's made of strips of Lycra, like a bandage. My sisters love a bandage dress, but I'm finding it nearly impossible to navigate. I tug at the bottom of it, hoping for a bit more coverage on my thighs. Why is the skirt so short? Why doesn't it have a back? Why are we pretending that it counts as clothes?

My phone and the ball of silver thread are in the small silver bag that dangles off my wrist. Even here, in the bandage dress, I'm on duty if my brother starts an earthquake.

Giggling comes from one of the stalls, and when the door opens, Acalle comes out, adjusting her skirt (as short as mine). Vortigern follows her, looking embarrassed. He is zipping his pants, tucking his shirt in. Also, he's a guy. In the ladies' room.

In front of the mirror, next to me, Acalle reapplies her

lipstick, which has smeared. She ignores him, and me. Finally, she looks back at him and points at the door.

"Get lost," she says. "I'll be down to see you later. Maybe."

Vortigern slinks out.

"What?" she says, looking at me. "I decided to keep him around for another day." Then she looks at me again more carefully, narrowing her eyes. "Aren't you looking virginal. Not for long."

"Shut up, Acalle." I'm not in the mood for it.

She laughs now, a real one. "You don't like this, do you? I always thought no one was interested in you because you weren't pretty." She says this easily, like there's nothing hurtful in it. Just a fact of life. Like some of us are tall and some are short and some aren't pretty.

She comes behind me, so we're both looking in the same mirror, and she loosens my chignon a little. We are sisters. There's no denying it. Her nose is thinner, her lips fuller, but our faces are remarkably similar. We have the same body. You could mistake me for her.

"You *are* pretty," she continues. "I mean, I'd shave a couple inches off my nose if I were you, some fillers in your lips, but you're completely acceptable. Hot, actually. You couldn't see it before now."

"I don't want to do this," I say.

"You're shy," she says.

"They're trying to make me do things . . . with Theseus . . . that I don't want to do . . ."

She squeezes my shoulders. "I saw that video, sister. I know exactly what you want to do."

I can't deny how I feel about Theseus, but . . . "I don't want it like this," I say. "Not on camera."

She reaches into her tiny handbag and pulls out a silver canister. She jiggles something out into her palm. It's a jumble of pills. "Here," she says. "Take one of the green ones—they take the eyes off."

"Don't you mean the edge off?"

"No, the eyes. You can forget that everyone is watching."

I look at her.

"Go on, take it," she says, putting the green pill in my hand. "That's how you make it through when you don't have Eros on your team."

I close my fingers around it, then drop it into my silver evening bag.

She pops the handful of other pills into her mouth and leans forward, drinking from the faucet. Then she sashays out of the bathroom. "Don't do anything I wouldn't do."

My hands are shaking as I leave the bathroom, remembering Acalle's face as she downed those pills.

I always thought my sisters liked this.

I find Icarus. "Icarus," I say. "Did you know that Acalle takes pills?"

He doesn't say anything.

I look out at the dance floor, where Acalle is leaned up against the bar, ordering a drink, her camera crew tracking behind her. Next to her, an older man on a barstool puts his hand on her backside. It's Polydectes, a very, very rich man from some random island. She giggles flirtatiously.

I have a sudden memory of Acalle in that one video with old Tyndareus of Sparta, when he kept saying no, that she was too young, and she kept taking off pieces of her clothes, until he finally gave in with a groan. Icarus and I thought Acalle's persistence was hilarious, and we wondered what it was that turned her on so much about poor goofy Tyndareus, who was older than my daddy. I understand now. She was taking pills. She did it for the show. For the *Paradoxes*.

"How long have you been pimping my sisters?" I ask.

"Hey, hey," he says, "pimping is a strong word. And it's not fair. You haven't been out with Acalle and Xenodice. I have. They like this fine. They like the boys. They like the clothes and shoes. They *love* being famous. Sometimes, to be famous, you have to do things that you would not otherwise wish to do."

Polydectes has backed Acalle up against the bar, and she rests a manicured hand on his shoulder.

"So you're telling me she wants to hook up with that guy?"

"You're worrying too much," Icarus says. "That's not one of the plotlines we've worked out. She'll get away from him in a minute."

"If she doesn't—or if it was a plotline you'd decided on?"

He has the decency to look embarrassed. "Look, she would be okay. If it was something she didn't love, she'd do it, then a week or so later, she would be off on a shopping spree and everything would be fine. She saves up a wish list for exactly that kind of situation. She has dresses on hold in her favorite stores. It's part of the *Paradoxes*. Acalle can take the good with the bad. She's happy. You'll see."

"How long have you known?" I ask again, looking him in the eye, refusing to be sidetracked. Refusing to unsee what I have seen.

He looks down at me, sadly. "I've always known, Ariadne. The question is, why haven't *you*?"

Why haven't I known?

Why did I stand by watching them, thinking about how much I hated my job, but thinking they liked theirs? I've always known that their lives are something I would never want. How can I have never understood that they might not want it, either? That sometimes they might hate the cameras, or the sex tapes, or the parties. I thought they wanted this. Maybe they do, but that doesn't change the fact that they don't have any choice about doing it.

They are doing what my mother wants. Making us famous.

A camera crew comes up to us, and a production assistant passes Icarus a pink-and-purple drink.

He hands it to me.

"Drink it," he says.

I take a sip of it, then nearly choke on the sickly sweet taste of it. I've finally gotten away from the muddy feeling that Daddy's martini gave me. I don't want to start again.

"This is terrible," I say.

"Best I can offer for now," he says. "You're going to need to drink it and look happy about it."

Icarus nods his head very slightly to the right and when I look that way, I see Daddy sitting in one of the banquettes that line the walls. He's pretending to listen to one of his cronies, but he is watching me. Daddy never stays at these parties for long. It's clear he's sticking around to make sure I do as I'm told. That I do what the gods demand.

"You are going to be convincing the entire world that you are doing something difficult and dangerous, that you are putting yourself forward in a way you have never done before," Icarus says quietly. "That means that you are going to need to act the part. Which means that you need to drink this liquid courage."

I nod at Icarus. "Fine," I say, then I take a long drink of the pink concoction, forcing myself to look happy.

"Good girl," Icarus says.

"Now what?" I say.

Icarus uses his phone to pull up the minute-by-minute ratings picture across platforms. "Okay," he says, "looks like we've had almost no drop-off from the drawing—and right now the only thing we're offering is a live feed of Acalle and Xenodice doing their Paradoxes thing. The drawing itself was up fifty percent over last year. Your very special episode is set to start in two hours." He looks at his watch. "So what we need is for you to find Theseus, get him to come with you to that room I showed you, and get some footage that I can edit into the end of the very special episode. If you'll remember the storyboard, right now, we have an empty space at the climax."

I have a mental image of the storyboard he showed me— Theseus and I together on a chaise longue. The lines I am supposed to say. What is supposed to happen after.

I'm thinking, *I can't do this, I can't do this.*

I don't say it.

"Now, let's find Theseus," he says.

He leads me across the room, me stumbling a little from the effect of the drink, to the edge of the writhing mass of people. He tells me something, but the music drowns his voice.

"I can't hear you," I shout.

He points across the room, and I see Theseus leaning against the wall with his hands in his pockets.

The way to him is blocked by a crowd of dancers.

He's standing in an alcove, where the music is probably less deafening. Hippolyta is practically snuggled up against him.

He's wearing a suit again, which I like, although I miss the flash of leg I got in the warrior costume. Hippolyta is wearing a very short gold backless dress that manages to look incredibly badass while also showing great expanses of skin. She is as tall as Theseus, and she holds her head high. She has a wide, warrior stance. I can't imagine what would happen to the idiot who thought that tiny dress was an invitation to touch her without permission. He'd be lucky to keep his hand. She touches Theseus's arm in a way that makes it clear he has permission.

"Go over there and talk to him," Icarus shouts at me.

"What?" I say, even though I did hear him this time. I want to make him suffer. He walks his fingers on his other hand for me to demonstrate, then points at Theseus and Hippolyta. Then he points at the camera crew and leans in close so I don't miss a word.

"See if you can generate some drama with the Amazon," he says.

The Amazon who could take me out with one swing? That Amazon?

"Then get him out of here," Icarus says. "We need to get you both to the room your mother made. So you can promise to help him. So you can show us some skin and blow the top off the ratings for this very special episode. Are you ready?"

"I can't . . . ," I say, and my anger and sadness and horror at my situation are there, right under the surface, ready to burst out, if Icarus gives me even the smallest amount of sympathy. Icarus must know it, too, because he doesn't tell me again how sorry he is.

"You can," he says.

I take a deep breath, then wade through the crowd of dancers, Icarus beside me, my bodyguards clearing a path ahead of me, while the cameramen follow behind. I can't walk like myself in this dress and these shoes. I fight the urge to tug down at

the hemline, knowing that it will draw attention to what I'm trying to get people to ignore.

Eyes are on me from every direction. In a way that I have
never felt before. It's desire. And anger. And possession. Even
with my bodyguards, people touch me as I pass them. As though
my tight dress gives them permission.

My skin crawls.

This must be what it is like for my sisters all the time.

Finally, we are through the crowd of dancers, and Icarus
steps back, my bodyguards making a space in front of me, and
there is no one between me and Theseus and Hippolyta. As soon
as I step into the alcove, the sound of the music drops. Theseus
and Hippolyta seem to be having a serious conversation, not
paying any attention to the debauchery going on around them.
Oblivious to the grinding dancers, the flashing lights, the missing clothes, the smoke.

I look back at Icarus, who looks back at Daddy, who is glaring at both of us from the banquette. Icarus gives me a funny
tail wiggle, then makes a shooing motion toward Theseus.

Theseus and the Amazon barely seem to have noticed me,
although I am hard to miss because I have an entourage. A camera crew. Bodyguards. Not to mention a bandage dress.

This is why I hate going out in public.

What is Theseus doing? I don't understand. Was I imagining our connection? Has everything been a trick? Why isn't he
saying hello to me?

I run through the possible opening gambits—*excuse me* feels small, like I'm intruding on their confab; a simple *Theseus* doesn't seem right, either, if he's trying to hurt my feelings.

"Are you going to ignore me all night?" is what I finally go with.

The Amazon turns her head slowly, like a cat lazily examining some item of prey. Theseus looks annoyed, like he's been interrupted.

Then his face quickly runs from irritated to surprised to curious to suspicious.

"Ariadne?" he says like he's genuinely confused.

"Bingo," I say. "That's my name."

"You . . ." He gestures at me, clearly encompassing my dress, hair, shoes, makeup, everything. "You look like . . ."

"She looks like her trashy sisters," Hippolyta says helpfully. "We thought you were one of them. They keep sneaking up on Theseus here, trying to get him out of his clothes."

"Wait, what?" I say, looking at Theseus. That hurts. My sisters have to know that I'm interested in Theseus by now. Why would they chase him? Because they are who they are. Because that would boost ratings, too. Everyone loves a triangle.

"Not that I blame them," Hippolyta continues, and nothing about her face suggests that she's kidding. "I, too, have been trying to relieve this young man of his garments." She rests her hand on his chest proprietarily. "To date, I have been unsuccessful." She leans in and kisses him on the mouth. "I am nothing if not persistent."

Before Theseus can respond, Hippolyta pushes backward,

spinning away from him. Her hips sway as she walks away from us. She turns back for a parting shot. "You are welcome in my room anytime. I will be waiting for you."

We both watch her walk away.

Theseus looks stunned for an instant, but then his attention turns to me, and I can tell he's not thinking about Hippolyta anymore. He's thinking about me. "Why are you dressed like this?" he asks. "One of the first things you ever told me was that you don't come to parties. Your sister said that, too. Why are you here?"

The cameras are rolling. Out of the corner of my eye, I can see Icarus looking nervous.

I could say anything right now. I know what my sisters would say. Xenodice would say—*I did it for you, do you like it?*—Acalle would say—*Don't you wish you knew?*

What do I say? I'm going to have to lie to him later tonight. I'm going to have to tell him that I will help him in the maze. That I will help him kill the Minotaur. I don't want to start lying now. I'm not ready.

Because the reality is that I would never, by choice, wear something that made it impossible for me to breathe, and these shoes are for sure not my idea of appropriate footwear, but being with Theseus? That is something I would do, no matter what.

It doesn't matter that my interests and the thing that I've been ordered to do happen to be aligned at this moment. Or at least that's what I tell myself.

So I tell him the truth. "My mother," I say, rolling my eyes.

191

"Most mothers are trying to keep their daughters out of these kinds of dresses," he says. "Away from this kind of party."

He waves at a couple behind us who are dancing in the most suggestive way imaginable.

I laugh. "My mother is not like most mothers."

"Fair enough," he says.

"Are you enjoying the party?" I ask.

He jams his hands deeper in his pockets. "It's not my kind of thing."

"Would you like to get out of here?" I say. "Go somewhere we can talk?"

He brightens. "I would like that better than anything."

He trusts me.

Theseus takes my hand, and I hate the twisting feeling inside me, knowing that I'm lying to him. "Lead the way," he says.

As we leave the party, we pass Daddy in his banquette. He raises his glass to me. I'm doing what I was told.

TWELVE

WHEN WE LEAVE THE PARTY, ICARUS AND MY bodyguards don't follow.

I'm carrying my six-inch stripper heels in one of my hands, since I can't walk in them. Exactly like Icarus showed in his storyboard. My other hand holds the silver evening bag with my thread and my phone.

"Where are we going?" Theseus asks, pulling me to a stop.

Oh gods, everything about this is new to me. If I were one of my sisters, this would be the chance to steal another kiss from him, but when I slow down and look at his face, Theseus isn't flirting. His face is troubled, serious. Clouded.

"I want to talk to you," I say, "and there's a room I want to show you."

"Will it be private?" he asks. I wonder if he means, *Will we be unmonitored, off the cameras?*

"We'll be alone," I say, answering a different question.

I take him on the elevator, up to the ninetieth floor. I lead him to the atrium. Up the floating stairs. I open the door to the crooked room.

He gasps in surprise at the room. "This is . . ."

"Amazing?" I say.

He nods. "Amazing."

I set my shoes and my bag down on the cube end table next to the red chaise longue.

Ambient music is piped in through hidden speakers. An unadorned man's voice, electronically manipulated, singing about a girl. Guitars over a droning hum. It is an intimate, surprisingly beautiful room, made for secrets.

We cross over to the tall, angled windows.

"It's a great view," he says, looking out at the harbor.

"Yes," I say. "Yes, it is."

Now is where I'm supposed to lead him over to the chaise longue. I'm supposed to say my lines—*I can't stop thinking about you. I can't stand the thought of you dying. I'll help you . . .*

I glance back into the room, back at the huge red piece of furniture. I'm fluttering inside, asking myself if I can really do this, and I find that I can't do anything. It's like my feet are stuck to the ground, my body encased in marble.

Theseus takes my hand in his.

"Thank you for bringing me up here," he says. "I've been wanting to talk to you about something."

"What is it?" I ask, my voice small, waiting for when he will ask again for help with the Minotaur.

"Is it possible that the drawing was rigged?"

"Rigged?" I say, confused.

"Manipulated."

I think of the wooden cards with the numbers branded into their surfaces. "That's impossible."

"Yet somehow it has happened," he says. His jaw is set, his eyes stormy. "It's my destiny to stop the murder of the Athenians. I'm sure of it. I can't do that if they are killed before me."

"You can't rig the drawing," I say. "They are pieces of wood. I've held them in my hands. There's no way to alter them."

"Well, there must be," he says stubbornly. "I'm supposed to go first. It's what the gods want."

"What if the gods don't want what you think they want?" I ask.

"They want me to end this. My whole life has led to now. I can't wait for thirteen more people to die . . ."

"You know this has been going on for ten years, right?" I say. "Your dad has been king this whole time—"

He cuts me off. "This isn't about my dad. This is about what it means to lead. I have to prove that I'm worthy of being their prince."

"No, you don't," I say, exasperated. "That's the whole thing with hereditary monarchy. You don't have to keep proving yourself. You already got those pirates. You killed the Cromwellian Sow—"

"The Crommyonian Sow," he interrupts.

"Whatever. The thing about being royalty is that you don't have to do anything to deserve it. You're born—and then you can do what you want. You're the king's son. You'll still be the prince even if you don't do this, right?"

He starts laughing, and it hurts right to my core, because it is a bitter, empty laugh with no joy in it. Not a sound I've ever heard from Theseus before.

"You don't understand anything," he says. His voice sounds infinitely sad.

I grab his hands. "Then explain it to me."

"I can't," he says, looking away.

I put my hand up to his cheek, turning his face back toward mine, and a wash of emotions passes over his face—anger, fear, sadness.

"Tell me," I whisper.

"Okay, fine," he says. "Until six months ago, I never had the slightest clue that my real father was Aegeus. I knew he was the king of Athens, but I had no idea that he had a connection to me. I believed my father was the god Poseidon. That's what my mom said, and she's the greatest. I never thought that she could be lying to me, even though everyone in town said that was a crock. As far as they were concerned I was a kid without a dad.

It didn't matter how well I did in school, or at sports—there was always that word, *bastard*."

As he's talking, his face reveals his empty despair and I think of the cameras that are rolling now, waiting to expose our naked bodies. But now, they are exposing Theseus's truth.

"Wait," I say. "You don't have to tell me this . . ." I drop my voice. "We're being watched."

"I want you to know," he says, looking up at the walls, and I know the cameras were never hiding from him. "I don't care who else does. I've held this for so long—like it was my fault. My shame. My secret. Not telling only protects the people who are at fault. I need to tell the truth, Ariadne."

So I grab his hand, and I don't let go.

"My mom and I, we live with my grandfather, and Grandfather, he says . . ."

He stops. He's probably never said this out loud to anyone.

"What does he say?" I whisper.

He spits out the words. "He says that he lets us stay there because of his charity. She works constantly, making sure everything is exactly how he likes it. And he never thanks her. My grandfather says it's what she deserves. Because of me. That if she doesn't do what he says, he'll send us away. 'Let Poseidon support his bastard.' Even though, as I found out, he knew the whole time that Aegeus was really my father."

On his face, I see a flash of the little boy he must have been and then it is replaced by grim anger, and I see the engine that drives Theseus. All that he has to prove.

"When did you find out?" I ask.

"Yeah, that's a funny story." Nothing about his manner suggests something funny. "When I turned seventeen, my mom took me out to a beach near the house. The beach where she always said she had met Poseidon. She told me I was going to find out about my future and my past. She asked me to move a large rock along a cliff face. It was heavy, but I did it. There was a cave back there. Guess what was in it?"

The way his voice sounds, I'm imagining something terrible, and I don't want to guess. "What was in the cave?" I ask.

"A pair of sandals and a knife."

"Why? I'm confused," I say.

"I was, too, until my mother explained. They belonged to my father, Aegeus, the gods-be-cursed king of Athens. He had hidden them for me to find. He spent a weekend in Troezen and hooked up with my mom. Later, when she found out she was pregnant, she wrote him letters, emails, texts. He never answered. Then after I was born, she wrote to tell him that he had a son. That's when he came back to Troezen to hide the sandals and the knife. He told her that if I could move the stone and get them, he would claim me as his son, but only if I was strong enough to do it myself. He wasn't interested in a weak son. He was worried that if I was weak, it would be easy for the Pallantides to take over."

"That's messed up," I say.

He shrugs. "Says the girl who leads kids to their deaths because her parents make her do it."

"My parents make me do it because the gods told them to,"
I say.

"Sure they do," he says, his voice full of sarcasm. "Haven't
you noticed that the gods mostly tell people to do stuff they already want to do?" He runs his hands through his hair. "You
want to know the most screwed-up thing? My mom told me that
she didn't even like Aegeus. She was only sixteen. He was over
forty. Aegeus was staying at my grandfather's house, and Grandfather made my mom take Aegeus out on the beach and get
him drunk and seduce him. Even though it was her first time.
My grandfather sold my mother's innocence for the chance to
have a *prince* in the family." The way he says the word *prince*
makes it sound dirty, like a curse.

His voice breaks, and his anger and self-hatred are there on
his face. Not packed away or hidden.

"That's where Poseidon came in," he continues. "After Aegeus left my mom on the beach, she felt like she was the one who
was dirty. Even though she was still a kid. She went out into the
sea to wash, and she could feel it supporting her, wanting her to
be okay. So later, when Aegeus wouldn't answer her emails or
letters or texts, she decided that Poseidon was my real father,
since the sea had been there for her when no one else was. That
way she never had to tell me the truth, that she'd been forced.
That I'd been abandoned. Her whole life, it's been ruined . . .
because of me . . . All she wanted to do was protect me. When
no one ever protected her." He spits out the last of his story.
"Now my grandfather is so happy. He's convinced that me being

a prince makes up for everything. Right before I left for Athens, he told me he was *proud* of me. Can you believe that?"

I am glad for the years with my brother, because there is no comfort that can cover Theseus's rage. Nothing I can say to make it better. I can just be with him. I wrap my hands around his clenched fists. I don't say anything and we sit together for a long minute.

Finally, I say, "I'm sorry your dad and grandfather are jerks."

"Yeah, me too."

He looks back at me. "Now do you see why I have to do this? My dad didn't protect me, and he hasn't protected these competitors, either. I can't leave them to it. Not when I can do something about it. From the first moment I knew who my father was, I knew that I would be the one to stop this."

It's so sad. So incredibly sad. I wish there was another way.

"It's my destiny to kill the Minotaur," Theseus says. "To end it. That's why I have to win. Come on, Ariadne, please, help me. I don't know why you don't want the Minotaur to die. I don't understand."

"I can't tell you," I say. "I have to do this. It's *my* destiny."

I shiver in the cold.

"Here, take my jacket," he says, stripping it off, then draping it over my shoulders. Then he takes my hands in his. "Ariadne, how does destiny work?"

I think about this for a long moment. "We do what the gods want us to. That's our destiny."

He pulls me in closer. "I don't agree. Our destiny, it's like a giant wave——we can let it beat us down. We can let it drown us. Or, we can try to get on top of it. We can make our own destinies. We can ride the wave.

"In the stories, people try and try to run away from their destinies, and they can't escape them. Then other people think they are fated to one thing, and an entirely different thing happens to them. The gods don't control us, Ariadne. They can't force us into a box unless we let them. We make our choices, and our destinies come to meet us." He reaches out and touches my cheek. "What would happen if you got on top of the wave?"

My whole life has been me getting beat up by the surf. And every time I stand up, another wave knocks me down.

"What do you want, Ariadne?" he asks.

"For this to be over," I say aloud. *For my brother to be healed*, I say to myself.

"No, what do you want for yourself?" he asks me.

"I don't know," I say. "I don't know."

"You have to want something," he says. He leans in close to me, his voice a whisper. "Isn't there anything you want for yourself?"

He rests his forehead against mine, so calm and still.

My heart beats in my chest like a bird trying to break free of its cage. These aren't questions that I'm allowed to ask. What would I want if I didn't have any duties? If the gods didn't control everything I do?

I want Theseus. I want to be free. I want to set my brother

free. I want to tear down the whole world. Knock it to the ground. Burn it and scatter the wreckage.

There is a force in me that is so scary and powerful that I don't know what to do with it. It feels like naming it would destroy everything I love.

"I can't . . . ," I choke out, twisting my hands.

"Too big?" he says as he takes my hands in his and keeps breathing slowly, resting his forehead against mine.

"Here's an easier one," he says. "If you could go anywhere, where would you go?"

I'm still frozen.

"Imagine a vacation," he says. "That's not hard."

"Alone?" I say.

"If you want to. Although I'd be happy to go with you."

I breathe in. I imagine it. Where would I go? "To a beach, maybe? A beach with no helicopters. No cameras. Or bandage dresses."

He pulls back from me and places his hands on my shoulders. He looks into my eyes. "Let me take you," he says. "This is no kind of life. You hate it. Help me, then let me take you away."

Far below us the streetlights show my proscribed routes, the buildings I can go into, in the city my daddy rules. Talos's giant head watching the entrance to the harbor. And beyond that, the darkness of the sea.

The lights of our city are so bright they keep you from seeing the stars.

Theseus turns toward me. His pupils dilate, and his look lights a fire in me. I'm blushing, and my pulse is racing.

I let him lean into me and kiss me again, longer this time. His lips are soft and dry, exactly like I remembered. The electrical energy that has surged between us is inside me now. His hands unbind my hair and take his jacket off my shoulders, and I'm unbuttoning his shirt. His hand slips under the shoulder strap of my dress and starts to pull it down, finding the line where the fabric meets my skin.

He nuzzles my neck, his hand dipping lower. "Help me in the maze, Ariadne, please."

This is it. This is the moment.

Yes, I just have to say *yes*.

It's one word. If I say it, I can find that red chaise longue and fall onto it with Theseus. I can do what my body is begging me to do. This is what Acalle and my mother meant by Eros. I don't care about the cameras. I don't care about the plotline. I don't care about the very special episode.

He'll never know it's a lie. Daddy will be happy. The gods will be happy. But.

Theseus will figure out that I lied to him, eventually. He'll go into the maze, thinking I'm going to help him. Then I won't. He'll know I betrayed him. His crumpled body would be in one of the turnings in the maze, waiting for me to stumble upon it.

What if I did help him? If I gave him my thread? If I told him the secrets of the maze?

Then I would be responsible for the death of my brother.

"I can't," I say, pulling away from Theseus and fixing my dress. "I can't help you."

This is absolutely, 100 percent, not what I'm supposed to say. This is not what I'm supposed to do. Even though I'm going to be in so much trouble, right here, in this moment, I find that I can't lie to Theseus. I can't pretend I'm going to hurt my brother. There's no way my destiny leads in that direction.

When the room starts trembling, for a moment I believe that it's coming from inside of me.

The planter of wheatgrass falls off the black cube end table with a crash. The mosaic tiles fall out of the walls. This earthquake is as bad as it has ever been. The whole building might be coming down around us, no matter how earthquake-safe the design.

"I have to go," I say, grabbing my bag off the table and running down the stairs, away from Theseus, away from everything.

Leaving my shoes behind.

I don't wait for Daddy to call. I can tell this is a bad one. The building is swaying in a truly alarming way.

In the maze, I rush past the obstacles, forcing down the bile in my throat at the feeling of the slick concrete under my bare feet. The whole time, Asterion's bellowing blocks out any other sounds, any other thoughts.

I sing like I always do, but he is so loud, he drowns out my voice.

He's running in the maze, somewhere.

I put my thread in the last hook. The one that tells the maze I've arrived at Asterion's room. So they can find my body if this is the one time I can't manage to calm my brother.

I come into his room, and it's as bad as I've ever seen it. Everything he has, all his treasures, are smashed and broken on the floor. The bull I made for him is shattered. The only thing left is our book and his blue blanket.

Asterion comes through the door and charges with terrifying speed, his head down, his horns leveled at me. He is like a freight train, and I barely manage to throw myself out of his way. He turns, breathing heavily, his massive head lowered in an attacking stance.

"Asterion," I say sternly, making it look like I'm not scared, even though I'm terrified. I have to remind him of who I am. Who *he* is. He doesn't straighten up. His eyes are red, and I can tell he doesn't recognize me. He is nothing but the Minotaur now. Nothing but bull. The force of his rage is turned on me, and for the first time in my life, I know what it must be like for the Athenians in the maze. Fear washes over me like an animating force, pumping my blood, ordering me to turn and run. Or to cover my head with my hands and cower in the corner. None of those things will help me. None of those things will remind him who he really is.

"Asterion," I say again, firmly. "Look at me."

He pauses, and his breathing slows. I hold his red eyes with my own, praying that his rage is receding, that he hasn't been swallowed by the bull. Gradually, his red eyes fade to brown, and the boy is back.

He groans and drops to the floor, curling into a ball, shaking with the tears he can't shed.

I kneel down, putting my hand on his back. "I know," I whisper. "I know."

Even though I don't. Even though I can never, ever know what it is like to be Asterion. Trapped here, underground. Trapped inside a body at war with itself.

He picks up the pieces of his pottery bull, and he holds it in his hands, looking down at it while I clean him up, bandaging the places where he's injured himself.

"We'll fix it," I say, closing his hands over the bull. "I can fix it."

We sit together on the edge of his bed.

I don't talk about anything like I normally would. No gossip from upstairs. I don't tell him about what numbers everyone drew. That the competitors will start coming into the maze tomorrow. Normal life is a million years away.

After a few more minutes, Asterion stands up and walks to the corner, where he finds his book.

He brings it over to me, opening it to the story of the Caledonian Boar. He points at the full-color page of the boar, with arrows and spears sticking out of its side.

What is he telling me?

He points at himself and then at the picture. Then he does it again, insistently.

"You are like the boar?" I ask. "Is that what you're saying?"

He nods.

I'm tired, he signs.

"You should sleep. It's really late."

No, he signs.

He doesn't mean that kind of tired.

He points at the boar again.

"What are you telling me?"

So tired, he signs.

He lays his head in my lap, and I pet his fur.

"Asterion," I say, looking at my brother. "Do you . . ."

What do I want to ask? I look around his room, his broken treasures, his shredded blankets. The walls, ripped and smashed.

"Asterion," I say finally. "What do *you* want?"

He holds both hands up, with the backs facing me, then flips them forward.

All done.

Then he points at himself.

I'm all done.

THIRTEEN

BACK IN MY ROOM, I TAKE A SHOWER TO WASH THE awful grime of the maze off my feet, then collapse into my bed.

When I'm awakened by my phone ringing, I am tangled in my covers, sweaty, disoriented. Again, I have been running through the maze in my dreams. Chasing Theseus. Chasing the Minotaur.

I claw myself to wakefulness, getting my phone off the nightstand.

It's Icarus.

I drop the phone back down and collapse on the pillows, heart racing, like I've barely gotten my head above the waves.

I didn't tell Theseus I would help him. I didn't show any skin. I'm going to be in so much trouble.

Not a thing I'm used to thinking.

I close my eyes again, not ready to face the day.

What was it Theseus said last night—*ride the wave*? That's for him, not me. I have too much at stake.

A text bubble crosses the screen—*Answer the phone, Ariadne, or I'll come down there and pull you out of bed myself.*

I would ask myself how he knows I'm in bed, but I don't. I already know the answer. I'm sure he typed my name into his system in the control room to find the video feed of me sweaty and gross in my pajamas.

I flip off the cameras that I know are in the ceiling somewhere.

My phone rings again.

I pick up.

"What's my penance now, Icarus?" I say, dreading whatever comes next. "What are they going to do to me?"

"Nothing," he says, "because I saved your butt. Seriously, you would owe me your firstborn child if I had any interest in such a thing. Get up here so I can show you what I did."

It takes me five minutes to get up to the control room. The screens are dark except for the monitor at his desk, which he's staring at intently. He doesn't look up when I come in.

"How bad is it?" I say, closing the door behind me.

"I salvaged it," he says, not looking up from his screen. "Do you understand how much trouble you could have gotten yourself into?"

"I know," I say. "Believe me, I know."

With a series of keystrokes, he rewinds the tape to the moment when Theseus and I come in the room. We are both breathless; the room is beautiful. Everything is as it was supposed to be.

"You had three lines, Ariadne," Icarus says, imitating a sexy voice that I can never imagine using. "'*I can't stop thinking about you. I can't stand the thought of you dying. I'll help you . . .*' That was it. Then a little something, something. But nooo . . ."

He presses a few buttons. "This wouldn't be a problem if I'd been there to redirect, but I wasn't there, Ariadne, and why not? Because I was worried about your sensibilities. Hades, why are you making this harder on yourself?"

"I don't know," I whisper. "I couldn't lie."

"Well, you are going to have to get over that, sister. It's not that the ratings are a problem—they were through the roof. That's why I never came in with the cameraman." He puts his attention back on the screen. "Here we are."

Our backs are to the camera, and it is a beautiful image. One I will hold in my mind.

"Thank you for bringing me up here," Theseus says. "I've been wanting to talk to you about something."

"We put a commercial here," Icarus says, "so we could leave out his speculation about the rigging of the drawing. That's not the kind of accusation anyone would appreciate being made publicly."

I look at Icarus curiously. "You couldn't rig the drawing, could you? Not with the cards being wood and everything?"

"No, of course not," he says, keeping his eyes on the screen. "Here we are."

On screen, Theseus is leaning in toward me, resting his forehead against mine, his voice a whisper. "Isn't there anything you want for yourself?"

My heart is racing remembering him, but I'm also confused, because this is much later in the conversation. He's already told me about his father. About being abandoned. About why he feels like he has to do this. Why he has to be the hero. I've had the most important conversation of my life so far, and Icarus has cut all of it.

"Pause it," I say to Icarus. "Why did you take out the stuff about his dad, and destiny?"

He presses a button and the screen freezes.

"It's too big, too much. We have so many plotlines going anyway, we can't add one with Theseus and Aegeus, especially since we can't tie it up with a bow."

"Because Theseus is going to die," I say carefully, trying out the words.

"Exactly," he says. "For maximum impact, people need to see them as a strongly bonded father and son, not an absentee dad and a kid with abandonment issues."

"That's not really fair," I say, defending Theseus.

"Hey," Icarus says, holding his hands up. "I'm telling you what drives ratings, and sad boys are not it. Metaphysical speculation and bad surfing metaphors also do not do anything for viewing numbers."

"It wasn't a bad metaphor."

"Sure," Icarus says. "You're only saying that because of the soulful look Theseus was giving you."

"You're laughing at me."

"Of course I'm laughing at you," he says. "If you had any sense, you'd be laughing at yourself."

I look hard at that screen, at Theseus holding me in his arms. I think about his question—*Isn't there anything you want for yourself?* A question no one has ever asked me.

"Why should I be laughing?" It comes out a whisper.

Icarus spins in his chair, grabbing my hands. "You can't get attached, Ariadne. Don't forget that."

His eyes are so serious behind his glasses, so intense. Revealing the boy I've always known. The one who would never admit that he missed his mother. The one who used to dream of flying away from here. He understands my dilemma, at least a little, understands how I'm torn between Theseus and my family.

But then the cold, clinical light is back. "You don't get to keep him." He turns back to the keyboard. "Okay, look what I did."

On the screen, I don't answer Theseus's question, don't tell him about wishing to be alone somewhere. Apparently, girls who don't like the cameras are also not good for ratings. Instead, Theseus kisses me, and I want to look away, but I don't. I watch him take down my hair, take his jacket off my shoulders.

The ghost of his touch passes over my skin.

Then his whisper. "Help me in the maze, Ariadne, please."

The place where I told him no.

Where I said, "I can't help you."

On the video, that's not my answer. Instead, I say, "Yes." My face is away from the camera, his head in my neck.

Then the screen fades to black. No earthquake to mar the proceedings.

I look at Icarus.

"I didn't say that," I say.

"Yes, you did."

"No, no I didn't."

"Well, I say you did, and as long as we can keep anyone from seeing the raw footage, which shouldn't be too hard since the very special episode has already aired and will only be seen again in eternal syndication, that is my story, and I'm sticking to it."

"How?" I ask.

He presses a few buttons, then calls up a snippet of a scene, from when we first came into the room and we're looking out the windows.

"It's a beautiful view," Theseus says.

"Yes," I say. "Yes, it is."

There it is. My yes to the view repurposed to my yes to everything I can't do.

"Icarus, I can't help him," I whisper, twisting my hands.

"Of course you can't help him. Who knows what your dad would do if you did."

"I don't want to lie to him, either," I say.

"That ship has sailed, sister," he says. "You simply don't have any choice. It gets easier, you know. With practice."

I don't want to practice.

I walk over to the inspiration board and touch the newest drawing he's pinned there. It's another self-portrait and this time the wings are made of silver, and the background is complete. He is soaring away from this tower, away from our island. The wings are carefully inked in, every feather detailed, and the land and the sea are so clearly rendered. But Icarus hasn't finished himself. He is only the whiteness on the paper.

"How is this what I'm supposed to be doing, Icarus?" I whisper. "Or you? How can this be it?"

His eyes are veiled. "You and I, we don't have any choices. We may be in a cage, but the bars are made of gold . . ." He stands up and puts his hands on my shoulders, looking down at me. "This is your destiny. It'll make it better for everyone if you lie back and enjoy it."

"What about your dreams?" I say.

Icarus looks at his picture for a long time. Then he tears it off the wall and wads it up, throwing it on the floor. I have known him for so long that it is like I am watching him flay his own skin.

"Yes, I had dreams, Ariadne, but then I had to wake up. I am a prisoner here. Forever. My father signed me into the contract when we came here. I can never work for anyone else. We don't have any choice," he says. "Neither of us."

He turns away from me and returns to his keyboard and monitor.

When he speaks next, his tone is normal, conversational.

"So, what are your plans for the rest of the day?"

"Going for a run." I pick up his tone myself. There's nothing else to say.

"And then?"

"I was thinking I would probably do what I always do."

"Hide in your room playing video games until it's time to lead the competitors?"

"Pretty much," I say.

"You're going to have to face Theseus again. You know that, right? You're going to have to continue this."

I'm not ready yet. "Can't we just hold off on today?" I say. "Surely you have enough programming."

He nods. "As a favor for you," he says. "My best friend."

He points at the screen. "You did good last night, even though you didn't do everything we wanted. That was hot, with you and Theseus. The Internet is on fire right now. Everyone is certain that it's true."

What if it is, I wonder, as I leave the room, remembering Theseus's arms around me. His lips on mine.

This time I go running away from the city, up the paths that lead into the hills that Daddy keeps free of development so that he can have his olive trees and vineyards, and the pastures where the sacred cattle graze.

I fight to keep my mind off Theseus. I try not to think of showing him the places that I love. The smell of the olive trees.

My security detail and I mostly have the paths to ourselves. Down a packed-earth path, not far from the pasture where my mother is supposed to have had her rendezvous with the white bull, I see a group of boys playing in the trees, climbing and jumping and throwing things at one another. They are twelve or thirteen, loud and rambunctious, still boys, but on the cusp of something else, and it hits me like a blow. This is where my brother should be. Here, in the sunlight. Not underground.

Alone.

I run back to the palace as fast as I can, making the effort to force out everything else.

As soon as I'm back in my room, I do nothing but slaughter harpies in VR for the next five hours.

When my mother and Mathilde arrive, I feel like I am in a cage I have no idea how to get out of.

The dress they have brought for me is transparent and gauzy with a very low neckline. No bra possible. A golden belt. A golden bag. My hair long and curling down around my shoulders. No jewelry. It's beautiful. But.

I object. "I can't wear this, you can see my nipples."

"There's no shame in a nipple, darling," my mother says.

Then we get to the shoes. My mother opens a box and pulls out a pair of peep-toe booties with towering heels.

"I can't walk in those," I say. "I want to wear something flat."

"Something flat?!?" my mother screeches, as though I've said I'm planning to lead the competitors in my underwear. Scratch that, she'd probably love it if I was doing it in my underwear.

"I will take them off," I say, steel in my voice.

We stare at each other, and I can see her trying to decide how serious I am.

"I will wear sneakers or I will go barefoot. I'm not wearing those."

My mother glances at Mathilde, and Mathilde gives a small negative motion. "If she is barefoot, it will ruin the ensemble. I see no reason to risk it. I told you the shoes would be too much. That is why I found the sandals."

"Fine." My mother pulls out a pair of bejeweled sandals that have ties that lace up my legs, and I nod. They will do.

Finally, they are done, and we stand together, looking at me in the mirror.

"You look so beautiful," my mother says, her voice full of surprise.

I do, but utterly unlike myself.

I ride with my mother and sisters to the stadium, barely paying attention to their chatter, even though I know they are talking about me.

At the stadium, I stand at the entry above the field, looking down the long path to the stage, lined with torches. Behind the stage are massive hammered steel doors, engraved with images of the Minotaur, that cover the concrete arch from floor to ceiling—the entrance to the maze—like a gate to the underworld.

I search for Theseus, finding him sitting in the fourteenth chair at the end of the line of competitors. He is so far away that I can't see his face clearly, but I can see the long lines of his body. His hands at his sides.

"Walk, Ariadne," Icarus's voice says in my earpiece.

I step forward, spotlights on me, the slow steady beat of a drum echoing, setting the pace of my march to the stage. The competitors stand. The crowd roars as my image is projected onto the Jumbotron. My arrival is as reliable as the pistol starting a race. Finally, someone will bleed. The crowd is excited. Vortigern is a good competitor. He is strong. He understands what he's up against.

It is so loud that it covers the sound of the beating drum. So loud it fills my head.

On the Jumbotron, they project Theseus looking at me. It stops me cold.

"Seriously, Ariadne, this is not hard. Walk," Icarus says.

I force my legs to move. Force my step to match the slow beat of the drum, which is burned into my muscle memory from the times I've done this before. Force myself to breath. To slow down my racing heart.

With every step, I'm closer to Theseus. Better able to see him.

His bare legs in his war kilt, his strong arms. Those hands.

His eyes, on me, watching me. Like I'm the only person in the world.

I nearly stumble going up the steps to the stage.

"Steady, Ariadne," Icarus says.

The crowd has hushed. The drumbeat is gone, replaced by the keening of a bouzouki.

I take a long, deep breath, tearing my attention away from Theseus. Toward the opening to the maze. I walk up the stairs slowly, calming myself with each breath. At the top of the stairs, I turn to face the crowd. To say the words I always say.

It is different now, because they can see me.

"Here are the bravest and most beautiful of Athens. They have come to face the mighty Minotaur. To discover the will of the gods—and their fate."

The crowd cheers.

"Take your place in line," I say to the competitors.

In a series of moves choreographed and practiced early today, everyone moves from their assigned places where they will watch *The Labyrinth Contest* to line up in two rows alongside the path that Vortigern will walk down, the path that will lead to the maze behind the stage.

At the front of them, Vortigern waits for me. Theseus is at the back of the line, closest to me.

I force myself not to look at him.

"Vortigern of Athens, are you ready to face the Minotaur?" I ask.

"Yes," he says. His voice is clear and strong. "I am ready to kill the Minotaur."

The crowd roars.

"Now the Keeper of the Maze will lead Vortigern to the Labyrinth," Daedalus announces.

The crowd cheers even louder.

I take Vortigern's hand in mine, and we walk to the steel doors. With a series of thunks and clicks, the locks disengage, and the doors glide open inwardly. We walk through into the cavernous tunnel, and the sound of the crowd in the stadium drops away.

I lead him into the darkness, the tunnel narrowing and sloping steeply down, and the motion sensor lights turn on, lighting his path forward.

Vortigern bounces on the balls of his feet.

"It's time, Ariadne," Icarus says in my ear.

I let go of Vortigern's hand.

"Wish me luck," he says.

I say, "Go, Vortigern," keeping my voice low and solemn. "Discover your fate."

He lifts his head and runs into the maze, and I turn and walk quickly back to the gates. The cameras aren't watching me anymore. Now they'll be focused on Vortigern. I walk through the gates, and they close with a clang behind me.

Once I'm back on the stage, I look out at the stadium floor. Sheets of fabric that had been pooled on the ground have been pulled up to make a giant scrim, visible to every seat in the stadium. This is where Vortigern's fight with the Minotaur will be projected, giving everyone here a front-row seat.

No one cares about me now; I can get out of here. In a matter of seconds, I'll be off camera, out of view. Then I'll get in the golf cart that is waiting for me, and it will speed me to the entrance, where a black SUV will return me to the palace. Back to my room. To my VR headset. My games. Oblivion.

So I don't have to see what happens.

So I don't have to watch my brother eat.

I walk through the line of competitors, keeping my head up. Not looking at them.

As I walk past Theseus, he grabs my arm.

"Ariadne, stop." He is not smiling now. "Where are you going?"

I should ignore him. I should keep walking. I have to get out of here before Vortigern gets to his first obstacle. I don't have much time.

"I don't stay for this part," I say.

"Don't tell me," he says. "You go back to your room and play video games."

I nod. "I have to go," I say, stepping away. But Theseus keeps his hand on my arm.

"Wait, Ariadne," he says. "You can't pretend you aren't part of this. Stay here with me. Watch."

I pull away from him.

"Stay." His voice is harsh. "It's the least you can do. If you are so set on protecting the Minotaur, at least you should see what he is. You should see what you are protecting."

"I know what he is," I say.

"Do you? Do you really?"

"Yes," I say, but my voice is not as certain as I want it to be. Do I know? Really? When was the last time I watched my brother eat? It was when I was a little girl with the cows.

"I can't," I say. "I can't."

"Stay, Ariadne," Theseus says. "You owe it to Vortigern. What are you afraid of?"

Theseus steps closer, his body next to mine.

"Competitors to their seats," a production assistant says, coming up from behind the stage.

I look at the spots where the competitors will be sitting, fourteen chairs in a row, one empty one where Vortigern was. Every night there will be one more empty chair. Unless one of them kills the Minotaur. One of the production assistants has set a small stool next to Theseus's seat. Icarus wants me to sit next to Theseus. He wants me to watch.

"Stay," Theseus says. His face is calm, and brave, and his eyes have that look in them. The one we share. The look of someone who has been swept up by forces they cannot control.

I cannot give him everything he wants.

However, I can give him this.

I nod and follow him over to the stool to watch.

FOURTEEN

DAEDALUS'S VOICE FILLS THE STADIUM. "VORTIGERN of Athens has reached the first branch of the tunnel."

On the screen, we see Vortigern face a branch in the tunnel.

"Which way will he go?" Daedalus asks. The music underneath is suspenseful, adding to the atmosphere.

From the left fork, a growl sounds, echoing off the concrete walls.

Vortigern hesitates.

Next to me, Theseus says, talking to himself as much as to Vortigern, who can't hear him, "Don't hunt the Minotaur yet, man. Wait until you have a weapon."

The maze is full of obstacles that can also be used as

weapons. Learning to use those weapons against the Minotaur is an important part of the competitors' training in Athens.

Vortigern doesn't do as Theseus suggests, turning instead toward the Minotaur's growl. As he moves forward, the motion sensor lights turn on, illuminating the path with their pale light only when he is a few yards away from whatever is next.

In the stadium, the camera shifts to the Minotaur. He is near his room, but he has caught Vortigern's scent. His eyes are dark red.

The camera switches to Vortigern still making his way through the tunnel.

Then we have video from the stands. Acalle, leaning forward and watching. She is biting one of her perfect fingernails. Has she gotten attached to Vortigern? Did Icarus warn her about that, too?

When we see Vortigern again, he's picking up speed, jogging.

Another roar echoes from deep in the maze, but closer than it was.

Next to me, Theseus whispers, "Don't run, man, don't run. There isn't any hurry."

The camera jumps to show us a dark pit ahead of Vortigern. He can't see it yet.

The lights flash on at the last possible minute, and Vortigern pulls up short.

Daedalus tells the crowd, "Vortigern has discovered his first obstacle—the Pit of Fire—a thirty-foot stretch of tunnel where the floor has been replaced with a fiery pit, ten feet deep.

Platforms are placed at eight-foot intervals. Vortigern's task will be to jump from platform to platform, without getting barbecued."

The screen shows a video of the obstacle. The bottom of the pit is covered in volcanic rocks, with jets of red flame shooting up.

Theseus says, "He should have gone the other way. There are no weapons there."

Vortigern looks at the obstacle, obviously trying to decide the best way to run it.

"The problem," Daedalus explains to the crowd, "is that while it is easy enough to reach the first platform, how will he get to the next one?"

"Look on the wall," Theseus says, beside me. "Look on the wall, you idiot."

Just then, Vortigern notices it, too. Tied to a cleat on the wall is a thick rope. Vortigern grabs it.

He leans back on the rope and lets himself swing forward, landing heavily on the first platform.

The crowd cheers loudly, and Acalle is smiling.

In the maze, another rope is tied to the wall beside Vortigern, and he manages the next platform and the next with relative ease. Now he has the flat ground of the tunnel ahead of him, but it is a bigger gap to get there than the others have been.

He backs himself to the edge of his platform, then swings out hard, throwing his body forward at the last minute with so much force that he ends up splayed out on the floor.

"Not bad," Theseus says, and the crowd cheers.

This is why I don't watch; I don't want to be rooting for these young Athenians. I don't want to be confused about my loyalties.

That's another lie.

I don't watch because I can't stand to see the Minotaur this way.

As if the producers are reading my mind, the next shot is not Vortigern, quickly making his way through the turns of the maze. It is the Minotaur.

His hot breath coming quickly.

He comes to a turn and is still for a moment, turning his massive head from side to side, sniffing the air. I try to see some sign of my brother in this face.

He isn't there.

I see only hunger.

The Minotaur takes off at a loping run and the camera switches to Vortigern, who is walking slowly through the tunnel, looking for dangers.

At another fork in the tunnel, Vortigern turns right. After he has walked for a few minutes, there is a whirring sound.

"What the . . . ," Vortigern says, taking a big step backward as a line of sharpened wooden stakes slams down from the ceiling, then retracts as quickly as it came down.

"Vortigern has found the Stake Wall," Daedalus tells us.

The image switches to a video of the obstacle. Five rows of stakes smashing down from the ceiling. Twelve feet separates each set of stakes, but they go up and down quickly at different rates.

"It will be up to Vortigern to make it through safely before he is found by the Minotaur . . ."

We see that the Minotaur has come to the same split in the tunnel that Vortigern passed a few minutes ago. The Minotaur raises his head, smelling the air. He takes the turn, following Vortigern, and the music increases in intensity.

"There has to be a pattern," Theseus says, watching intently. "There has to be a system."

Vortigern stares at the stakes as they go up and down. Sometimes there is barely a second between them, not enough time to make it through, but other times they stay up long enough to run under them and face the next set, rising and falling in their turn.

A roar echoes through the tunnel.

Vortigern turns and sees the Minotaur standing at his full height.

Beside me, Theseus whispers, "Come on, Vortigern, it's four fast, one slow, two fast, one slow, man. Get out of there. That's no place to make a stand."

Vortigern must not have figured it out. The next time the stakes come down, he grabs one of the lengths of wood, pulling hard and ripping it from its mounting in the ceiling. He turns to face the Minotaur, holding the stake out as a weapon.

In the stadium, the crowd roars.

This is why they came. This is why they are here.

Vortigern is trapped, and the Minotaur knows it.

His bellow of triumph fills the tunnel, its amplified reverberation filling the stadium above.

I want to close my eyes. I want to look away.

Vortigern brandishes his stick at the Minotaur.

"Come on," Vortigern shouts. "Come and get me!"

Beside me, Theseus sighs.

In the maze, the Minotaur's eyes never leave Vortigern and his sharpened stick. Then, exactly as he did with me last night, the Minotaur drops his head and charges.

Vortigern holds his stake steady, pointing it right at the Minotaur's heart. At the last minute, he dodges to the side, using the stake to stab the Minotaur's chest, then running past him.

My hands cover my mouth.

A gash opens up the Minotaur's chest, blood staining his skin.

His roar is full of rage.

The Minotaur spins, focused on Vortigern.

They have traded positions. Vortigern has the open tunnel behind him, and the Minotaur is in front of the Stake Wall.

Beside me, Theseus says, "Run."

Instead, Vortigern runs at the Minotaur, holding his spear in the attack position. At the last minute, the Minotaur shifts to the left, avoiding the spear and using his right horn to gouge a long cut in Vortigern's unprotected left flank, the cut drawing blood and worse from his gut. The force of the Minotaur's blow slams Vortigern into the narrow tunnel wall, and the spear drops from his hand.

Vortigern reaches for the wound, as though he could possibly close it with his hands.

With a savage push of his arms, the Minotaur sends Vortigern backward into the space where the stakes have risen up into the ceiling, and before Vortigern can roll, before he can protect himself, the line of stakes comes down, the sharpened wood slamming into his soft body.

Vortigern is screaming and screaming as the stakes impale him and blood soaks the ground.

Around me in the stadium, the people are cheering. They got a fight. They got what they wanted.

I look down the row of competitors, their faces numb.

The camera shows Acalle in the stands. She is pale, tears making mascara run down her cheeks.

"Get out of there, Ariadne," Icarus says in my ear, urgent. "Don't watch this."

I nod. I can't see this. I've seen enough.

I stand, but Theseus grabs my wrist.

"Wait," he says. His eyes on me are fierce. Certain. "You have to watch."

"I can't," I whisper. I am shaking like sails in the wind. My teeth are chattering with the awfulness of what I have seen.

"Stay," Theseus says. "You owe Vortigern that."

Every part of me is pushing to be away from here. "Why would he want me to see this?"

"Then stay for me."

His gaze is clear, serious. Honest.

"Stay with me, please."

I sit back down on the stool and look up at the screen. Feeling Theseus's hand tight in mine.

The Minotaur pulls the limp body of Vortigern out from under the stakes. This boy who was alive, awake, strong, moments ago is limp and dead.

The Minotaur bends down over Vortigern's body, and when he rises up, his snout is covered in blood.

In my mind, I am not here, in the stadium. I am in the pasture with the cows. When my brother tore their flesh with his teeth and his horns. His face covered in blood and gore.

His eyes are the color of dried blood, full of hunger as he bends again to Vortigern's body, as he lifts his head and crows in triumph.

There is nothing of the gods in this.

I gag, vomit rising in my throat. I know I will be sick right here if I don't get away. I yank my hand out of Theseus's and bolt away from the stage. Theseus is behind me.

A cameraman pulls out of the line, ready to follow me, but in my earpiece, Icarus says, "Leave her. Let her go."

Out of the stadium, I rush toward Temple Row. I have to get back to my room. Block out what I have witnessed. Lose myself.

I make it to the Temple of Zeus before I cannot go any

farther. I vomit prolifically on the pedestal under the statue of the Thunder God. The Father God.

His lidless eyes look down, watching me the whole time.

I kneel in front of Zeus, retching and heaving.

My heart races in my chest as I try to force away the image of my brother's snout coated in blood and gore.

I am crouched before the statue, hands on my knees. Hollow inside, the pile of vomit staining the white marble of the pedestal.

"How can this be what you demand?" I whisper to the god who I kneel before. "How can you have made my brother into this?"

Footsteps come up behind me, but I don't turn. Is it my bodyguards, coming to take me back to my room? Icarus coming to bring me back in front of the cameras?

Then a hand rests on my shoulder, and I know, instantly. It's Theseus.

He gently moves my hair away from my face.

"Come on," he says. "Let's get you up."

I'm still wobbly and shaking as I stand, and we walk around to the back side of the statue, where there is a marble fountain. The water bubbles up from a sacred spring, and you are supposed to wash before entering the temple. I hold my hands under the cold clear water, then take a drink, swallowing the bitter taste of my own sick.

Together, Theseus and I sit on the bottom step of the temple, looking out at the back of Zeus and the row of temples beyond.

"Now do you see?" Theseus asks me quietly. "Do you understand what you are supporting? What you are making possible? It's horrible, Ariadne."

I nod. "Yes, I can see it."

"Then why are you still part of it? Why won't you help me end it?"

"You don't understand," I say, shaking my head back and forth.

"Then tell me," he says. His voice is rising. He is angry with me. "Why do you have to protect that monster? Why can't you help me?"

My throat is closing. I've never said these words out loud to anyone.

He grabs my shoulders. "Why, Ariadne?" He's shouting now. "You owe me the truth!"

The words are stuck inside me. I try to force them out. "He's my brother," I whisper, so soft he can't hear me. Finally, it erupts from me. "The Minotaur is my brother!"

The pressure of Theseus's hands lessens. "Your what?"

"My brother," I say more quietly. "The Minotaur is my baby brother."

I can tell he doesn't believe me. "How is that possible? How can that be? He's a *monster*."

I hold out my hands, begging him to understand.

"It's more than that," I say. "He's more than that."

"How?" Theseus looks bewildered.

"You know about my mom with the bull?" I ask.

He nods.

"So after that, my brother was born. He was a baby. A little baby. With the head of a calf. More than a monster."

"You saw what happened, Ariadne, he *is* a monster."

"It isn't his fault," I say in a small voice. "He doesn't have any choice," I try to explain. "He has to eat people. He can't help himself. It's like a sickness. He hates it."

"What if you could cure him?" Theseus asks me. "What if you could end this?"

How can he not have been listening? "What do you think I've been trying to do?" I say, my voice rising. "I'm not doing this for fun! I do exactly what the gods demand, and in return, they will set him free."

"When?" he asks quietly. "How many times do you have to do this before you get what you want?"

My shoulders slump. "I don't know. The gods don't talk to me. How could I know?"

He takes my hand in his, turning it over and tracing a line on my palm.

"Maybe they don't talk to you because you are asking the wrong questions."

There is no way the gods want this. It can't be right. If the gods don't want this, what do they want?

I let Theseus wrap his arms around me. I let myself be lost for a moment as he holds on to me.

Then I hear Icarus. "Ariadne, come to the control room, now. I have to show you something. It's important."

I stand up.

"Where are you going?" Theseus asks me, keeping my hand.

"I have to see Icarus," I say.

"I'm coming with you."

I know Theseus isn't allowed into the control room, but I don't care. Right this minute, I don't want to be alone anymore.

In the control room, Icarus is sitting in a chair, looking at a piece of paper in his hands.

It's a picture of himself with wings. He's spread out the wrinkles and is staring at it.

He looks up numbly and doesn't comment on Theseus's presence here, in the most secure place on Crete, except for the maze itself.

"What's going on?" I ask.

He takes a deep breath. "I have to show you something, but I really don't want to."

"What is it?" I ask.

He turns in his chair, putting the picture down on the desk. Then he picks up a small flash drive.

"Okay, look," he says. "My dad has a hidden safe in our rooms, and he keeps these flash drives with records of things that he thinks are important—things he'll use if he ever needs to. He calls them insurance."

"Insurance against what?" I ask.

"He signed a contract to come here, but the flash drives keep everyone honest."

"Blackmail material," Theseus says.

Icarus shrugs. "I prefer the euphemism, but you can call it that, if you must."

I look at the flash drive in his hand. It has a tiny printed label reading: MINOS 10- ARIADNE.

"Why do you have it?" I ask.

Icarus runs his hand over his eyes. "You have to understand. I've never looked at the flash drives. I didn't want to know. It always felt better that way, safer, too. But then, after today, seeing you watch the Minotaur—I had to know . . ."

Icarus is never like this. So faded.

"What did you see?" I ask, reaching for the flash drive, but before I can get it, Icarus grabs my wrist, holding it tightly.

"Ariadne, you have to understand: I didn't know. I promise you, I never knew."

He inserts the flash drive into his computer and an image comes up on the widescreen in front of us.

It's Daddy and Daedalus, in Daddy's office. But you can tell it's from a long time ago, from their clothes and the lack of gray in their hair.

Daddy leans back in his chair. "What are you telling me, Daedalus?"

Daedalus paces back and forth. "I'm telling you that the oracle is clear. You are going to have to sacrifice the white bull. The gods sent it so that you could sacrifice it to honor them."

That's our bull. The one that rose from the sea.

Daddy slams his hands on the desk. "It's mine. It came onto my beach. To show that I was right in my war with Athens. Now you're telling me that I'm supposed to sacrifice it?"

"Listen again to the oracle, Your Majesty," Daedalus says, and you can tell he's modulating his voice, forcing himself not to get too excited, too pushy, which is the surest way to find yourself stuck as Xenodice's lead pedicure tech. He pulls a piece of paper from his pocket, the small sheet you are given after visiting the Oracle at Delphi, and he reads, *"The gods granted you a gift in victory over Athens. As his due, Poseidon demands a monumental sacrifice in turn."*

He lays the paper down, carefully, with the reverence that it's due as a sign from the gods. "That means this bull."

I look at Icarus. "Daddy always says the gods didn't want him to sacrifice the bull . . ."

"Shhh," Icarus says.

On screen, Daddy frowns. "I won't sacrifice it. It's mine. It's the proof that I was right in attacking Athens. I'm not killing it."

"Your Majesty," Daedalus begins.

"Enough. The gold we take from Athens will have to be enough for the gods. I'm done with this conversation."

The feed fades to black.

"So it could have ended then," Theseus says, his fists clenched.

I'm shaking my head. "It can't be right," I say. "Daedalus must have misunderstood the oracle. If the gods wanted Daddy to sacrifice the bull, he would have done it . . ."

Another image starts.

We're back in Daddy's office. Daedalus and Daddy are in evening wear.

"Where is my wife?" Daddy asks. "Why is she not at the party?"

His voice is louder with each word.

Daedalus looks very nervous. "She tried to jump the paddock fence again, Your Majesty. To see the bull."

I blush in my seat. This is when my mother first fell in love with the bull. I remember her face in my room the other night, when she got me ready for the drawing. Her fascination. Her certainty. Her words—*How could I have been wrong when the gods made it so?*

Daddy is very still. Not saying anything, waiting for Daedalus to continue.

"If I may offer a theory," Daedalus says.

"Go on," Daddy says.

"The gods must be causing this, Your Majesty. It will be abated if we sacrifice the bull."

"What have I told you about this?" Daddy's voice is controlled, but his face is red. He is far angrier at this suggestion than he was at the fact that my mother was trying to make love to a bull. His anger breaks through in a rage as he stands. "We are not sacrificing that bull. Take more from Athens. Give that to the gods."

Even through the screen and through the years, I lean back, away from his rage.

Daedalus holds up his hands, staying remarkably calm. "Your Majesty, by our calculations, Athens has paid us as much as they possibly can without causing the full collapse of their economy."

"What difference does that make to me?" Daddy asks, his voice quiet.

Daedalus bows. "As you say, sir. What about your wife?"

Daddy collapses in his chair. "Figure it out, Daedalus, do whatever you need to do to make this go away."

"The wooden cow," I say in a whisper.

Because my father was so stubborn, so unwilling to admit that the bull was supposed to be sacrificed to the gods, he let Daedalus build that wooden cow.

A new video starts.

Daddy is pacing the largest dining room, while Daedalus stands very still holding a piece of paper. A vase full of flowers is broken on the floor.

"Get on with it," Daddy says angrily. "Things are worse and worse. What have you figured out?"

"My theory is that since your wife . . ." Daedalus pauses, taking a breath. Then pushes forward. "Since your wife consorted with the white bull, prior to her pregnancy, this creature is the product of that union."

"Half bull," Daddy says, looking daggers at Daedalus. "Did you know that this was possible when you set all this up?"

"No, Your Majesty, I did not," Daedalus says. "But the wooden cow was the only way, without sacrificing—"

"Don't say it," Daddy says. "I don't want to hear another word about sacrificing that white bull."

"Yes, sir," Daedalus says. "This creature is new to science. I am calling it a Minotaur. It means Minos's bull."

"I know what it means," Daddy says thoughtfully, a growing sparkle in his eyes. "It is a new species, you say?"

"Yes," Daedalus says. "New and uniquely dangerous. And getting more so by the day. Surely you have seen the reports: the slaughter of the cattle with Ariadne. The incident with a member of the kitchen staff who had been sent down to take a meal."

"You got that hushed up, Daedalus, there is no reason for anyone to know . . ."

"He ate the boy, Your Majesty."

"Yes, yes, I know. Get to the point, Daedalus. What does the oracle say?"

Daedalus reads the oracle's message, carefully, leaning backward, away from Daddy's rage. "*The gods granted you a gift in victory over Athens. As his due, Poseidon demands a monumental sacrifice in turn.*"

"It's the same as the last time." Daddy slams his fist on the table. "They can't even have that bull now. It was more trouble than it was worth—refusing to breed with my cattle and tearing up the fences—Heracles captured it. I sent it to Athens. I would be shocked if anyone will be able to kill it."

"I killed it," Theseus says. "I killed that bull."

"Shhh," Icarus says.

"I no longer believe the gods are asking for the bull, Your Majesty," Daedalus says. "I think they desire another sacrifice. A greater one. I think they are asking you to sacrifice the Minotaur."

Daddy's eyes narrow dangerously.

"You think they want me to sacrifice my Minotaur?" Daddy asks, his voice thoughtful.

Daedalus nods. "Yes, sir, I do."

He is silent for a long time. Leaving Daedalus to stand and wait.

When he speaks again, there is a strange light in his eyes. "I have a task for you, Daedalus. I think you will like it."

Daedalus steps forward.

"I need for you to build me an underground maze," Daddy continues. "As large as you can make it. The largest in the world."

Daedalus has a familiar hungry look. The excitement of a new project.

"When?" he asks.

"As quickly as you can," Daddy says. "Money is no object."

Daedalus gets a faraway look, already laying the plans.

"I'll send you a list of specifications," Daddy says. "Oh, and Daedalus, bring Aegeus of Athens to Crete. I need to talk to him."

"What about the Minotaur?" Daedalus asks. "Do you want me to contact the priests about the best way to sacrifice him?"

Daddy's lip curls. "Daedalus, you have no vision. We aren't going to *sacrifice* the Minotaur, we're going to use him to glorify Crete."

The television goes dark.

"See?" Theseus says, looking at me. "You see? The Minotaur is meant to die."

"That can't be right," I say.

"Wait," Icarus says, holding his hand out as the next video starts. "It gets worse."

Daddy is in his office with Daedalus standing behind his chair when Aegeus walks in.

"My father," Theseus whispers.

Aegeus is gray-haired, with a very nice suit and a heavy gold pendant over his tie. He has an expensive watch on his wrist and a heavy ring on his finger. He looks tired behind his tanned skin and white teeth.

"What can I tell you, Minos," Aegeus says to Daddy. "You have bled us dry. We have nothing more to give."

His gold pendant and watch suggest there might be a bit more they could give.

"I have an offer for you," Daddy says, leaning forward. "A mutually beneficial offer."

Aegeus has a greedy look. "What is it?"

"We have a new monster in Crete," Daedalus says from his spot behind Daddy.

"A Minotaur," Daddy says, savoring the word. "It requires human flesh to keep it calm. As food."

Aegeus looks disgusted, but he quickly masks it. He is clearly interested in finding out what they are offering.

"What does this have to do with me?" Aegeus asks.

"I need fourteen teenagers, once a year," Daddy says.

"To feed your monster," Aegeus says thoughtfully.

"My Minotaur," Daddy says. "Only the bravest and most beautiful would be acceptable. Send them here, as competitors, to fight in a maze that Daedalus is finishing. A fight to the death."

Aegeus drums his fingers on the chair, thinking. "Why fourteen?" he asks.

"Because I like fourteen," Daddy says. "Seven girls and seven boys. It's a lucky number."

"He can't—" Theseus says, then stops himself, because we know that he did.

"The competitors . . . ," Aegeus says. "Must they be of the true, old, pure blood of Athens? Of the nobility?"

Daddy rubs his hands together. "I am sure the Minotaur will find the blood of new Athenians as tasty as he does the oldest families. As long as they are residents of Athens, brave and beautiful, that will be enough. And you can keep your gold."

"We are quite depleted in gold now," Aegeus says, his face crafty. "I am not sure that we have the funds to hold a competition to find the bravest and most beautiful. Or to get them to Crete . . ."

Daddy leans in, leading Aegeus. "I'm sure we could find

some kind of stipend. A stream of funds that would make things easier."

Next to me, Theseus growls.

"My people could never know," Aegeus says. "My brother is always scheming against me. If he knew about this . . ."

"Not to worry," Daddy says, smiling. "Daedalus will handle the transfers. It will be invisible."

Aegeus holds out his hand. "Done."

The screen fades to black and Icarus pauses the video.

Beside me, Theseus's fists are clenched on the arms of his chair.

"He sold them." He says it quietly. "He sold them. One hundred and forty-one kids so far, and how many more in future years?" Theseus jumps up. "Why didn't he argue? Why didn't he fight? Why didn't he make war against Crete to stop it?"

Icarus stares at the screen. "I don't know," he says.

"I . . . I . . . ," I say, not knowing what to say, what to do. There must be more here than we have seen. Some private message from the gods. Some reason why this was allowed to continue.

"Ariadne," Icarus says, putting his hand on my shoulder. "There's more."

I am shaking my head. "I can't watch it, Icarus. I can't . . ."

"You have to watch, Ariadne," Icarus says. "It's about you."

Theseus takes my hand. I let him hold on to it, dreading what

I will see. I force myself to breathe, force myself to sit up higher in my chair. I'm not a child. Whatever is coming, I can handle it.

On the widescreen, Daedalus paces back and forth in front of Daddy's desk, his hair wild from running his hands through it. They both look the same as they did in the video from Aegeus's visit, so it must be around the same time.

"*The Labyrinth Contest* debuts tonight, Your Majesty, but I'm not sure we're going to make it. The earthquakes are damaging every quarter of the city." He stops walking and stands in front of Daddy. "Every time we get near the gates to the maze, he rattles the foundations of the palace. For the sake of the gods, Your Majesty—you are going to have to sacrifice him before he brings the city down around us. The only thing that calms him is Ariadne."

"I will do no such thing," Daddy says. "I'm not giving up on this. We are having *The Labyrinth Contest*, and we are not sacrificing my Minotaur. You told me the answer weeks ago, we just have to have the balls to see it through. If the only thing that calms the Minotaur is Ariadne, then she will be the one to lead the competitors to the gate. We will make her the Keeper of the Maze."

Daedalus looks down at his hands. "She is a child," he says quietly.

"She is my daughter," Daddy says, his face firm. "She will do as she is told. Bring her here."

In the next image, I am standing in front of my daddy's desk. Six years old, in my chiton. My long hair curled and tied back with a bow. Holding my mask in my hand. I look like a baby, my hands still dimpled.

Daddy walks around the desk and kneels in front of me, putting his hands on my shoulders. "The gods have a plan for you, sweetheart," he says. "And for your brother. He can do more good for our family this way." He wipes a tear off my cheek with his thumb. "Be brave, my sweet girl. Remember, it won't be forever. The ways of the gods are mysterious. Only they know what they will do."

These are the words I've heard countless times.

"How long will he be down there?" I ask. "How long until he is cured?" The questions I've always asked.

"We can't know," Daddy says. "We must trust the gods."

My little lip starts to tremble. "But, Daddy, Asterion is . . ."

I shudder hearing his name aloud outside of the maze, and my transgression is clear on Daddy's face.

"Ariadne." His voice is stern, full of disappointment.

I hold out my hand and he slaps it, hard. Then he pulls me in for a hug. "Remember, darling," he says. His face is shadowed. "We must never, never say his name."

"Yes, Daddy," I say, my voice muffled.

Daddy stands and motions to his desk, where a wrapped gift is waiting. "Look, I got you something."

"A present?" I ask, brightening.

I can remember it. That gift, on the table. Wrapped in silver paper with a blue bow. Something for me. On the screen, I tear into the paper, and inside, there is a new gaming console. A VR headset and ten games. I can remember my excitement. By that time, I had already started playing video games. But this was top of the line. Something I had been wanting for months. I remember thinking how jealous Icarus would be of it.

"When can I play it?" I ask on the screen.

"Soon," Daddy says. "Tonight. In a few minutes, you will lead one of those competitors we met to the gates of the maze in the stadium. As soon as you are done, Daedalus will take you back to your room, and you can play games as long as you want."

"What will happen to the competitor?" I ask.

"That is nothing you need to worry about," he says. "Now, let's put that mask on."

My little girl's face is covered by the blank white of the mask.

Icarus turns off the widescreen and pulls out the flash drive and gives it to Theseus.

"I made a copy. I thought you might want to have this one."

Theseus slips it into his pocket. "There's one more thing," Icarus says. "You remember how you asked me if the drawing could be rigged? If the numbers could be changed? And I said no?"

I nod. "I remember. Because the cards are made of wood with numbers burned into them. They couldn't be changed."

"Yeah," he says. "You need to look at this." He hands me a card. I flip it over and over in my hand. It is blank. There is no burned-in number on the face of it.

"There's no number on it," I say. "I don't understand."

"Yeah," Icarus says. "Neither do I. They always have a number on them. So why doesn't this one?"

I stand up, pulled out of my chair by an invisible string. "I have to talk to my father."

"What are you going to say to him?" Icarus says.

I push my fingers against my palms, my fingernails digging into my skin, pressing against the slowly healing scrapes from my fall in the maze. "I have to know if it's true. I have to hear him say that it was a lie."

"Be careful," he says.

"Icarus," I say, reaching toward him, grabbing his hand with mine. "What are *you* going to do?"

"I don't know," he says, then he gently moves my hand away. "Get out of here. Go do what you need to do."

FIFTEEN

BEFORE THESEUS AND I STEP ONTO THE ELEVATOR, I look down at the blank wooden card. My whole life, these cards have been sacred. Kept in a golden box inside a special inlaid cabinet. Blessed by the priests before the drawing. They are given to me in the burlap sack immediately before the ceremony, then returned to the box after we are done.

They are relics.

Because they show the will of the gods, I have been told to revere them—not as symbols of godly power but as a tangible sign of the divine.

Now I know that isn't what they are. They are tools for our manipulation.

I grip the card, as though if I understand this, I will understand everything else.

I realize that the outside of this card won't tell me anything. It's a trick. A scam. I need to see the inside. I need to see the guts of the thing.

A week ago, a day ago, an hour ago, it would have felt like sacrilege to even roughly handle this small card.

But now?

A fierce joy rises in me as I grip each end of the card between fingers and thumbs and bend it, forcing the shape to warp and stretch, and, finally, break.

With a snap the card cracks in two, revealing what I had already guessed—a wafer-thin sheet of light diodes and electronics, sheathed in a translucent wooden veneer.

One thing pretending to be something else.

Like my life.

I hand one of the broken halves to Theseus.

"It was a lie," he says. "None of it had to happen."

I stare down at my hands, gripping the broken piece of the card. Shaking.

"How can they have done this?" I say, reeling at the scale of it. "How can they have used me this way? For so long?"

Theseus pulls me in closer to him.

"I know," he says. And he does.

He has been betrayed, too. Lied to. By his father, his grandfather. Even his mother. Now he has the fresh betrayal that his father sold his people. That the Athenians never had to come here. That he never had to volunteer.

"I don't know what to say."

"I'm glad I met you," he tells me. Then he turns me to face him, looking into my eyes. He reaches out and runs a calloused thumb down the side of my face, and I let myself lean in toward his hand, toward the strength of him.

The silence rests between us, as he waits for whatever I'm going to say.

I nod. "I feel—" I say, but I stop myself. I'm not used to talking about what I feel. I don't have the words.

"What is it?" he whispers, putting his other arm up to my shoulder, holding me.

"Like I'm at the edge of a cliff. Like I'm going to throw myself off. Like I'm never going to stop falling . . ."

"I'll catch you," he whispers, then leans in to kiss me. In that moment, wrapped in his arms, his lips on mine, I believe him.

The pleasure of kissing him, of feeling his arms around me, of touching him, fills me with a golden glow, like the sun rising over the waves.

We break apart and look at each other, both full of wonder.

"I've never—" he starts.

"—felt this before," I finish.

"I was going to say, met anyone like you," he says. "But that's true, too."

He kisses my forehead gently.

"Are you ready to go to a dance party?" I ask.

Theseus looks down at his competitor's uniform—the warrior kilt and open vest. "I'm not exactly dressed for it," he says.

"Not to worry," I say. "With those legs, you'll be welcome anywhere."

Theseus and I spot Daddy in his favorite banquette, looking out at the writhing bodies on the dance floor, nursing a martini. I try to read him, wondering what he is thinking—he is proud of this, because he owns it.

I leave Theseus at the bar, accepting one last kiss.

Daddy makes room for me on the bench, and the wool of his tuxedo jacket is scratchy against my bare arm. I take in the smell of him. Gin and tobacco and cologne. Daddy. Comfort. Home.

I close my eyes for a moment, steeling myself. I can do this. I can stand up to him. I'm not going to be afraid of him anymore.

"Daddy," I say.

"What is it, baby?" he asks, looking away from the dancers and back at me.

"Can I talk to you for a minute?"

"Sure," he says. "Let's go in the private dining room."

We head to a door hidden in the panels of the wall. It opens into a small dining room, drenched in red. Scarlet fabric on the walls, wine-colored carpet on the floor. The chairs upholstered in a crimson paisley.

Daddy's bodyguards and the two priests follow us into the room.

"Have a seat, sweetheart," Daddy says. "Whatcha got?"

"I want to talk to you," I say.

He rests his hand on mine across the table, and I think about everything that I have just seen, and I want to pull my hand away. But I don't.

"I know what you're going to say," he says. "I saw that you watched the boy go into the maze today, and that must have been hard. There's a reason I don't want you to watch."

I nod, ready to interrupt.

"I'll tell you," he says, "it made for great television. There isn't a person in the global viewing audience who doesn't believe you'll help that boy now. The look on your face. The horror. That was a good job, baby. I'm proud of you. I had no idea we had a little actress on our hands."

Acting. Like what I'm doing right now, as I pretend that everything is okay. As I pretend that my whole world hasn't been blown to pieces.

I take one of my hands out of his and put it into my pocket, touching my silver thread and, beside it, the blank card Theseus and I broke.

"Daddy," I say. "I have to ask you something."

"What is it, sweetheart?"

I remember the questions I've asked before: When will this end? Why did it happen? When will my brother be cured? None of these are my question now.

"Daddy," I say, holding on to the moment, knowing somehow that I'm about to break something. "Why didn't we sacrifice the white bull when it came out of the sea?"

The indulgent smile on Daddy's face slips.

"You know why," he says. "Why would the gods have given me something so amazing, only to have me kill it?"

"Praise the gods," the priests chant from the corner.

"How could you be sure that the gods didn't *intend* for you to kill it?" I ask, keeping my voice level. Like this is a normal conversation.

"Excuse me?" He pulls his hand from mine and stands.

I know that if I continue, I will never again be his favorite, never again be the best of all of us.

How could I live with myself if I don't?

I remember Theseus down in the accommodations asking me what I really wanted. I couldn't tell him. I couldn't say out loud that I wanted to break the world. That I wanted to tear it down.

And that's what I'm going to do.

"How do you know what the gods wanted?" I say. "How do you know that they didn't want you to sacrifice the bull? How do you know that they wanted to use *The Labyrinth Contest* to heal Asterion—"

"Don't say that name." He cuts me off.

"How do you know?" I continue, keeping my voice calm.

"I had a dream," he says.

And I know, with the certainty of a cold clear night when

you can see every star, that it was a lie. I know it as soon as I think it. It was always a lie.

"What about the oracle?" I ask. "Did the oracle tell you to have this contest?"

"The oracle," he says, his voice very low, a pulse beating next to his eyebrow. "The oracle. Yes."

"Is that exactly what it said?" I ask.

"Of course it was," he says, dismissive. Everything about him is saying *Leave it alone, Ariadne.*

I keep myself so calm. I'm not leaving it. Not this time.

"Are you sure?" I ask, making him lie again. "Are you sure that was what the prophecy said?"

"Of course it was," he says, pacing away from me. He doesn't want me to see that I'm getting to him. He doesn't want to show his rising anger.

"Really?" I ask. "Because I know that it said, '*The gods granted you a gift in victory over Athens. As his due, Poseidon demands a monumental sacrifice in turn.*'"

My father's face is very red now, nearly purple, the pulse still beating next to his eye.

"Where did you hear that?" He stalks around the table toward me.

"It came to me in a dream," I lie, standing up from my chair, keeping my voice sweet, normal, like this is something we could talk about. "You were supposed to make a sacrifice. You were supposed to sacrifice the bull."

"A dream?" he says, his voice incredulous.

I nod.

"Well, here's what I'll tell you," Daddy says. "The gods wanted a sacrifice and that's what they got. I'd call a hundred and forty-one seventeen-year-olds a world-class sacrifice."

"It wasn't a sacrifice of anything you cared about," I say. "The gods wanted you to give up something of yours. That's what they wanted."

"The gods!" he roars. "The gods want what *I* want."

"Praise the gods," the priests chant in the corner.

"Get out!" Daddy yells, and the priests quickly leave the room. No question who they serve.

"What about Asterion?" I ask.

I have a wrenching, dawning sadness that this whole time I have been following a trail that other people laid out for me, never looking from side to side. Never asking any questions. I thought I was special because I hid from the cameras, because I was my own person. But I always only did what I was told.

"What about my brother?" I say.

"Gods, Ariadne, you are not a child anymore. It's not your brother. I don't care who its mother is. It's a monster, or have you not noticed that by now? It's never been anything but a monster, and it never will be. Its name isn't Asterion, it's the Minotaur—Minos's bull—and you'd better not forget it. The gods made your mother rut with a bull . . . a stinking bull . . . so that I could have the tool of my vengeance."

He steps forward and grabs me by the arms, his hands tightening. "Look at me," he says.

I lift my eyes up to his face, and I look at him. Somehow, it feels like I'm seeing him for the first time. His sharp eyes, always assessing, weighing and measuring and counting. Who owes him. What he can get. He doesn't love me, I realize with a shock. Not as a person. Not as Ariadne. I'm another thing he owns. Like the Minotaur.

"No matter what you think, this contest is never ending. Aegeus will keep sending me competitors, as he is paid to . . ."

"So it was never about vengeance?" I ask. "It was never about Androgeous?"

He laughs now, a nasty laugh. "Oh yes, it was always about Androgeous. I will have vengeance for my son. Eventually, you'll understand how much better it feels to screw someone over when they are begging you to do it. Every year, the old man is asking me when he's going to get paid. And you know the best thing? His precious Theseus is competing, and Aegeus can't stop it. He keeps calling me and leaving messages, 'Please spare my son,'"—he uses that voice he puts on to signal weakness, a high-pitched voice. A female voice. "He's offered to pay me millions, more than he's ever taken in payment from me. More than I ever got in tribute to let his son go, but I won't take his money. Because I have something better. I get to watch *his* son die."

He beams. "He can't ever stop this. He'll have to watch his son die, and he can't complain. He'll send me fourteen more competitors next year, without complaint. Because I can tell his people that he's been taking my coin all these years to keep those kids coming, and he won't have a kingdom anymore."

Daddy still has his hand on my upper arm, and he tightens it.

"Here's what is going to happen," he says. "The people will see a grand battle between a hero and a monster. They will see you helping Theseus for thirteen days."

I cannot move from his grip on my arm. His hand will leave a bruise.

Daddy's phone rings and he answers it. "What?" he shouts, keeping it on speaker.

It's one of his bodyguards. "Heracles booked his flight for tomorrow."

"Heracles is coming," I say. Not asking the question, just taking it in. "I thought you were going to keep him away from Acalle."

He shrugs. "I thought about it, but then I decided that wasn't what I wanted to do. Your mother thought everything with your sisters had gotten tame and maudlin with Acalle crying after that Athenian died today. We need to distract her. It'll be better this way. Everyone likes some drama."

I don't respond.

"Now listen," he says, turning back to me. Like things are fine between us. "I watched that episode last night, of you and Theseus, and it was good. But we're going to need more. I don't want any more of this modesty crap. Next time you're with Theseus, I need skin. Bare skin. We promised the advertisers nudity. At least to the nipples, so I'm going to need to see it."

I don't say anything.

"Do you understand?" Daddy asks.

"Perfectly," I say, leaving the room.

Because I do. For the first time in my life, I understand exactly what is going on.

When I get to the bar, my face must show Theseus that I'm in shock, because he doesn't ask me anything. He takes me by the arm. "Let's get out of here," he says.

Then I see Acalle leaning against the bar, her earlier tears gone and dress changed, but she does not seem entirely herself. A sadness pulls at the edges of her. Xenodice is next to her, clearly trying to cheer her up.

I realize that I can't leave Acalle not knowing that Heracles is coming tomorrow. That he's going to find her.

"One second," I say to Theseus, and he follows me over to the bar.

"Hey, Acalle," I say, tapping her arm.

"Hey," she says, pulling me into a hug. It is a real hug, not our normal air kiss routine.

"You okay?" I ask quietly.

"Yeah," she says, smiling ruefully. "I forgot rule number one: Don't get attached. We can't keep them."

She looks Theseus up and down appreciatively, then turns back to me.

"You should remember that, too," she says, her voice low. "Don't ever forget, Ariadne. None of this is real."

Vortigern's death was real, and the other competitors who came before him. Asterion's pain is real.

Theseus squeezes my hand. Whatever is going on between us is real, too.

"Some things are real," I say just as quietly.

She lifts her chin. "Not for me."

"Hey, listen," I say, wishing I didn't have to tell her what I'm about to. "Heracles is coming. He booked a flight for tomorrow."

"Daddy said—" and she stops. For a second, I see her hurt, her knowledge that my father knows that she's afraid of Heracles but doesn't care. Then she tosses her hair and laughs. "Between you and me, it will be quite the ratings contest. I wonder what Xenodice will have to do to get ahead of us."

Xenodice perks up, hearing her name. "What?" she says.

"Nothing," Acalle says. "It's nothing."

"It isn't," I say. "You don't have to do this . . ."

Acalle has a sad, empty smile. "I think I actually do," she says. "You do, too."

She lifts her drink off the bar and downs it in one smooth motion, then holds her hand high in the air. "I think I need to do some dancing!"

Xenodice shrieks.

And like that, they are gone.

Together, Theseus and I weave our way through the crowds of dancers.

My mother is waiting outside the doors to the ballroom. Her

sleeveless dress is long and red with a plunging neckline. Her nails are painted the same dark red, as are her lips. Her hair flows across her shoulders and down her back, a sheet of gold over her tanned skin. In the plush white and gold of the hallway, she is the only colorful thing.

As always, there is not an ounce of extra fat on her; she is as streamlined as a sports car, and as hard.

She looks at Theseus and me together, holding hands, and her eyes narrow.

"If it isn't the stars of the hour," she says. "The viewers can't keep their eyes off you. I told you that you were meant to be a star."

Yesterday, I would have argued with her. I would have told her that I wasn't doing anything to be a star.

Not now.

I don't care about arguing with her. I just want to hear the truth from my mother. I've never mentioned Asterion to her. Not since she barricaded herself in her room when he was born. The taboo that was placed on his name when I was a little girl has kept me from ever saying anything about him. From asking her if she even remembers him. I don't know what she thinks about any of this.

She is part of this. As much as anyone.

When my father didn't sacrifice the bull, she was the one who fell in love with it. She was the one who was humiliated. She was the one whose son is now trapped in the maze.

Is she a victim? Or a perpetrator? I have to know.

I ask her the same question that I asked my father. "Why didn't we sacrifice the white bull when it came out of the sea?"

If my question has fazed her, it doesn't show. "Daedalus wanted to," she says, "but your father was sure that it was a sign that he was still favored by the gods. Something too precious to be killed."

"And what about you?" I ask. "What did you think?"

She walks a few steps down the hall, toward a massive mirror in a gilded frame.

She looks at herself in the mirror, touching the blond hair at her temple, while Theseus and I stand barely out of the frame.

"What did I think?" she says. "On the day we received word that Androgeous had been killed in Athens, I begged the gods for vengeance. Your father led our armies off to Athens and defeated them. They paid their tribute in gold. That wasn't enough for me. Not nearly enough. Then the white bull rose from the sea. I knew it was the sign that the gods would answer my prayers for revenge."

Her eyes have a distant, secret look, and I'm embarrassed for her. I dare a glance at Theseus, and he looks like he would like to be anywhere but here.

"When I felt that passion for the bull, I knew it must have come from the gods, that it must be a way to carry out my vengeance. I begged Daedalus to help me."

I wonder if she's talked about this to anyone in the years since it happened.

"When I got pregnant, I picked the name Asterion, and I hoped I would have a boy who would grow into a strong man who could avenge his brother. A man who could rule Crete and rub Athens under the heel of his boot."

She straightens, apparently satisfied with her appearance, and then she turns her attention back to me.

"But he was a monster . . ." Her mouth twists, giving a glimpse of the howl of pain that she hides inside herself. Then she swallows it, and her face is perfect again. "I saw him, and I knew the gods would take their vengeance another way. If he keeps killing Athenians for another hundred years, it will not quench my thirst for their blood."

The distance between her calm, even, conversational tone and her bloodlust is chilling.

Theseus's anger radiates like heat off his body, and my mother must sense it.

"Do you want to know why, Athenian?" my mother asks, speaking to Theseus for the first time.

He doesn't answer, but that doesn't stop her.

"You Athenians took something that I can never have back. My boy. My son. My hero."

She drops her hand to her bracelet, running her fingers over the charm with the image of Androgeous. The only charm on a bracelet that could hold many. Funny that I never noticed that until now. Icy numbness grows in my stomach. What about my sisters, Asterion, me?

"Androgeous was worth more than the rest of you put

together." My mother's voice is low and secret, but full of power. This is her truth.

Theseus grips my hand, and I can feel his desire to defend me. But I squeeze his hand and give a slight shake of my head. I don't need for him to.

"I would give anything to have Androgeous back," my mother says now, her voice husky. "Anything; however, it is impossible. Since I cannot have my son, I will have vengeance."

Her voice is loud, but it drops again. "I would give all my other children to see my vengeance over Athens, and it still would not be enough."

Theseus and I have stepped away from her as she has been talking, as though the venom in her words could actually spill out and burn us.

I am shaking.

I always knew that I wasn't her favorite. I knew that. But I thought my sisters were. To hear that she would sacrifice any of us? It hurts more than I would have believed.

There is a sliver of ice at the heart of my mother. Has it always been there, or was it born when Androgeous died?

My mother comes close to us, her face proud.

She leans toward Theseus, smiling at his outrage.

"Now, Theseus of Athens." She runs her manicured hand across his bare chest, her red nails like blood against his skin. He shoves her hand away, and she laughs.

"Push me away if you like, but you are the sweetest tool of my vengeance. Because you have made my daughter want you."

She moves to me, touching the side of my face with her fingers, cold as ice.

"Darling," she says, but there is nothing affectionate in her voice. It is like a snake sliding over dry leaves. "You will make my vengeance complete. You want this boy, I can see it. You want to help him. And that will destroy Athens. Aegeus is watching: his hopes are raised. Nothing you can do will stop the Minotaur. When Theseus goes into the maze, he *will* be killed. Aegeus's son will be taken from him, just as he stole mine."

She drops her hand from me and turns, going through the doors, back into the party.

SIXTEEN

THESEUS AND I RUSH TOGETHER THROUGH THE PALACE, not speaking. I'm not sure either of us knows what to say yet.

I see everything around me with new eyes. The gilded hallways. The people who turn their backs as I walk by. The cameras mounted to the ceiling. They are all the bars of my cage.

Together, Theseus and I go to the massive fountain in front of the new hotel. We sit together on the side of it. It is still and peaceful now, in the silence before it begins its next display.

He wraps his arms around me.

A jet of water shoots up, red light refracting through it. Followed by another, and another, the splashes echoing on the still water.

"Gods, Ariadne, I don't know what to say. That was terrible. Your mother . . ."

I let him hold me close. It doesn't fix what I've heard, but I'd be lying if I said it didn't help a little.

The notes of the music start for the fountain display. In honor of *The Labyrinth Contest*, they are using the theme as the music this week. The first drums start their beat, the spouts of water shooting up in time, the red lights staining the water.

"That's not even the worst thing that has happened to me in the last hour," I say to Theseus.

He runs his hand over my hair. "Seriously? Because that sucked."

"Yeah, I know. My conversation with my father was worse."

He draws back from me a little, looking in my eyes. "How?"

The strings and horns have started on the theme, filling in the melody, but it's still slow, still building.

"He called the Minotaur an it," I say. "Asterion. He called Asterion an *it*. He said he's not really my brother. When I finally asked him the right questions, my father"—not Daddy, never Daddy again—"said the gods want what he wants. This was always about revenge. Never about my little brother. I believed . . . I believed that if I kept doing what I had been doing, Asterion could change . . ."

"I'm sorry, Ariadne," Theseus says, and I'm incredibly grateful that he doesn't say that he told me so, even though he did.

"I should have known." I choke out the words. The truth. "I should have guessed that it was a lie."

266

Theseus starts to say something, but I stop him.

"They told me that I was special, and I believed them. I let it keep happening . . . I never asked . . . I never thought . . . I never knew."

Theseus holds my hands, gently. "You know now, Ariadne. So what are you going to do about it?"

The fountain show has reached its climax, the music is blasting, and the water is waving and churning.

I think of Asterion last night, his signing.

All done. I'm all done.

The fountain finishes its show, the music stopping, the jets stilling. The only sign of turbulence is the ripples on the water. And even those fade.

I look over the still water. Past the new hotel. Up at the fields and hillsides beyond. At the trees where I imagined my brother playing. At the cattle in their pasture.

I close my eyes. My family was supposed to sacrifice the bull, but they didn't. They were supposed to sacrifice the Minotaur when Asterion changed, and they didn't do that, either. So Asterion has suffered, for eleven years. My parents will let him suffer for a hundred more years if they can. My parents won't end this. The gods won't end this.

"If we don't end this, no one will," I say.

"How?" he asks.

We can't risk talking about it here. We can't risk being overheard.

"Trust me," I say.

Theseus grabs my hand. "Will you come down to my room with me?" he whispers in my ear. "I'm not sure you should be alone."

That is what I want to do, more than anything.

But the word stops me—*alone.*

I think of a lonely figure, curled into a ball on a concrete bed in the middle of a bare room, at the center of an empty underground maze. The person who has suffered the most.

My brother. Asterion.

He was injured today. His chest torn with that wooden stake. I would have been there hours ago to clean and bandage it, if things were normal. He's down there, hurting. Waiting.

I'm going to hurt Theseus by telling him. I can't help it.

"I want to come with you so much," I say, pulling away.

"Then come." He presses his lips to my neck, right behind my ear.

"I can't," I say, making myself sound firm. Serious. "I have to go."

I take a step away from him so the sweet smell of him can't pull me back.

"You're going to the maze," he says. "To the Minotaur."

"He needs me," I say. "I'll meet you in the lobby at eight. We'll go talk to Icarus."

I give Theseus one last kiss, then leave him standing in front of the fountain.

Back in my room, I change into jeans and rainboots. Then I make the long trip down to the maze. When I make it to

Asterion's room, he's backed up in the corner, curled into a ball, quietly moaning. His brown eyes are full of pain and a desperate sadness. He is dripping wet from the water that Daedalus has sluiced through the maze, so any gore has washed off his body and his fur. He is shaking from the cold.

I unlock the cabinet, taking out my supplies. He comes to sit on the edge of the bed, and I dry him off, then clean his wound and bandage his side. Neither of us speaks.

Finally, once I have him tucked in, I say, "I love you, Asterion." I kiss his furry head.

He is asleep before I stand up from the edge of the bed.

I wake up clear-eyed in the light of day. I throw my toast in the fire and say my prayer, probably for the final time, but changed a little. *Please free my brother.*

I meet Theseus in the lobby and we go together to the control room.

The competitor who is supposed to go today is the short bulky boy with a crew cut, the one whose fear was clear on his face the first day. I don't think he will protest if Theseus takes his place in the line. Not like Hippolyta, who would probably push Theseus out of the way.

The hard part will be convincing Icarus to help us.

We find Icarus staring at his monitor, dark circles under his eyes, and I tell him and Theseus my plan.

"You know a hundred and forty-one other people have tried

to fight the Minotaur, right?" Icarus says. "The odds of Theseus surviving this are not good."

"Theseus isn't going to be killed in the maze," I say.

"You know that how?" Icarus says.

"It's his destiny," I say.

"Ariadne, we've just established that destiny is a manipulative pile of trash, have we not?" Icarus says, running his fingers through his hair.

I grab his hands. "I know, Icarus, but I don't have anything else to do. Asterion is miserable, desperately unhappy. I can't let him go from the maze, you know what he will do . . ."

Icarus shudders, thinking of the bloody consequences of that.

"I can't leave without him. More than that," I say, "Asterion doesn't want to be the Minotaur anymore. He is so tired of the killing. I hope that if Asterion is sacrificed, he can be saved."

Icarus stands and starts pacing, his hands pressed to his temples. "So you and Theseus go in the maze tonight, instead of the second competitor. Then let's say you kill the Minotaur. Then what?"

"I'm taking her to Athens with me," Theseus says.

"If we can manage to keep the cameras on, and keep the whole world watching," I say, "my father will have to give Theseus the prize. He will have to let us go—"

Icarus interrupts me, pinching the bridge of his nose. "No, Ariadne, he will have to let Theseus go. You, he will lock away."

I shrug. "You said it yourself, Icarus. We're already in prison. I don't care what the bars are made of."

Icarus grabs my hand. "Ariadne, this is a nice jail, with gold and cushions and cameras. I've seen your father's real jails, even if you haven't, and believe me, they are not nice. He tortures people. I don't mean like he tortures them by making them be in shows they don't want to be in. I mean like he cuts off their fingers. And toes."

Everything he is saying is true. I know it is. It doesn't matter. "Icarus, I can't live like this. Not anymore. I don't think you can, either."

He has taped the picture of himself with wings back on the inspiration board.

"Don't tell me that nothing has changed after seeing what we saw yesterday, knowing what we know, Icarus, because I won't believe you."

He rolls his eyes. "Give me a few days to forget about it. A few days to meditate on my own potential punishment."

"If we do it right, he won't catch me," I say. "Also, he won't know you had anything to do with it."

"You don't have to stay here," Theseus says to Icarus. "If we make it through this, I'm taking Ariadne with me. You could come, too."

Icarus laughs. "When I make my triumphant return to Athens, it will not be on an overcrowded boat full of second-rate reality stars." He looks at Theseus. "No offense."

"None taken."

"Also, I can't leave my dad," Icarus says.

"He's part of this, too," I say. I'm not as angry at Daedalus as I am at my dad, but it's pretty close. "He's kept the whole thing going."

"It's not the same," Icarus says. "When he signed his contract, he might not have understood what he was going to have to do, but he is stuck here. So am I."

"Okay, okay, you won't come with us," I say. "Will you help us? Keep the cameras rolling, no matter what. If people are watching and the ratings are going up, my father won't stop us. So you keep the audience engaged."

He nods. "Yes. That I can do." He starts shuffling through the papers on his desk. "Have you thought about what you're going to do when you get away? Do you have a phone that your dad can't track? Do you have any identification so you can get a job or a life once you leave here?"

I'm embarrassed. "Um, no. I guess I hadn't thought of that."

He gives Theseus a hard look. "You were going to take her to Athens, but you didn't think of this?"

Theseus shrugs.

Icarus turns back to me. "Having a phone your dad can track would make for a short-lived escape," he says, disgusted. "Thankfully, you have a friend who does think of these things." He shows me a tiny square of plastic with embedded electronics. "Give me your phone." He efficiently opens my phone, takes one card out, and installs the new one. "It's paid for a year. Now you're just Ariadne, a girl from Kydonia, nobody special." He brings me in for a tight hug. "Except to me."

"Kydonia?" I say, naming a medium-sized city, farther down the coast in Crete. "Icarus, I don't know anything about Kydonia."

"Neither does anyone else, sweetheart," he says. "Better yet, nobody cares. If you start talking about Kydonia, you'll just put the whole world to sleep."

"How did you do this?" I ask him. "I hadn't even told you what I was planning."

He pushes me out but keeps his hands on my arms. "I've known you a long time, sister. I knew there was no way you could stay here after what we saw last night."

He looks back and forth between me and Theseus, then says, "Thank you is generally considered to be the appropriate response when someone gives you something . . ."

"Thank you!" I say.

"You're welcome. I need one thing in return."

"What is it?" I ask.

"Be a girl today, okay? Go on a run with him." He nods toward Theseus. "Have a picnic. No video games."

For one blissful morning, Theseus and I act like an ordinary boy and girl who like each other. I try my hardest to ignore my bodyguards following us. The cameramen. Trailing us even tighter than my minders is my fear that this will be the last day I ever spend with him.

I take him on a run, going back into the hills behind the palace. I show him the trees and the mountains.

We eat a picnic at the base of the mountain.

Then I take him to a small circle of trees at the edge of the road that leads back to the palace compound.

I breathe in the smell of Theseus. When he brings his mouth to mine, it is like a tuning fork has been rung inside me, echoing through me, making my whole being sing. I want to do this for hours.

I want. I want.

I want to do this until I can forget every other thing that has happened. I want to be two bodies twined together, two souls joined, two people without history, without responsibilities.

His hands slide down my back, lifting me to him. Letting me feel him.

Our kisses are powerful, angry even, like we could kiss away what we've seen. Like this could prevent everything that will happen next. My lips are swollen, my cheeks burn from the pressure of his stubble on my face. It hurts a little, but it's a wonderful kind of hurt.

"I have to go get ready," I say.

He nods.

"I'll see you in the stadium," he says.

"I'll be there."

SEVENTEEN

IT IS FOUR O'CLOCK WHEN I GET BACK TO THE FAMILY hallway, but I don't go to my own room. I find Acalle's instead. I knock on the door, and she answers it, surprised, her phone in her hand, her face hidden behind a mud mask, her shortie robe thrown over her bra and thong.

"Hey," she says, her hardened mask cracking as she breaks into a grin. "What's up?"

"Acalle," I say, stepping into her room, "I need your help."

Her room is a feminine explosion of pinks and reds and animal prints. Pillows and gauze and gold, every surface covered with something valuable and beautiful, a shelf crowded with stuffed animals. The room smells like her, spicy and sweet.

"Sit down," she says, heading into her spa bathroom. "Let me get this off my face, and then you can tell me what's going on."

She leaves the door open as she peels off the mask, and I look around for somewhere to sit. Her overstuffed chair is covered with scarves and shoes, and the vanity chair has about twenty dresses thrown over it. The bed makes the pillows on my bed look restrained, but I find a spot at the end. She comes out of the bathroom, wiping the last of the mask off with a cotton ball. I don't remember the last time I saw Acalle without makeup. She is still so young. I forget.

"What do you need?" she asks.

I take a deep breath. I don't want to lie to her, but I can't tell her everything, not with the cameras watching. "I want you to dress me for *The Labyrinth Contest* tonight. I want you to style me."

"Why?" she asks.

"Because you get me, in a way that they don't," I say. "I know that I need to look beautiful, but I want to look like myself, too. I want to be able to walk. I want to have a bra on. I don't want to pretend to be someone I'm not."

She looks at me carefully. "Why would Mother and Mathilde let me do that?" she asks.

I look up at the cameras mounted to the corners of her room. The cameras that have filmed so much. Identical to the cameras in my room, which have only ever taken video of a girl playing video games in a VR headset.

"You can put it on the show," I say, keeping my voice clear.

So I don't sound unsure about this. "You can use it on the *Paradoxes*."

"Wait," Acalle says. "You're letting us put you on the *Paradoxes*. For real?"

"Yes," I say. "We can have a girl party or whatever."

"Yes!" Acalle punches the air. "Yes!"

She pulls out her phone and starts furiously texting. "Let's get this going, we don't have much time."

"The show doesn't start for three hours," I say.

"Yeah, that's what I said. No time at all."

She texts my mother and Mathilde to let them know the great news. She texts Icarus to tell him to send a crew, and she texts Xenodice for backup.

Five minutes later, Xenodice arrives in the room, squealing and carrying a bulging bag of clothes and shoes. A cameraman and a lighting tech follow directly behind her and start setting up. Xenodice dumps the clothes out on Acalle's bed, where they mix in with the pillows and scarves and other clothes that were already there.

Acalle snaps a picture and shares it with her millions of followers. Then she looks at me. "Are you ready?"

"Ready as I'll ever be," I say.

She holds the phone high over her head and coaches me. "Turn to the side, now straight on to the camera, chin down a little, don't smile, but don't not smile, you know. Smile with your eyes."

"That doesn't make any sense," I say.

"Try . . . ," she says, sounding frustrated. "Xenodice, stop photobombing. You'll get in there, too, I promise."

She snaps the picture. Then shows it to me. I don't hate it. "Perfect," she says. Then posts it, #sisterbonding, #makeovers, #Paradoxes.

Xenodice starts rifling through the clothes on the bed. "What are we going to put her in?" she asks. "This?"

She holds up a bandage dress. I look at Acalle. "No bandage dresses," I say.

Acalle grabs Xenodice's arm. "We're styling her to look like Ariadne, not like us."

"Of course she's going to look like Ariadne," Xenodice says. "She *is* Ariadne . . . Duh . . ."

"I know that," Acalle says, purposefully keeping her voice calm and slow. "We need to style her in what Ariadne would wear if Ariadne was stylish . . ."

"Thanks, Acalle," I say.

"Don't give me that. You know you're not stylish. You do it on purpose."

"Jeans and a hoodie?" Xenodice says, sounding confused. "Sneakers? What are we going to do with that?"

Acalle takes a deep breath. "We're going to *elevate*."

"Oh," Xenodice says, like she's finally understanding. "Like take the things she likes, and make them pretty . . ."

"Exactly."

Acalle looks me up and down, thinking. "Do you have a jumpsuit in there?"

"Acalle, I don't know about a jumpsuit," I say, thinking of any number of awful things that might meet that description.

"You shush," Acalle says. "You don't know about any of this. Trust me."

Twenty minutes later, I decide that Acalle is right. We have been through about thirty jumpsuits of various types, and we have ended up with a navy blue one, wide legged, with a golden belt. I have a bra on, thank the gods, and real underwear. Acalle even found a pair of gold sneakers.

Acalle styles my hair long and down my back, with a pair of golden earrings that hang to my shoulders but feel like they weigh nothing.

Xenodice puts my makeup on, but thankfully she uses a light hand. I look at myself in the mirror, the two of them standing behind me. The cameras filming us. I am happy with what I see, for once.

I want to tell them that I love them. I want to say that I'm sorry for the years that I didn't understand what they were going through. I want to say goodbye.

Instead, I say, "Thank you," and I hope that it is enough.

I am standing at one end of the stadium, where I have stood 141 times. My ball of thread in my pocket. The stadium is full to capacity. The scenes of me and Theseus have millions of views and ratings numbers are way up, near season three numbers. Everyone hopes that by the end of the two weeks when Theseus is supposed to go into the maze that we will surpass the first season.

What no one knows is that there won't be another two weeks.

The stadium field is a lake of fog and flashing lights.

Icarus's voice comes into my ear. Tonight, he's talking to me on the secure channel between our phones. "Ready?"

"Yes," I say.

Wind machines on the edges of the field come to life, blowing away the fog, and the drumbeat starts, beating out my stately pace.

"Now," Icarus says.

I walk out onto the field, head held high. A spotlight finds me immediately.

The crowd stands and roars.

The wind machines blow my hair back and make the legs of my jumpsuit swirl around me as I stride down the long field, head held high.

The competitors file out in their black and gold, each standing in front of their chairs. Thirteen of them, with one empty seat, where Vortigern used to be. In the next chair is the crew cut boy, the one who is supposed to go tonight.

I look at Theseus. He nods at me and I smile, not breaking my stride.

I climb the stairs, looking beyond the stage at the heavy doors that lead to the maze.

I turn to face the crowd. I know what I am supposed to

say—introduce the competitors, give a standard line about the will of the gods—but I am not saying it. Not today.

Instead, I raise my arms, and the noise of the crowd drops.

"People of Crete," I say, my voice echoing over the loudspeakers. "People of the world."

The Jumbotron shows the people in the stands, my family in their box. My sisters are typing furiously on their phones—social media blast. My mother's face is calm and serene. My father looks pleased. Elegant and royal.

"We've surpassed season two," Icarus says in my earpiece.

Good. I want the whole world watching.

"One hundred and forty-one," I say. "That is how many Athenians have died. In revenge for one prince of Crete."

On the Jumbotron they show the crowd again, leaning forward, watching.

"But it has gone on long enough," I say. "It is time for the Hero of Athens to have his turn in the maze. It is time for him to fight the Minotaur."

The Jumbotron switches back to my parents, and my father's face is murderous. He knows what I am doing. He knows that I have betrayed him. He walks out of the box. He will be calling the security team now, trying to figure out if they can stop me.

I have very little time.

"Theseus of Athens," I say, and Theseus stands. "Are you ready to face the Minotaur?"

Theseus waits for the hubbub of voices to die down, the calls of "Not Theseus!" or "It isn't his turn!" or "What is she doing?" or, very loudly from Hippolyta, "That's not fair!"

"I'm ready," Theseus says, stepping toward me.

"They're coming for you," Icarus says in my earpiece. "You'd better get moving."

When I look at the edges of the field, soldiers are filling the entrances, getting ready to rush the stage. But the crowd has started stomping, building a new cheer—"Theseus! Theseus!"—their feet and clapping hands drowning out everything else.

My father won't dare interrupt this right now, not with the whole crowd involved, not with the ratings rising and rising.

I don't have long.

"They're calling for commercial," Icarus says.

I know we have to move. If they can get a commercial, they'll pull me back, and this will have been wasted.

"Theseus," I say, my voice full of command. "Come with me."

He stands and walks to me, then pulls me in for a kiss, in front of the whole world.

Together we walk quickly to the gate to the maze.

I pull the thread from my pocket and press it to the doors. They swing open, and we're through. Then the doors swing closed behind us, and the roar of the crowd drops away.

The motion sensor lights turn on, and Theseus turns to look at me. "Will anyone follow us in here?"

"What do you think, Icarus?" I say.

I get a laugh in my earpiece. "Not likely," he says. "Your father doesn't pay anyone enough for that."

"How does it look out there?" I ask.

"Up here?" Icarus says. "Well, I'm hooking you and Lover Boy into a livestream on twenty different channels, every one of which has suspended their programming, and *The Labyrinth Contest* has the highest ratings since season one. Your parents should be very proud."

I laugh. "I have a feeling they won't be."

"Oh, me too, sister," he says. "Me too. Get going. You are talking too much. If I didn't know better, I'd think you didn't want to do this."

I square my shoulders. "Oh, I'm doing this."

Theseus can't hear Icarus's end of the conversation, but he's watching me.

"Are you ready for this?" he asks.

I sigh. "As ready as I'll ever be."

I put my thread into the hook by the door, and we start walking forward.

"What does that do?" Theseus says, curious.

"It's my thread," I say. "It turns off the obstacles. It's how I navigate the maze."

He turns to watch it spool out behind me.

As we walk down the steep tunnel, the sights and sounds of the maze rise up to meet us. Water drips from far below, and the smell grows stronger.

I look at Theseus. He's pale. "Are you okay?" I ask.

"Sure, sure," he says. "It's the smell."

"Yeah," I say, and I would say you never get used to it, but I guess you do a little, because Theseus looks like he is going to puke and I only feel a tingle in my nose.

"What do we do now?" Theseus asks.

Normally, I would be long gone by now. Already putting on my VR goggles.

"We find the Minotaur," I say.

As we walk forward, the motion sensor lights make islands of light in the silent darkness of the passage.

"Wait," Theseus says, grabbing my hand and pulling me close to him. "Ariadne, before we do this, I want to say, you're the bravest person I've ever known."

He kisses me quickly, and that kiss carries the weight of our connection. I let myself be lost in this feeling, knowing that this is something new in my life. Something I've never had before—a connection not based on blood or friendship or common interests but on something different, something elemental. It's the feeling I had that first day I met him, a kinship at the heart of us, like we're a pair of magnets drawn together.

We break apart, and I can hear a new sound, so low it's barely audible, a rumbling growl, echoing off the concrete walls of the maze.

"That's Asterion," I say, clutching my thread tightly. "Let's get going."

I follow the directions to get to the heart of it, right and then two lefts, right and then two lefts. I hope that the directions that work in the part of the maze where I usually am still hold true here, in this quadrant where I've never spent any time.

Theseus catches me before I step forward into a tar pit.

An obstacle. We were not looking for obstacles because my thread disarms them.

"Icarus," I say, "why are there obstacles?"

"I don't know," Icarus says, and I can hear the sound of typing as he's searching his systems. "Oh Hades, Ariadne," his voice returns. "They've disabled your thread. The obstacles are online."

"We have to face the obstacles," I tell Theseus, and my nerves are obvious in my voice.

I rack my brain, thinking about the obstacles, forcing myself to remember what is down there. I've been involved in planning sessions, but I wasn't really paying attention. It never occurred to me that my thread wouldn't work when we went in the maze.

"I've never done any obstacles," I say.

"We'll be fine," Theseus says. "Obstacles are good. They'll keep us on our toes."

I take a deep breath, trying to believe him. We walk the tiny ledge that runs alongside the tar pit.

I don't look down.

"Listen," Icarus says in my earpiece. "I've got people banging on the door to the control room. I'm going to have to be radio silent for a while, okay? I'll try to get your thread back online."

"Good luck," I say, then get back to carefully moving through the tunnel, watching for obstacles. My thread trails behind us.

"Why do we still have that if it isn't disarming the obstacles?" Theseus asks me.

"We have to hope Icarus will turn them back off," I say. "Also, I don't know about you, but I'd like to get out of here when this is over."

We round a corner to the right and Theseus pulls me up short, pointing at a thin line in the poured concrete floor. "Obstacle," he says.

When we make the next turn, there it is, in front of us. A ten-foot stretch of wall with spring-loaded crossbows bolted into the concrete. The springs are set off by pressure points in the floor, so one wrong step will result in an arrow flying through whatever part of your body is in the way.

"Arrow wall," Theseus says. "I studied this one on the tapes. It took out a lot of competitors last year. Everyone was trying to avoid the spots on the floor where the arrows would be set off."

"But they moved every run," I say, remembering.

"Right," he says. "I have a strategy." He points at the wall. "The arrows are arranged where the lowest ones can get you in the calf, and the highest ones will get your head, so the only thing to do is to get lower than the lowest."

"Crawling?" I say.

He pushes his hand toward the floor. "Lower. We're going

to have to basically slide along the floor to avoid getting hit. That way, when the arrows are sprung, they will fall on us but not stab us."

"Are you sure they won't skewer us when they fall?"

"No," he says, "I'm not. Do you have a better idea?"

I shake my head, looking down at the floor, where the concrete has been stained with the blood of previous competitors. "No, I don't."

I clutch my ball of thread in my fist as Theseus drops to the floor. "Here we go," he says.

He begins slinking forward on his stomach, and I lie down on the cold concrete and do the same. As I inch forward, I realize that I can't look to see where we are going or what Theseus is doing without putting my head in the path of one of the arrows aimed at calf height. My eye level is at the soles of his shoes as I creep forward, waiting for the arrows to begin falling on us.

It doesn't take long.

I hear the clatter of arrows as Theseus goes ahead of me, but I don't dare look up to see if he's been hit. He doesn't groan and his shoes keep moving, which seems like a good sign.

Arrows launch from the wall, but each time they slam harmlessly into the opposite wall or the floor beside me. I dare a small peek up after an arrow falls, and I can see that Theseus is almost to the end.

I breathe a sigh of relief.

Then Theseus cries out in pain. I start to raise myself up to see what has happened to him, and he calls out, "Ariadne, don't move."

Glancing at the wall ahead of me, I see an arrow, its point sharp and shining, right at the level the top of my head would have been if I had raised it an inch higher. I pull my head down, and the low arrow flies from its position as I pass. It clatters beside me.

That is the last one, and when I pull myself to my feet, Theseus is leaning against the wall, holding his shoulder and breathing hard.

"What happened?" I say.

He pulls his hand away from his shoulder and it is covered with blood. "No big deal," he says. "One of the taller ones grazed me."

I look at it. I have a lot of experience bandaging wounds from the years of taking care of Asterion, and I can tell it isn't deep. "It will be okay," I say.

"I know," he says, keeping the arrow in his hand.

"I'm glad you paid attention to *The Labyrinth Contest*," I say, thinking about what would have happened if I'd stumbled into that.

He grabs my hand and we walk on, knowing that we're lucky to be alive.

As we go farther down, Asterion's breathing gets louder, echoing through the maze.

We turn again, and again, and then I can hear another

sound, a *whoomp, whoomp, whoomp* sound, like a very slow-moving helicopter.

"The Pendulum," Theseus and I say together. Many of the obstacles change year after year, but the Pendulum has been here since the beginning.

We round the next corner, and there it is. We're close to the heart of the maze.

When I come to comfort Asterion, the Pendulum is safely held back against the wall, a ten-foot-tall bronze decoration that I barely notice as I walk by.

Now it swings back and forth across the path, its bronze sides honed razor sharp. It goes back and forth, back and forth, like a metronome. There is no strategy to the Pendulum. All you can do is outrun it.

"You go first," Theseus says to me.

I roll my thread under it, so I will have it on the other side.

Then I wait, bouncing on my toes, until the Pendulum has reached its highest right-hand position and I start running as it begins its descent toward the opposite wall. When I make it past, the wind of the Pendulum's return blows my long hair forward. As fast as I am, I barely made it.

Then I wait while Theseus gets ready for his turn. He's bigger than I am, which gives him even less room to maneuver. He gives himself a running start, then slides under it, barely making it. I breathe again once he's through.

We turn and then turn again, getting closer and closer to Asterion's room.

The last camera is mounted on the ceiling, and beyond it, the light from Asterion's room seeps out into the hallway. "We're here," I say.

The sound of his breathing fills the space around us, but I still don't know where he is.

I blink at the brightness in Asterion's room after the darkness of the maze.

No sign of Asterion.

Theseus looks around at the room, taking it in. I can see his horror. I am seeing the room through his eyes. It is a shock, the desperate misery of this room—the torn and stained upholstery, the dented metal cabinet where I keep his supplies. Asterion's blue blanket.

"What's this?" Theseus asks, picking up something off the floor.

I take it from him, cradling it in my hands. It's half of Asterion's book. He's torn it in half. He's destroyed it, like his other treasures. I lay it down and pick up his blue blanket.

The floor under us vibrates with the rumbling of an earthquake, and a low growl fills the space around us.

"Run, Ariadne," Theseus says, keeping his voice calm. Theseus has turned away from me and is facing the door. He has dropped into a fighting stance.

Asterion fills the doorway, his head down in the attack

position, horns leveled at us. The rage and blind hatred in his eyes make me take a step backward.

There is no sign of my brother. Like a raging bull, Asterion stomps his foot on the floor, and the walls tremble around us.

He and Theseus size each other up.

"Get out of here, Ariadne," Theseus says. "I don't want him to hurt you."

Would Asterion hurt me? I have had a glimpse of what the Athenians must feel like when they face the Minotaur, but this is even worse. I don't know if I could stop him, even if I wanted to. I don't think he remembers who I am.

I would leave, but I can't. Asterion is blocking the door.

Asterion bellows a call of fury. Theseus is an intruder in his room.

Asterion runs at Theseus.

Right before Asterion's horns hit, Theseus sidesteps out of the way, and I remember, Theseus fought the Cretan Bull— he's planning to fight Asterion the way you would fight a bull.

Asterion's momentum carries him past Theseus and he slams into the wall, shaking the foundations. I hold Asterion's blue blanket, feeling its softness between my fingers.

Asterion pounds the floor with his foot and makes another pass at Theseus, and again, Theseus jumps out of the way. Asterion is faster this time, and Theseus's sidestep is more of a leap than a graceful step.

They aren't fighting yet, they're testing each other out, looking for weaknesses.

Theseus holds his arms out. "Is that all you've got?"

Asterion passes again, and this time, when Theseus sidesteps, he grabs one of Asterion's horns and leaps onto his back.

Asterion bellows and shakes Theseus like a dog with a rat. He carries Theseus through the door, out into the main hallways, where the cameras are watching.

Theseus is holding on tightly, trying to choke Asterion. If Theseus had been fighting another man, this would have worked, but with Asterion's bull's head on his body, his neck and shoulders are too wide for Theseus to get his arms around.

Then Asterion raises up to his full height and slams backward, crashing Theseus into the wall. Theseus loses his grip and slides down the wall.

Asterion takes several steps forward, then turns to look at Theseus.

Theseus returns to his fighting stance, but he is wobbly on his feet, his eyes bleary. I can already tell what is going to happen. When Asterion comes at him again, horns down, Theseus doesn't make it out of the way in time. Asterion knocks him into the wall.

The sound of Theseus hitting the wall is horrible, and he lays on the floor, stunned, for a moment before he tries to get to his feet. Before he can, Asterion grabs him and throws him against the wall again.

This time when he hits the floor, Theseus doesn't try to stand. He can't.

I watch as Asterion stands to his full height and roars in triumph. His eyes are red with rage; he is snorting and growling, and snot drips from his nose. He is a monster. He is the Minotaur.

I know with a sudden certainty—Asterion is going to kill him. Here in this hallway, on camera for the whole world, in front of me, Asterion is going to kill Theseus.

He's going to kill him and eat him, like he did Vortigern.

It's like when I was a little girl and he killed the cows. He tore them with his teeth and horns. He devoured them. And I watched.

I came in here thinking that I would kill the Minotaur if Theseus did not, but I know for sure that I am not strong enough to defeat this monster. Not like this. Ten people couldn't do it.

I remember Asterion's eyes after he scared me, how sad he was, how sorry. He doesn't want this.

All done, he said. *All done.*

My brother is not here, in this monster. This cannot be the way I get him back.

I stand in the doorway, clutching his blanket. He may have forgotten who he is, but I haven't.

"Asterion!" I scream. "Asterion, stop!"

Asterion reaches to pick Theseus up again, but I run at the two of them, grabbing Asterion's arms. The last time I tried to stop him, I was too weak to do anything. But I'm not a little girl anymore.

He shoves me backward and I fall to the floor, but I get up again.

I grip his arm. "Asterion," I scream into his ear. "Asterion!"

I'm pulling at his hands, trying to get him to step back from Theseus.

I'm crying and screaming and holding on for dear life. I'm praying out loud to the gods. "Please let him hear me." I'm calling his name. "Asterion, please, please remember me. Asterion, I love you. Please remember who you are. You're my brother. You're my brother."

I feel the change in his breathing, the moment of stillness. His head is still down, he is still full of anger, but he backs away from Theseus.

Theseus is collapsed against the wall, battered and bloody. He watches us with eyes that are already swelling.

"This is my friend," I say to Asterion.

The redness fades from Asterion's eyes, but he doesn't leave his fighting stance.

"Asterion," I say, "this is my friend . . ."

He unclenches his fists and makes the sign. *Friend?*

"Yes, he's my friend."

He looks at me, seriously. *Ariadne love friend?*

Do I? Do I love Theseus? I look at him, pulling himself to his feet, watching us carefully. He can't understand what we are saying, since Asterion is signing, but his bruised face has a mix of curiosity and concern, and I can feel him asking me what is happening, what is about to happen, and I see that flash of connection between us. The way he gets me.

"Yes," I tell Asterion. "Yes, I do."

Asterion looks at me carefully, turning his big head slightly. *Ariadne love me?*

I take his hand in mine. "Yes. I love you. Always."

What Ariadne want?

I stand there looking at him, holding his hand. I look down at his blue blanket, clutched in my other hand. "I want you to be happy, Asterion. I want you to be free."

He is standing in front of me, at his full height, looking down at me. He puts his hand to my cheek. *I love you.*

Tears are running down my cheeks. For the first time in our lives, he is the one who is comforting me.

Goodbye, he signs. *Goodbye.*

Gently, he nudges me on the shoulder, pushing me away. His breathing is settled. His eyes are their own sweet brown.

Ariadne go.

He pushes me a little harder this time, and I stumble backward. He turns toward Theseus, lowering his head, getting ready to charge.

Theseus is back on his feet. He is ready.

Theseus uses the wall as a springboard to throw himself at my brother, grabbing him by the horns.

In slow motion, Theseus uses the force of their combined momentum to twist Asterion's head. The sickening crack is louder than a gunshot as Theseus breaks my brother's neck. Together they fall to the floor.

Theseus is the only one to stand. His face exultant. He has won.

Asterion lays on the floor, his body twisted, neck broken. His sweet brown eyes open and staring.

I cry out and run forward, toward Asterion. As I do, something strange happens. When I touch the brown hair of his bull's head, the air around us starts to shimmer, and my brother's body starts to change, like a reverse time-lapse video of a flower's growth. Slowly, his body transforms, the monstrous shape of the Minotaur shrinking and changing into a brown-haired thirteen-year-old boy.

My Asterion. His hands are no longer torn and battered by the walls of his prison. His skin is no longer burned and scarred.

His eyes are the same as they have always been.

"Ariadne," he says, his voice a whisper, and he smiles up at me. My whole life, I have never heard his voice.

Tears stream down my cheeks as I touch his face. I was right. This worked. I have him with me. I can take him out of the maze.

"Let's get you out of here," I say, looking around me for something to carry him out on. "We can make a stretcher. We can . . ."

I look up at Theseus, desperately. "Theseus, help me get him up. Help me carry him."

Theseus is battered and bloodstained. He has bruises on his

face and his arms are crisscrossed with gouges. He looks exhausted. He shakes his head. "We shouldn't move him."

Asterion's body is twisted and broken on the floor, and I realize that Theseus is right. We can't move him without risking injuring him more.

"We'll get help," I say.

"Ariadne," Asterion says, and his voice freezes me. It's softer than it was, barely audible. "Don't leave me."

"No, no," I say, crouching next to him. "I won't leave you."

"Ariadne, I . . . ," he starts, but then he seems to be looking at something far away. I'm losing him.

"No, no, no," I say. "Stay with me, Asterion. I'm right here."

With great effort, he draws his attention back to me. He lifts his hand to my cheek.

"I love you," he breathes out. "Thank you."

With that last word, his eyes lose focus on me, and his body stills, the life in him slipping away.

He is gone.

He is dead.

The gods betrayed me. They betrayed us both.

I feel the warmth leave Asterion's body, and I look at his eyes, unchanged, shining out of a boy's face.

Tears rise in me like an electrical storm, and I can't stop them. I hold Asterion in my arms, and I can't let go.

I'm crying and crying, and I don't know that I will ever stop.

EIGHTEEN

"ARIADNE. ARIADNE."

Someone is calling my name, but it's like I'm down a hole, deep in the ground. Nothing can reach me. Out there, aboveground, it sounds like someone is howling. Screaming. Like a wounded animal.

I am lost.

"Ariadne," the voice says again, but I won't let it distract me.

I clutch Asterion to me.

Even while I hold his lanky boy's body to me, my fingers in his curly hair, I miss the shape of Asterion as I've known him for so long. I miss the softness of his fur. I miss the bulk of him. This is what I always dreamed of, having him back as the boy he would have been, but the boy I loved was the Minotaur, too.

I close my eyes tightly, breathing in the smell of him. That has not changed.

I pray and pray and pray. This is wrong. Bring him back. Wrong. Wrong. Wrong.

"Ariadne, please." A hand rests on my shoulder. "Ariadne, please. I need you."

I finally open my eyes. I realize that the keening howl is coming from me.

Theseus kneels beside me. "Ariadne, we have to get out of here," he says.

"I can't leave him like this," I say, looking down at the broken body of my brother.

Theseus nods. "We'll take him with us."

When I wrap his blue blanket around Asterion's naked form and gently close his eyes, a sparkling light surrounds us. Asterion begins to change, his body fading, becoming instead many points of light, like tiny blinking stars. The stars swirl around us, and the corridor sings with a sound like ringing bells. A joyful sound, of freedom.

Then he is gone. His body dissolved into the air, and the blue blanket flutters to the ground.

The glowing light fades, and the maze comes back to its grim darkness.

I pick up the blanket—all that is left of my brother, but that isn't true. Those ringing bells tell me that he is somewhere else. His voice, thanking me, tells me that, too. This isn't the ending that I wanted. But Asterion is free.

I tear off a small piece of the blue blanket and put it into my pocket.

Then I reach a hand out to Theseus. "Let's go."

Beyond us, the Pendulum swings back and forth, my ball of thread resting on the floor in front of it. As we walk toward the obstacle, I gather the energy to run past it. Asterion would never want me to stay in the maze.

"Ariadne. Ariadne." I hear Icarus's voice in my earpiece. "Thank the gods. I've finally got you back online. What happened in there? We got the video of Theseus killing the Minotaur, but after that, my cameras blew out. What's going on? Did Asterion . . ."

He leaves his question unfinished, waiting for me to answer.

"He's gone," I say, hoping that it is enough.

The Pendulum slows, then stops. With the Minotaur defeated, *The Labyrinth Contest* has a winner. There is no longer any reason for the obstacles.

"Let's get you out here, then," Icarus says. "There are eighty thousand people waiting."

Theseus and I trudge back out of the maze in silence, both lost in our thoughts. I'm in a daze. I can't even believe that the world is still the same.

Finally, we reach the end of the maze. I push my rolled thread against the metal gates, and they swing open. We walk through them holding hands, the cheers of the crowd reverberating around us. Confetti and balloons fall from the ceiling.

The stadium floor has been cleared, and dancing girls gyrate enthusiastically while little children in matching outfits wave giant ribbons high in the air. The Jumbotron intermixes shots of the crowd with replays of our run through the maze. I never thought a Cretan audience would be pleased with this outcome, but everyone must have gotten wrapped up in the excitement, because they are dancing and cheering—glowing with the knowledge that they've witnessed history.

Then the Jumbotron shows my family. My mother looks stunned and frozen, while my father is talking on his phone, his eyes full of rage. Then they realize that they are being broadcast, and they both paste false smiles on. My sisters, who had been staring at their phones, jump and dance for the millions of people watching.

Seeing my father's face raises the hair on my neck. He is never going to willingly let me leave Crete. I look around for the exits, thinking about how I can get out of the stadium before he has a chance to get me. Then I notice soldiers and plainclothes security staff coming out onto the stadium floor in twos and threes.

This isn't over yet.

Daedalus comes onto the stage with his microphone to do the first-ever post–*Labyrinth Contest* interview. Cameramen and the crowd of competitors surround us, slapping Theseus on the back, asking questions. I feel the push of the crowd trying to get me apart from Theseus, and I fight it. If we get separated, I'm screwed.

"Theseus," Daedalus says, and we are projected onto the Jumbotron for the crowd. "What can you tell us about your time in the maze?"

I have to find a way to talk to Theseus.

"Excuse me," I say, interrupting Daedalus. "Can I borrow him for a second?"

I don't give him a chance to answer before I whisper to Theseus, "There are soldiers coming everywhere. How can we get out of here?"

Theseus smiles at Daedalus and the cameras. "Here's what I'll tell you," Theseus says. "I'd love to chat. But really what I want to do is go back to Athens."

"You can't leave now," Daedalus says. "What about the awards? The parties?"

"I think I've attended enough parties for a lifetime," Theseus says.

Then he turns to the competitors in the circle around us. "Come on, guys. Let's go home." He looks up at the cameras. "If you're watching down there in the harbor, get the *Parthenos* ready. We're headed to Athens!"

The competitors let out a loud cheer, and Theseus and I step around Daedalus, with his microphone, and walk down the stairs to the stadium floor.

The competitors follow behind us as we march out of the

stadium gates toward the harbor, forcing the cameras to follow us. People line the sides of the harbor road, cheering and taking our pictures, as the stadium empties and thousands of people crowd the road.

There is an ebullient mood around us, but I don't feel it. Everywhere in the crowd, I see soldiers in uniform. The black suits of the security detail. When I look up at the roofs of the temples, snipers have been posted. I stay close to Theseus and the competitors, hoping that my father wouldn't go that far.

I am wondering what to expect when we get to the ship, when I remember that I have Icarus in my ear. "Icarus," I say. "What's going on at the harbor?"

"We're scrambling to have some kind of ceremony on the pier," Icarus answers. "I've officially been demoted because of this disaster, so I can't help you much. But listen, your dad is going to try everything he can to get his hands on you. Don't leave Theseus's side, and whatever you do, *don't* get off camera."

I tell Theseus what Icarus said.

"I'm not letting go of you," Theseus says. "Not now. Not ever."

I am a nervous wreck the whole of the three-mile walk to the harbor.

When we get there, my family and a selection of international media organizations are gathered around a makeshift stage on the pier. They must have driven down from the palace, skipping the parade.

On the jetty, the crew of the *Parthenos* scrambles around on board, getting ready to depart.

Theseus and I push through the security line, and the cameras follow us as we walk up to the stage.

Icarus comes to meet us, looking professional, no hint of anything more. "We'll need to do the award ceremony, and then we can let you get out of here. Right, Dad?" He turns and looks at Daedalus, the confirmation that he has been demoted.

"Absolutely," Daedalus says, his voice avuncular. "Now, Ariadne, if you'll come stand here with your family."

He grabs my arm, pulling me away from Theseus.

My father is glaring at me, while my mother looks catatonic. Xenodice is too busy snapping selfies to notice, but Acalle's face turns pale. The cameras are watching us, but if I go with Daedalus, no one will think anything about it, and I will not get another chance to escape from Crete.

The only way I can stop this, the only way to control it, is to use the cameras that surround us. I have to *make* them care.

"No," I say, pulling my arm back, saying it loudly, making a scene. "I'm not going with you. I'm not going back to the palace."

The reporters perk up, paying attention now. The cameras turn to focus on me. I reach out for Theseus's hand, and he pulls me close, like we're dancing.

"I'm going with Theseus," I say. "I'm going to Athens."

At that, the reporters start shouting questions. A princess of

Crete leaving with a prince of Athens is front-page news. I have to hope that the public relations disaster that would happen if my father tried to pull us apart now will be enough to get me on the boat.

"Surely you don't need to be in the photo op," Daedalus says softly, through clenched teeth. "I'll make sure you get back to him."

I keep my voice as low as his. "You've been lying to me since I was six years old. Why should I believe you now?"

Then, knowing that the cameras are watching, I turn to Theseus and kiss him.

The crowds who have lined up beyond the security fences on the pier and down the road cheer for that, the media's camera shutters click, and their lights flash.

"That's enough," my father says to Daedalus. "Let's get this over with."

Daedalus sets up the shot, while the hair and makeup people come to powder Theseus's nose and fix my hair. Then Theseus and I are standing beside my father, smiling at the international media, while my sisters give Theseus a giant check.

Behind his false smile, my father radiates menace.

He shakes Theseus's hand perfunctorily. Then he pulls me in for a hug. The cameras snap the picture of fatherly affection, but I hear his voice in my ear. "Don't think this is over, Ariadne," he says. "I will find you. I *will* bring you back. You will be punished. You are mine. Don't forget it."

A chill runs down my spine.

I pull myself out of my father's arms and turn to Theseus. "Can we go now?" I ask.

He nods, and together we walk off the stage, toward the black-sailed ship, the competitors coming behind us.

I'm getting ready to board, when Icarus comes over to me.

"Watch out," I say. "You don't want to be seen talking to me."

"You're my best friend," he says. "They can't get me in too much trouble."

"I'm not sure about that," I say. "What are you going to do if they figure out that you helped me?"

"They won't," he says, but I'm not so sure.

I don't know what to say. There is so much. For my whole life, Icarus was my only friend. And I'm leaving him behind.

"Icarus . . . ," I say.

He lightly touches my hair.

"No drama, sister, no drama."

"I wasn't going to be dramatic," I say.

"Oh yes, you were. I can see it."

He pulls me in for a tight hug. "This isn't goodbye," he whispers into my ear, and I think of the drawing taped to his inspiration board—Icarus with his wings.

"Okay," I say. "Not goodbye."

I walk onto the ship and I don't look back.

The giant bronze head of Talos watches our exit from the harbor.

NINETEEN

THE CAPTAIN GREETS US AS WE COME ABOARD THE
Parthenos. She has short white hair, and her gray eyes are pale in
her deeply tan face. Everything about her is crisp and command-
ing from her starched white shirt to the bars on her shoulders.

"Get us to Athens as fast as you can," Theseus says as we follow her into the enclosed helm station. It's very high-tech, all
black and glass and leather and flatscreen monitors. The only
things that suggest a sailboat are the wood finishes and the view
of the Mediterranean out the angled windows.

"It's a sailing ship, not a speedboat," the captain says, pointing at a display of our route between Crete and the port of
Athens. "It's a hundred and seventy nautical miles. Even with
our best speed, it will be at least eleven hours."

"Eleven hours?" I say, incredulous. "My father's ships are much faster than that."

"Yes," the captain says, turning to look at me. "They have more firepower, too. If they are coming for us, there's nothing we can do about it, so I suggest you both relax. I doubt even Minos will attack this ship when we are carrying the champion back to Athens. Especially not with *them* watching." She points out the window at the small flotilla of boats that surrounds us—a combination of the media in their speedboats and pleasure craft trying to get a better view. High above in the sky, helicopters hover. She gives me a piercing look. "Frankly, given what I know about Minos, this is probably the safest you'll be for a long time."

When Theseus and I leave the helm station, we walk down a narrow flight of stairs and enter the belowdecks living area, which if it wasn't for the rolling of the floor underfoot and the curved ceiling, you would think is a fancy cigar bar, not a boat.

The remaining competitors have taken up most of the space on the dark leather sectional sofas and all the cream-upholstered mahogany chairs at the dining table. A spread of bread, cheese, fruit, and sausages is on the table, but no one has touched it yet. The chattering voices go silent when we enter. No one moves to make any room for us on the sofa. Everyone looks at us with undisguised hostility while the uncomfortable silence stretches out.

I'm tired and dirty and sick of wearing this jumpsuit. My dad wants to lock me up. I'm on my way to a city I've never been before, where most people, including Theseus's dad, are likely to hate me. I've left behind my best and only friend. And my brother is gone.

Seriously, I don't have time for this.

"If we're all going to stare at each other, can I eat while we're doing it?" I ask. "Because I'm starving." I take a hunk of cheese and some bread off the table.

The silence is broken.

"Theseus, you cheated," Hippolyta says, standing. "You used this *princess* and cheated."

Other voices chime in.

"I didn't get my chance to go into the maze."

"I needed that money."

"We were all supposed to have a chance to kill the monster."

It's funny how when the numbers were given out, some of these people looked like they were going to lose their cookies over going into the maze, but now they're each convinced they would have been the one to win.

The voices get louder and louder, and a tornado of negative energy swirls around Theseus. I can see that he's trying to fix it and make it right, but I have no idea how he can. I also can't think of anything that I could say to help.

I want to escape this room and take a shower, and chill out, but I have no idea where to go. I don't know which room is Theseus's, and it wouldn't help my case to pick a random competitor's room. So I just eat my bread and cheese and wait.

Theseus's voice is conciliatory. "Look, everybody, I know that didn't go how it was supposed to."

"Darn right it didn't," one of the boys says.

"Enough," Hippolyta says. "Let Theseus speak."

Theseus stands tall. I know him well enough now to know that he's running through the possible ways to play this situation—how much of the truth should he tell? He holds his arms out, palms up. "I know that it looks like I went into the maze out of turn."

"Looks like? There's no looks like, you did!" one of the competitors shouts, but the others silence her.

"Ariadne, show them the card," he says.

I pull the broken card out of my pocket and give it to Theseus.

"Pass this around," he says. "As you can see, it isn't wood. The drawing was fixed. No one knows what order the gods would have wanted us to go in, because Minos didn't play fair."

The competitors pass the card around, commenting on the wires and electrodes.

"That still doesn't justify you going in on your own," Hippolyta says. "You should have given the rest of us an opportunity."

Theseus nods. "I understand. You wanted your chance in the maze." He says this as though any one of them could have succeeded, even while we all know that the odds were terrible. "However, you will come back to Athens as heroes in your own right. I bet the sponsors will be lined up for you. Famous forever as the competitors who survived *The Labyrinth Contest*."

"What about the prize money?" someone calls out. "We won't get any of that."

Theseus looks thoughtful. "What if I share the money out among us—with a share going to the each of you, one to Vortigern's family, and one to Ariadne."

"Theseus," I say, grabbing his arm. "You don't have to—"

"Why should you give our money to a princess of Crete?" Hippolyta says loudly. "She did nothing."

Theseus gives my hand a quick squeeze. "Ariadne has given up everything to come here. She deserves a share as much as anyone. Either she is included or no one is." He looks around at the group. "What do you say?"

Hippolyta looks for support, but no one will meet her eyes.

Finally, someone says, "I say half a cake is better than no cake."

The rest agree with varying degrees of enthusiasm.

Finally, only Hippolyta is left. She looks me up and down, disgusted. She says, "I will take my half a cake. But know, I could have defeated the Minotaur without the help of that princess. I am sure of it."

"I'm glad you are," Theseus says. "Because there is no way that I could have done it without her." He reaches for some cheese and a bunch of grapes. "Now, if you'll excuse me, I'm going to take a shower."

I follow him into his cabin.

It is luxurious, with walls of lacquered wood and a curving

ceiling. The bed has been made with pristine white sheets, and two orange towels are folded up on the end of it.

"Theseus," I say, "I can't take that money. My brother died, you can't pay me for that. It's blood money."

Theseus grabs my hands. "Look, Ariadne, it's your father's money and he didn't want to give it to me. Do you seriously think that Asterion would want you to go out in the world with no money? Or to be dependent on me? How is that freedom?" He pulls me in close. "Why don't we get cleaned up and then we can talk about it."

I look down at my bedraggled jumpsuit. "I didn't bring anything to change into."

"If you'll get in the shower, I'll go find something you can borrow."

My shower is blissful, and when I come out, wrapped in my towel, he has a spare T-shirt and red shorts from the crew. I change while he's showering, and then curl up on the bed. Outside the portholes, the sunset has streaked the sky with orange.

I pick up a book from the nightstand—*A History of Athens*—then put it down, then pick it up again. I look at my phone, hoping for a message from Icarus, the only person with this number since I have a new identification card, knowing I'm unlikely to have one. I resist checking to see what the newsfeeds are saying about the end of *The Labyrinth Contest*. I don't want to think about that right now.

I'm picking up the book again when Theseus comes out of

the bathroom. He is wearing jeans and a T-shirt for the first time since I met him, and his curls are wet and tousled.

My breath catches.

"Mind if I sit down?" he asks.

"No, no," I say nervously, scooting over to make room for him.

He wraps his arms around me and I lean into him. It doesn't look like any of the injuries Asterion gave him are permanent, but one of his eyes is black, and his face and body have cuts and bruises.

"*A History of Athens*, huh?" he asks. "Reading up on your new home?"

"I'm too distracted to read," I say, and I lean over him to set the book back down on the nightstand.

He runs his finger along the side of my ear, and I shiver.

"Why are you distracted?" he asks.

"You know the answer to that," I say, and my lips are nearly touching his.

And then they are.

For the first time, I am kissing Theseus with no one watching us. It is wonderful.

It doesn't last long.

We only get a few kisses in before there is a loud banging at the cabin door.

We pull apart, like we're in trouble.

"Prince Theseus," a voice calls. "I need to speak with you."

Theseus runs his hand through his hair, only making it messier. "I guess I should answer that."

We make ourselves presentable before opening the door.

The captain is standing outside, raising her hand to knock again. "Your Majesty," she says. "I must speak with you."

"Just Theseus, please. What's going on?"

"I have an urgent communication from your father."

We follow her through the living areas. The competitors are on every piece of furniture—playing cards, making out, eating. Many of them glare at me as we pass. I definitely have not won them over yet.

We go up a flight of narrow stairs to the helm station. Once we are crowded into the tiny room, the captain turns to Theseus. "Your father wants you to call him."

Theseus takes a deep breath. "Okay, that's what I'll do. Captain, if you'll excuse us."

The captain looks at me. "Your father insisted that you be alone when you call."

"Thanks for letting me know," Theseus says, but he doesn't ask me to leave. "If you'll excuse us."

The captain shakes her head, but steps out of the room. Theseus closes the door.

"I'll sit where he can't see me," I say, taking one of the leather benches in the corner of the helm station and drawing my knees up to my chest so I am out of sight of the monitor.

Theseus dials his father's number. He stares at the screen while it rings. He wears that bleak look, and I realize that he is still trapped in his own maze. The Minotaur is gone, but Theseus's story isn't over.

When Aegeus's face appears on the screen, he is harried and anxious looking, his gray hair untidy and his shirt rumpled. A wide, false smile takes over his face when he sees Theseus. "My son! Thank the gods."

"Hello, Father," Theseus says, putting on his own pretend smile in return.

"Listen, son," Aegeus says, leaning forward, "are you alone?"

"Yes," Theseus says, not looking in my direction, giving no clue that I am here.

"The ship will stop on the island of Adamantas in a few hours," Aegeus says, rubbing his ear. "You must drop an item of cargo there. It is incredibly important."

"What cargo is that?" Theseus asks.

Aegeus drops his gaze and his voice comes out a whisper. "The Cretan princess. Ariadne."

Cold fingers run up my spine, but I don't make a sound.

Theseus raises his eyebrow. "You can't be serious."

"I am deadly serious." Aegeus leans in toward the camera. "You must leave her."

"She saved my life, and you want me to abandon her?" Theseus's voice is devoid of emotion.

"Not abandon, son, not abandon," Aegeus says, putting his hand to his upper chest, all wounded innocence. "I would *never* ask you to abandon the girl. I'm merely saying that she should be returned to the bosom of her family."

When I think of being left on Adamantas for my father to find, panic rises in me. I can't go back. I think of my father's face as we were leaving. His words—*I will* bring you back. *You will be punished. You are mine.*

A flush has risen across Theseus's face, and his hands are clenched. "Father, I'm not doing this."

Aegeus's eyes shift, like he's looking for some new way to convince Theseus. "You must. Listen to me, son, if you don't give her to her father, he will come to Athens and take her. He has already told me that he will." He reaches his hand out toward the camera. "We barely survived the last Cretan attack when Androgeous was killed. We're in no position to defend ourselves now—"

Theseus interrupts. "That isn't true. Call up the national guard. Get the people ready. Tell them to defend Athens. They'll do it."

Aegeus runs his hands over his eyes. "I will not ask the people of Athens to go to war to defend a Cretan princess. And it is not only Crete that we have to worry about. I just received intelligence that the Pallantides are plotting a surprise attack sometime this week. We are trying to learn more, but it's complicated. I don't have the forces for a two-front war, Theseus. I'm doing everything I can to protect you."

"What about Medea?" Theseus asks. "Where is she in this?"

"Gone. She left with Medus today." He shakes his head quickly, a look of desolation on his face. "I don't know if I can manage without her." He chokes up but forces himself to keep talking. "She says the situation is hopeless. She doesn't think you are brave enough to leave the girl behind. If Ariadne of Crete comes to Athens, everything is ruined, Theseus. *Everything.*" Fat tears run down Aegeus's cheeks and he presses his fist to his mouth.

I don't like Aegeus, but I have no pleasure in his misery. What am I asking Theseus to do by bringing me to Athens? What is he risking?

Theseus holds his hand out toward Aegeus, trying to calm him. "Father, Father, listen," he says. "It isn't that bad. We can defend ourselves against both of them. Don't worry. We can handle the Pallantides. We've done it before. We have our sources, we'll figure out their plans. You concentrate on getting the defenses ready for an attack from Crete. We're stronger than you think. I promise."

But Aegeus doesn't stop shaking his head and sobbing. "You must leave the girl behind. You can't bring her here . . ." He draws in a deep shuddering breath. "You must do this."

Theseus crosses his arms. "I won't."

Aegeus takes a shuddering breath. "So, you choose selfishness. Is that what you are telling me? You are still a boy. I am making this decision for you. I will send a message to the captain and the crew, and they will carry the girl to Adamantas."

My heart is racing now.

The captain is waiting outside the door to the helm station. What will I do if she tries to take me by force? There are eleven people on the crew. Is Theseus strong enough to stop them if they decide to get rid of me? Would any of the competitors fight the crew for me? What if I jumped off the ship and asked for help from the media? Would they see me in the dark? I look out the windows at the dark sea. There is nowhere for me to go.

"Father, wait," Theseus says. He slides Icarus's flash drive out of his pocket. "Don't do this." He holds up the flash drive. "I know you have been taking money from Minos for years. I have proof of it. I have the video."

Aegeus's mouth is gaping, and he shakes his head back and forth.

Theseus continues. "If you contact the captain or do anything to hurt Ariadne, I'll show it to the world. How would you like it if everyone knew that you'd been paid for sending competitors?"

"You don't understand," Aegeus says, his voice a whine. "Our country was bankrupted. There was nothing. The people were going to overthrow me if I didn't *do* something. Minos's money has paid for schools. For roads. For that lovely ship that you are sailing on right now. Without the income from Minos, the Pallantides would have taken over years ago."

"It's blood money, Father," Theseus says.

"No, son, listen to me"—Aegeus drops his voice, like he is telling a secret—"Minos has promised me a fortune if we get the girl back to him. Enough to make up for the loss of *The Labyrinth Contest*. If you leave her, and we take his money, we will benefit. Athens will benefit. But if you bring her here, Minos will come for her. I'm sure of it. It will be like it was with his son—he will burn Athens to the ground."

"I'm not doing that, Father," Theseus says.

"Son, Theseus, listen to me," Aegeus says, and his eyes are wild. "Drop the girl on Adamantas, then raise the white sails on the ship, that way I'll know that it is done. It is our only hope."

With that, Aegeus disconnects the call.

I have a shaky feeling, but I fight it. I didn't go through everything I just went through to be handed to my father like an animal for sacrifice. I stand up. "I'll jump off this boat before I go back to my father."

Theseus wraps his arms around me. "It's not happening," he says.

"If the captain and the crew try to take me, how will you stop them?"

"My father won't risk that." Theseus runs his hands up and down my arms. "I promise you, whatever happens, I'm not leaving you for your father to find. I swear it."

"What about if my father attacks Athens? What will you do then?" I ask in a small voice, wondering what helping me has gotten Theseus into.

"Ariadne," he says, pulling me in closer. "I'm not my father. Athens has been weak because he's weak. The people don't follow him, because he doesn't know how to lead. That's not true with me. Athens won't be so easy to beat this time."

He is using his Hero of Athens voice, and I shiver.

"Theseus, I don't want to be a bone that you and my father

fight over. I don't want to be the cause of a war between Athens and Crete."

"You won't be," he says, running his hand over my cheek. "I'll introduce you to my mom. You'll get to see the city. I'll take you to my favorite gyro place. It's going to be okay. I promise."

When Theseus and I leave the helm station, he seems relaxed and calm. In command.

The captain is waiting for us. "Do you have any orders?"

"No," Theseus says. "Continue on to Athens. What time should we arrive?"

"On our current course, we should be there by morning," she says.

Theseus nods.

Neither Theseus nor I wants to go back to his room. Instead, we go up to the bow of the ship. There is an area inset into the deck ahead of the mast, with benches and cushions, and we snuggle together, listening to the sounds of the waves and looking up at the night sky. It is like nothing I've ever seen before. In the darkness, I can see the Milky Way, bright behind the stars. Theseus tells me the names of the different constellations.

Then he leans over and kisses me tenderly.

After a long time, Theseus raises himself up on one arm and looks down at my face, pushing my hair back from my cheek.

"You are so beautiful," he says, and I believe him.

"You are, too," I say, and I run my palm across his chest.

Then we are moving together, gently.

And the only eyes on us are the stars.

* * *

I wake up with a jerk, confused about where I am. It takes a second to remember that I am on a ship. The sky has brightened to a pale gray. Before too long it will be morning, and we will be in Athens, where a bunch of trouble is waiting for us.

Theseus kisses me.

Then he points over my shoulder. "Look," he says. "Look there."

The lightening sky reveals that we are no longer out in the open sea. An outcropping of land extends into the water, and on a high cliff at the end of it, a lonely marble temple stands. Just then, the sun peeks above the horizon, flooding the temple with golden light. Our ship glides past, and I am stunned by its silent beauty.

"It's Cape Sounio," Theseus says. "The Temple of Poseidon."

The columns make a stark outline against the sky. The sails of our ship are black against the spreading pink of the dawn. The flotilla of smaller boats has stayed with us overnight. They bob in the water surrounding the *Parthenos*.

I look back up at the Temple of Poseidon and see a flash of movement, high on the cliff.

"What's that?" I ask. "Look."

Theseus follows my pointing finger, and we both make out the small figure, a shadow against the bright light of the rising sun. It is a person, running toward the cliff.

As the sun gets a little higher, I see the outlines of five or six other people around the temple. They must have seen the running man, too, because they go after him, but he is faster.

He is almost to the edge, not slowing down, not stopping.

Theseus and I gasp in horror as the runner plunges off, then falls the long distance down to the ground, his arms and legs wheeling, still running in the air. Then his body is lost in the jumble of boulders below the cliff.

I cry out. "Oh gods!"

I'm shaking with horror, and Theseus's face is pale in the morning light.

He pulls me in close to him.

"Can we do anything?" I ask.

"No one can do anything now."

I don't understand. What kind of despair would drive someone to throw themself off a cliff? How can it be that one minute someone is alive, and running, and in the next they are gone? I wish you could rewind the film—take the runner back to the top of the cliff—but you can't.

As the *Parthenos* moves up the coastline, I hear sirens, and a few of the small boats speed off toward the base of the cliff to investigate.

"We'll be getting there in an hour or so," Theseus says finally. "I should probably get changed."

We are walking back toward Theseus's cabin when the captain stops us. "I need to talk with you both," she says. "Privately."

We go into Theseus's cabin and he closes the door behind

us. The captain stands, holding her hands at her sides, her pale eyes solemn. "I am the bearer of terrible news."

"What is it?" Theseus asks.

"Your Majesty," the captain starts.

Theseus holds his hand out. "Like I said before, *Theseus* is fine. You don't have to call me that."

The captain takes a deep breath. "I'm afraid that I do. King Aegeus is dead. You are now the king of Athens."

Theseus looks shocked. "Dead? How? When?" He looks at me. "We just talked to him last night. How can he be dead?"

The captain runs her hand over her eyes. "We received word moments ago. Your father . . . he threw himself off the cliff at Cape Sounio. He died instantly, they say."

I grab Theseus's hand as his shoulders droop. An ache grows in my chest.

"Why?" Theseus asks, his voice numb. "Why?"

"He demanded to be taken to Cape Sounio at sunrise so that he could see your ship, and when he saw it, he—" She stops.

"It was the sails," Theseus says, his voice breaking. "It was because I forgot to change the sails."

"It isn't your fault, Theseus," I say, holding tight to his hand. Because this is my fault. Theseus's father killed himself because *I* am coming to Athens. Theseus didn't change the sails because he didn't do what his father ordered him to do. He didn't leave me on Adamantas. My hands are shaking. One more death added to my tally. Gods.

Theseus looks up at the curved ceiling, tears running down

his face. "Father, why couldn't you trust me? We were strong enough to protect Athens together. Why couldn't you wait?" His last words are a whisper. "Why did you leave me to do this alone?"

I think of everything that Theseus is facing—becoming king with no experience; the Pallantides' planned attack; Medea, who will not keep her hands out of this if she thinks there's any chance for her to benefit; and my father and the whole Cretan navy coming to take me back. There is nothing I can do about the Pallantides or Medea, but I can protect Theseus and the people of Athens from my father.

I look down at Theseus's hand in mine. It is strong and substantial, calloused from work. I love the feel of it. I know that he would do anything to keep me safe.

I take my hand out of his.

"You can't bring me to Athens," I say to Theseus. "You can't."

"I have to protect you," he says. "I promised."

I shake my head. "Theseus, you're the king of Athens now. You have to protect the people, too. And you can't keep them safe if the first thing that you do brings the firepower of Crete against you." He starts to say something, but I stop him. "Theseus. I can't be responsible for bringing death and destruction to Athens. I can't. I've had enough of that for two or three lifetimes."

"I don't want to lose you," he says, grabbing my hand again and holding tight to it.

"I'm not giving you up so easily," I say, touching the side of his face. "I have a new phone now, with a number that can't be traced to me. We can stay together, and when things settle down here, you can come and see me."

Theseus rests his forehead on mine. "It's not fair," he says.

"I know." A lone tear rolls down my cheek, but I brush it away. I put my hand on his chest, and it feels like our hearts are beating in time.

He leans in and kisses me, holding me to him. "Where will you go? What will you do?"

"I don't know," I say, shaking my head.

The captain clears her throat and I jump. I'd forgotten she was there. "I have an idea," she says.

She leaves us for a minute and then comes back with a pair of scissors.

Theseus looks at her skeptically. "Scissors?"

I look at the captain's short white hair and feel the weight of the long braid that runs down to my lower back, and I know what she's thinking. "You want to cut my hair."

Theseus gasps and reaches his hand out toward my hair, thus confirming that it is my best feature. "Your hair?"

"Gods, Theseus," I say, "it's just hair. It will grow back." I'm saying the same thing to myself, by the way.

The captain looks at him, irritated. "With that long dark hair, she might as well have a tattoo that announces she is one of the Paradoxes. Plus, this will mean she won't have to worry about her hair while she's getting settled. Luckily, I cut my own hair, so I have the tools we need." She touches her own cropped hair. "It really is much easier wearing it short."

Theseus stares wide-eyed at the captain's hair. "It's going to be that short?"

I smile. "Theseus," I say. "It's going to be fine. It's called a pixie cut. It's cute."

He shakes his head, disbelieving.

"Not this short," the captain says. "That would draw too much attention to her. A bob. Sit down," she tells me, and I take one of the low chairs.

The captain holds the scissors to the nape of my neck and they make a sawing sound through my thick braid. Finally, she cuts it loose, and my head feels light on my shoulders.

The captain hands me my two-foot-long braid and I look at it while she continues trimming my hair. "What do I do with it?" I ask.

Theseus looks like a fish that has been pulled out of the water. He is actually making gasping sounds. "Theseus," I say, "you're freaking me out now. It's going to be okay."

"This is necessary," the captain says sternly. "You are a king now. Kings make sacrifices."

"Yes," Theseus says, taking my braid out of my hands. "I'll just hold on to this."

"We can't glue it back on," I say, smiling. As more of my hair falls to the floor, I feel like a weight is lifting off me.

"We're done," the captain says, and I walk over to a mirror in the wall.

I can't stop smiling. I touch my hair. It's chin length, and it swings when I move my head. I still look like myself, only younger, sweeter, happier, and I don't look anything like my sisters.

"I love it," I say, turning to the captain. "Thank you."

"Where will she go?" Theseus asks. "Where can she be safe?"

The captain turns to me. "What are you qualified to do?"

"Do?" I ask. "Like, for a job?" I think about my life so far. "I can deal with *very* difficult people. I can bandage cuts and bruises. I'm a decent tour guide."

She looks thoughtful. "I have a friend who runs a taverna on Naxos. I bet he'd be willing to take a chance on you."

"Naxos?" I ask. It's one of the islands in the archipelago that fills the sea between Crete and the mainland, but since there are 227 inhabited islands, I don't know much about it other than that.

"It's the biggest island in the Cyclades," she says. "There's windsurfing, beaches, great food. There aren't that many year-round residents, but the cruise ships and ferries stop there, so you won't stand out as a young woman passing through. You'll be another backpacker looking for seasonal work. Most important for our purposes, Naxos isn't controlled by Crete or Athens or any other great power, and the people like it that way. If someone comes looking for you, no one will be likely to give you up."

I have a lightening feeling in my chest. Like this might really work.

"Do you think my father could find me there?" I say.

"Sure, if he was looking for you," she says. "But he isn't likely to be looking for you there. Think about it—as far as he'll know,

327

you came to Athens. When you don't show up here, he's going to be looking for you on the mainland."

The walkie-talkie strapped to her belt goes off. "We're approaching the port of Athens," a voice squawks.

"Take the sails down and go to motor power," she says into the device. "I'll be up in a minute." Her tone quickens as she turns back to me. "Here's what we're going to do. The *Parthenos* can't take you to Naxos, it would be too obvious. Stay here and wait while Theseus and the competitors leave. When we leave the *Parthenos* for supplies, come with us, you'll blend in with your uniform. At the market, you can buy some clothes to change into—then go to the ferry terminal and get a ticket to Naxos. Ferries run every day."

"I don't have any money," I say.

"Yes, you do," Theseus says. "Remember, I'm giving you a share of my prize money."

"Theseus, I can't," I protest.

"You can." He gets his wallet out and hands me an enormous wad of cash, then folds his fingers over mine. "This is yours. Put it in your pocket so you don't lose it."

I nod, blinking the tears out of my eyes. I look at the captain. "Why are you doing this for us?"

She shrugs. "I hate bullies, and I hate seeing girls get yanked around by their families. It will be my good deed for the month."

Her walkie-talkie goes off again, and she salutes Theseus, then leaves.

Theseus brushes his hand across my newly shorn hair. "It

feels nice. I'm getting used to it." He kisses me. "I'm going to miss you so much."

I wrap my arms around him tightly, hiding my face in his neck. "This isn't goodbye," I say. "You'll know where to find me."

Theseus kisses me like he's never going to let me go.

Then the *Parthenos* comes to an abrupt stop. I draw back from Theseus, putting my hand on his cheek. "You have to go now," I say. "Your people are waiting."

He changes into his suit, then there is a knock at the door.

"Call me, text me," he says. "Promise."

"I will," I say. Then I push him toward the door. "Go, Theseus, you have a destiny to claim."

The door closes behind him and I go over to the windows to watch him meet his people. The port of Athens is gritty and industrial, the low buildings faded, their windows broken. The air smells like diesel fuel and raw sewage. It is as different as it could be from my father's shiny city of gold and glass. On the dock, there is a sea of people, well-wishers and sightseers, but also a crowd of media with their cameras and microphones. I watch the competitors walk down a ramp onto the dock, where they merge with the cheering crowd.

Now hundreds of people are shouting Theseus's name. The din of voices overtakes the calling of the seagulls.

Theseus walks down the ramp, looking strong and confident in his suit.

The crowd cheers as he passes. They will follow him anywhere.

TWENTY

I GO OUT INTO THE CITY WITH THE CREW.

The crowd has dispersed, but the docks are still full of people. No one pays any attention to me. In the market, I get supplies for my new life—clothes, a toothbrush, and a tote bag. In the market bathroom, I change into jeans, a T-shirt, and a hoodie. The only things left over from my old life are my golden sneakers, my phone with its new identification card, and the silver thread and piece of blanket in my pocket.

I say a quick goodbye to the captain and follow her directions to the ferry terminal.

It is the strangest feeling, moving through the crowd with no one noticing me. No one following me. No one pays any attention to me as I wait in line to buy my ticket and board the ferry.

I find a seat at the bow, among a mass of people, no one looking at me, and watch as the lumbering, slow-moving ferry pulls
out of the harbor, the engine a low hum.

It's only when I'm settled into my seat, feeling the salt spray
on my face, watching the churning waves, that it hits me what
I'm doing. I'm going to a new place, where I've never been before. Where I don't know anyone. Alone.

I pull my phone out of my pocket. There are no messages
from Theseus or Icarus, the only two people in the world who
know this number. I open the newsfeeds for a second and see
Theseus crowned in Athens, followed by *Is there a future for Crete after
The Labyrinth Contest?* I quickly shut it down, my heart racing. It's too soon.

I look out at the sea, but then I feel like someone is looking
at me, and I have a feeling of dread. I look up, and there are
three girls in sundresses. They see me looking at them. "First
trip?" one of them asks with a smile.

"Yes," I say, feeling overwhelming relief. They don't know
who I am. They're just being nice.

"You had that rookie look of panic," another one says. "Don't
worry, you'll have a blast traveling."

"Where are you headed?" the third girl asks.

I tell them Naxos, and they say that they are going to Mykonos first, then heading to Naxos in a day or two. They are on a
gap year traveling the world. They ask me where I'm from, and
when I tell them I'm from Kydonia, they clearly have no idea
where it is. Which is what I am going for.

"Where are you staying on Naxos?" they ask.

"I don't know yet. Where will you stay on Mykonos?"

"In a youth hostel," one of the girls says. "We heard it has an infinity pool and everything."

"I'll believe that when I see it," another one says. "You don't know where you're staying?"

I shake my head.

"You really are a newbie!" She pages through a guidebook. "Look, there's a hostel right next to Naxos town; grab a bed as soon as you get there, before it fills up."

"Thanks for the tip," I say, not wanting to seem any more like an idiot, but I think—*A bed? Do I get anything else?*

The announcement goes out that the ferry is making its stop on Mykonos, and the girls gather their things. "Maybe we'll see you on Naxos," one of them says.

"That would be nice," I say, and I mean it.

Once they are gone, I use my phone to look up what a youth hostel is, and I text Theseus to tell him that I made it to the ferry. I don't want to bother him on such an important day, but I don't want him to worry, either.

Soon, the ferry pulls into Naxos. I look out at the little town as we come into the harbor. Rows of white houses rise up the island hillside. Multicolored fishing boats bob in the late afternoon light.

I get off the ferry, following a crowd of tourists. For the first time in my life, I walk around without my bodyguards. I explore the cobbled streets of Naxos, letting my feet take me wherever I want. I go up the whitewashed stairs, smelling the flowers that grow up the sides of the buildings. I'm just a girl in a town. People smile at me, but it's the way that people smile at other people on a beautiful day—like we're all sharing the pleasure of being alive. I'm hot in my jeans and T-shirt, and I decide that I'm going to buy a sundress like the girls on the ferry.

But first, I need to find the youth hostel that the girls mentioned. It is a whitewashed building close to the beach, and I am going to be sharing a room with five other people. It's super-cheap, though, and they have free storage for my tote bag.

I get a sandwich, then go to find the taverna that the captain recommended. It's on a cobbled street, two blocks back from the harbor, near a bookstore. It is whitewashed, with a bright blue awning draped in electric-pink flowers. Through a gap in the buildings, I can see the sea. Tables and blue-painted chairs are set up outside, and they are crowded with families and backpackers and older tourists enjoying a meal. A waitress in an apron with a long braid down her back moves quickly between the tables.

The food smells delicious.

There is a HELP WANTED sign in the window.

I run my hand through my new short hair and then open the door. A bell jingles as I enter. The inside is dim and cool after the heat outside. Ten tables are lined up along one of the stone walls, and a long bar is on the other side. At the entry, there is a coffee station and a freezer full of gelato.

"Grab a seat anywhere," a tall guy with blond-streaked hair

says. He looks a few years older than I am, and he is carrying a full platter. He looks harried. Every table is full, and other than the bartender and the waitress outside, he looks like the only person working.

"Actually, I'm looking for a job," I say. "Someone I know from Athens said that you might need someone."

A broad grin breaks across his tan face, showing perfect bright-white teeth. "Stay there. Seriously, don't move. I'll be right back."

He gets the food to his table and then comes over to me and holds his hand out to shake. "I'm Dionysus. I own this place, and the windsurfing shop down on the beach, so I'm back and forth a lot. But we're short-staffed at the moment, so I'm doing everything."

"I'm Ariadne," I say.

"Ariadne, what brings you to Naxos?"

"Looking for a change," I say.

"Anything happen at home?" he asks, then stops himself. "Sorry, that was a personal question—you don't have to tell me. If you ever need to talk, I understand complicated families."

"No, I'm fine," I say. "Just ready to see a little more of the world."

He nods. "Sure," he says. If he doesn't believe me, he's polite enough to not say so. "Do you have ID?"

I give him my phone, and he scans it with his. I cross my fingers, hoping that Icarus did everything right. Dionysus's phone makes a chime that sounds positive and I breathe a sigh of relief.

He hands my phone back to me. "Perfect, Ariadne of Kydonia. Can you bus a table?"

"Yes," I say. "Definitely."

Which is technically true. I *can* do anything, and he didn't ask me if I had ever bussed a table before.

He brings me an apron, and I meet the waitress I saw outside—her name is Irene, she's nineteen, from Sparta, came here for a month and stayed on; she smiles at me in a distracted but friendly way—and then I start bussing tables. It's hard work and I'm constantly getting it wrong. But Irene and Dionysus aren't too hard on me. They really must be desperate for the help. The hours fly by, and I have no time to think about anything but not dropping the trays of glasses and plates that I'm carrying back to the cramped kitchen.

As the sun sets, a musician sets up outside, and the taverna is full of music and laughter. We keep working for hours. The lights come on in our street. Irene and Dionysus grin at me as we pass each other in a dance that I am learning. People look at me in passing, but only as the girl who is clearing their table.

Late in the night, the three girls from the ferry show up at the restaurant.

"Ariadne!" they call, greeting me like I'm an old friend. The infinity-pool hostel on Mykonos was full, so they hopped another ferry to Naxos and will go back to Mykonos next week. They are staying in my hostel.

After midnight, the last customer leaves and I give my apron back to Dionysus.

"How was your first day?" he asks.

"Great," I say, and I can't stop smiling. I know I should be nervous or concerned about my performance, but I'm not. The music and the food and the joy around me have taken any nervousness right out of me.

"We open at ten tomorrow; I'll see you then," he says.

Irene waves to me as she walks down the street to her own apartment.

The girls from the ferry have waited for me, and we walk together down to the hostel, laughing and talking the whole way as the girls recount some of their craziest adventures since they left home six months ago.

We get to the door of the hostel, and I look out at the beach, the moon hanging high in the sky over the sea.

"Are you coming?" one of the girls asks.

"I'll be up in a minute," I say.

I pull my phone out of my pocket. There's a message from Theseus—*I miss you already*. And one from Icarus—a picture of himself with wings. I smile, then slip my phone back in my pocket.

I take my shoes off and walk down to the silent beach. My footprints are the only marks in the sand.

Is this what a bird feels like the first time it flies? This is what I dreamed of. This is freedom.

The waves roll in and out, tickling my toes. I put my hand in my pocket, touching the blue blanket and ball of silver thread. I think of my brother. The peaceful look in his eyes as he lay on the floor of the maze; his hands, healed from their scars. He gave up his life so that I could be free. Free to be my own person. To find my own life.

And I did.

I stare up at the stars spangled across the sky, and it feels to me like they are singing the same song I heard when Asterion disappeared.

I know he is up there, watching me. And he is happy.

AUTHOR'S NOTE

I HAVE LOVED GREEK MYTHOLOGY SINCE I WAS A KID, but I started thinking about the myths in a new way with the rise of reality television. I started to wonder how the most salacious elements of the myths became public knowledge. This brought me to one of the weirdest and most shocking things in mythology: Pasiphae and her wooden cow. How did the word get out about *that*? Which made me imagine the mythological paparazzi, and that led to everything else. For this story, I have tried to stay as close as I could to the commonly agreed-upon points of the myth of the Minotaur, but in some cases, I've switched chronologies or events for story reasons. The biggest change is that in the myth, Theseus leaves Ariadne on Naxos because the goddess Athena tells him to. Also, the myth doesn't say that Aegeus is taking money from Minos, but it doesn't say that he isn't, either. Which is to say, don't use this version of the story on your ACT. However, the sea north of Crete is now called the Aegean because Aegeus threw himself into it, so there are many things that I drew straight from the myths. I loved finding the connections between our world and a story that was first written down over two thousand years ago.

ACKNOWLEDGMENTS

WRITING CAN BE A SOLITARY ART; EASY TO HOLD CLOSE to you, quiet and secret, but I'm terrible at secrets. I have always wanted to collaborate and create with other people, and this book has let me do that. For that I'm eternally grateful.

Janine O'Malley has been the editor of my dreams. She made my book better on every page, and it would not be what it is without her. Working with Janine and Melissa Warten has been a gift. They loved and understood this book from the beginning.

To my amazing, absolutely brilliant, and tail-kicking agent, Kerry Sparks, I cannot express my gratitude enough. I love knowing that I have someone in my corner with your literary taste, business savvy, and eye for fashion. Thanks also to Sarah

Bedingfield and Elizabeth Fisher at Levine Greenberg Rostan and all the rest of the LGR team.

To Joy Peskin and the entire FSG Books for Young Readers team, thank you so much for all your support for this book.

Two different critique groups were instrumental to making this book. To my DFW Writers on the Square, Amy Kelly, Denise Dupont, and Kellye Abernathy, thank you for every time you pushed me to make it weirder. And to Mervyn Dejecacion, thank you so much for inviting me to join a critique group. It has made all the difference. To my fellow Arkansas writers, Melissa Bacon, Monica Clark-Robinson, Elle Evans, Heather Breed Steadham, Angelle Gremillion, Amelia Loken, Stephanie Vanderslice, and Annmarie Worthington, you believed in this book before I did. Thank you.

Some writers keep everything close to their chest, never sharing anything, and others force their families and friends to read everything. I'm definitely of the second variety. To my parents, John and Valerie McNee, and my sister, Elaine Kemp, thanks for supporting me every step of the way. To Camille Hemmer and Jenny McCallum, thanks for reading so many drafts. To Kirsten Sanford, thanks for being my friend forever. To my husband, Russell, thanks for never giving up on me, even when the road seemed unsure. To my boys Will, John Henry, and Grant, you make everything better. For the rest of our family and dear friends (you know who you are), thanks for listening to me talk about the motivations of imaginary people, and helping me figure out how to put this story out into the world. I could not do this without you.

Last of all, I want to thank some wonderful teachers who set me on this road. Judy Goss, thank you for teaching me about writing and showing me what a writer's life can look like. The late Susan Taylor Barham was a spark of light in this life. She was the teacher sponsor for my high school senior trip to Greece that first got me thinking about Knossos. She believed that I belonged among the company of writers, and she would have absolutely loved every minute of this.